C0-AYC-109

ALSO BY NICK JAINA

Memoir

Get It While You Can

Essay

Lessons from Fighting the Black Snake at Standing Rock (with Leslie Orihel)

Chapbook

How to Enjoy Dance

HITOMI

a novel

NICK JAINA

Published by Modern Mythology Press
PO Box 8521
Emeryville, CA 94608
www.modernmythologypress.com

Hitomi / Nick Jaina
ISBN: 978-1-64826-764-2
Library of Congress Control Number: 2020902441
First printing in the year 2020

Edited by Cooper Lee and Jennifer Lewis
Copyedited by Des Hewson and Jessie Carver
Cover painting and book design by the author
Vintage botanical illustrations courtesy of Tom Chalky
Author photograph by Bradley Cox at the Casino Bar in Bodega, CA

Printed in Wisconsin by Worzalla on Sebago Tradeblock Antique paper
Cover stock printed on Mohawk Via Felt
Set in Hoefler Text with headings in Georgia and Bodoni 72

nickjaina@gmail.com
www.nickjaina.com

for Leslie

"It isn't enough for your heart to break,
because everybody's heart is broken now."

— Allen Ginsburg

HITOMI

PART ONE

1. The Apartment

MAYBE I COULD BE the world's foremost expert on the smallest things, brought into court to testify on the grandeur in a single speck of dust. Big things are always exploding. Small things hold their center.

It was early September in the part of Brooklyn named for a flying elephant. I rang the buzzer on an apartment building.

"Kxxkkch kcchxx." A voice came through an old speaker.

I wasn't sure how to respond.

"I . . . Uh," I said. "I'm the guy. Tom's son?"

There was silence.

A pigeon fluttered his wings and tried to land on the railing next to me. He seemed to forget that he only had one leg, stumbled around, abandoned his plan, and flew off.

The buzzer sounded.

Up four flights of stairs an old man opened his door. A dog yapped behind him. In the little crack of the opening, I could see the clutter of his apartment, and I caught the Fear. Capital F fear, like something they should make an educational film about: *Fear will kill you faster than diabetes.*

I thought of running away. What would it be like to drive all the way from Indiana and then run at the sight of a few piles of boxes and magazines?

"Come, come," he said to me.

At least there will be a piano, I told myself.

I walked inside and the dog leapt up and punched me in the groin. Like a cheap joke to get the audience to pity me, except nobody was watching. Dennis, the old man, didn't see it either because his back was turned.

"Come now, Farfle, not everyone loves dogs," he said. "Would you like a cup of maté, sir?"

"Um," I said, still recovering.

"It's a tea that tastes like dirt, *but it's the most exotic dirt you ever had*," he said as he raised his hands up like he was talking about a cruise to Bora Bora.

"I usually wait until the afternoon to drink dirt," I said.

I think I gained a bit of his respect with that comment. Maybe. He turned back to the kitchen.

"It takes me some time to get around," Dennis said. "The effects of the medication are the same as the symptoms of the disease."

He pulled at his leg like he was removing it from tar and then shook it. I thought of what my best friend Robert once told me about little kids: "You have to let them make their own peanut butter sandwiches because it builds their self-esteem, even if they make a mess."

That flashed in my head: a two-year-old on a high chair making the messiest peanut butter sandwich and smiling. Dennis hadn't yet made it to the kitchen.

"I hear you have a piano?" I said, as though it were the smallest trifle of a detail. Maybe it would distract him from the maté and move things along.

"Yes," Dennis said as he started to turn around. "Hammerstein himself once played on it."

"Really?"

"Maybe Rogers. The one who didn't really know how to play piano."

The sun broke through the clouds, illuminating the view out the window behind him. Tugboats skirted down the East River.

"You should know," he said, "this drawer is broken, so be careful when you pull it out. I need to get some wood putty so it can hold a screw." He got stuck pulling a kitchen drawer halfway out and couldn't get it back in. "God damn it."

"So, my room is down here?" I asked.

"Yes, I'll show you."

I followed him down the hall. More magazines, more boxes, unplugged and unshaded lamps unable to participate in anything. I looked back at Farfle, and he seemed to hint at a jailbreak.

"I'm not always like this," he said. "It's just this stupid machine." He looked down at his body.

"Can I help?" I asked.

"No," he said, a little too sharply, then caught himself. "No. Just give me time."

He showed me my room. There was a mattress on the floor in front of a window that looked out on a fire escape that was doing its absolute best to completely obscure the view of one of the great cities of the world.

Who was doing favors for whom, I wondered. I often lose track. It was a free apartment in exchange for dog walking and other unnamed duties, and a free apartment in New York is something to behold. But still it felt like I was doing a kind act. The apartment smelled like the glue on the back of stamps. I did not want to investigate this further.

"Down here is that piano you're always talking about," he said.

I followed him to the end of the hall, where I saw an absolute American tragedy in black and white. I was hoping the piano would be on my side. Could potentially be part of the jailbreak. Instead the piano was old and dusty and some of the keys were broken. It had been overrun with books and magazines. Everything was packed in like it belonged there, would always be there, and would fight you if you tried to move it. This piano was the saddest I had ever seen. It had given up waiting for another Rogers or Hammerstein to come along. It had succumbed to being a piece of furniture.

We were trapped, me and the piano. I couldn't find another place I could afford to live. Farfle was at my hip the whole time, and I scratched his head deeper the more I worried. He accepted all the attention he could get, this mutt with scraggly hair who was just big enough to not be one of those annoying little dogs, but small enough that I could lift him up and carry him somewhere should I ever need to.

Like to run for freedom—

"So, what do you do, young man?" Dennis asked. I was flattered that he thought I was young, but I suppose it was true I was about half his age.

"I don't know," I said, as I shook my head. And then I realized he wasn't asking my advice on how to fix this piano, but rather what I *did*, like with my life. I closed my eyes.

"I'm writing a book," I said.

I had never said that sentence out loud before, but after seeing the decrepit piano I decided to accept Robert's advice and write a book. Someone had to document the forgotten pianos of the world.

"Well," Dennis said, "if you need any help getting around the city, I have a scar on my knee that is a perfect map of the subway system."

He perched there with a smile. I didn't know how to react. Was he hitting on me? Was this all a setup for a creepy man who wanted me to rub lotion on his thighs while he watched Rhianna music videos? My face got red and my voice disappeared. Farfle stood there motionless in between us, wondering from whom to seek attention. Frail, wobbling Dennis, or me, sweat on my forehead, pale faced, leaning on the piano like it was a crutch.

"Not a fan of *Harry Potter*, I see," he said as he broke his frozen posture and hobbled back down the hall.

"Oh," I said. "Ah. Ha."

The weakest imitation of a laugh. I had lost his respect.

I had a very modest amount of money in the bank that would last me perhaps three months of writing in New York if I could maintain a good relationship with Dennis and keep my rent free.

I know the naiveté of that statement, having lived in New York before. I know you can take one wrong step in that city and lose a month's rent. I know you can fumble around in the back of a café, thinking you're about to step into the bathroom, when actually you open the door onto a pyramid scheme, and you are given brochures with detachable tabs that take your account numbers and start sucking your savings until you have to sell a kidney.

I knew this. At least there was a piano in the apartment.

No. I had to let go of the idea of the piano. It was a painful reminder at the end of the hall. It was a drawing of an open meadow. Just a drawing. Not even a good one.

Besides, pianos are too big. Focus on the small things.

Consider the flower: radiating colors in different dimensions. Silently bending with the wind. Picked by horny lovers. Molested by bees. Peed on by dogs.

Okay, stop considering the flower. Consider the decades-old blob of gum on the sidewalk of Jay Street. Things that are so small they can never let you down. Consider the one-legged pigeon. Consider the dripping paint in the graffitied letters on the awning. Consider the tear in the awning. The patch of gray sky poking through.

New York City has great abundance, probably from all the money it has fleeced from people accidentally choosing the wrong door in the back of a café. This abundance means that free objects are often left on the side of the streets, as though they were thrown overboard from a sinking ship. For example, I found a free writing desk six blocks from Dennis's apartment. Farfle investigated it by sniffing all around. I didn't have anyone to help me carry it, that wounded soldier, and leaving it might mean losing it, so I started to push the desk by myself, moving one side and then the other—a hobbled, awkward journey, with Farfle frustrated and whining.

I got it five blocks along, then sat on a curb to catch my breath on the final block when a man offered his help. He didn't even ask how far away I lived, and for all he knew I was going to Sag Harbor and he was now roped into a miles-long journey carrying a desk with a stranger.

We got the desk to the steps of the apartment. We looked at each other and he asked me, "What floor?"

"Fourth?" I said with a question mark. Like it was negotiable. Like I could live on the second floor if it were more convenient.

"Alright then," he said.

We hoisted and pivoted that desk to the fourth-not-the-second floor and slid it into my room, Farfle barking our arrival to all who cared. I shook the stranger's hand and asked if I could make him a maté.

"Glorious, wet dirt," I said with a smile as Dennis sat in his easy chair ignoring us.

The man said he had to go.

After he left, I unpacked a clay pot I brought from Indiana, and I saw that it had broken into two pieces. I found some glue in that kitchen drawer and put the pot back together. Dennis ignored all this too. I stood there holding the pot in my hands while it dried.

My phone started buzzing with texts from my friend Melissa, who should have been in the Caribbean with her new husband and not texting me.

First text:

No one can find Robert. Have you heard from him?

What did that mean? Where were they looking?

The next text:

We're scared

And then:

Please call

I held on to that pot, afraid to let go. I heard the sirens of a firetruck as it raced down the block. My hands were occupied with the clay pot. The smallest of things. I could only see the lights bleeding through the white linen curtains. They spread emergency red and distress blue across my bare walls, and because it had started raining, the light was pockmarked by the droplets that were stuck to the windows. The truck kept on its horn.

Let's not be dramatic. Robert wasn't missing. Robert was away. Robert sometimes went away. I understood this. He needed time to think alone, out in the forest, but other people in his life didn't ever accept it. They were insisting on putting up MISSING signs.

I had seen Robert just two days before, at Melissa's wedding in Indiana. I had seen him all summer. He was Robert. He'd saved my life in a hundred different ways.

I talked to Melissa on the phone. She was convinced it was different this time. He was supposed to be cat-sitting for them when they went on their honeymoon. Now they were going to cancel their trip.

"Are tickets to Saint Kitts something you can donate to charity?" she asked.

"Just find someone else to watch the cats," I suggested. "He's forgetful sometimes, but he's not in peril. And cats are fine. They can manage."

I guess that did have me worried, that he would forget to feed Melissa's cats.

I sat down to write at my new desk in my red notebook, one I had stitched together by hand. I tried to start writing what I had promised Robert: a book of failures, of me playing piano in a crowded bar, all the people chatting, me sitting there imagining a spotlight of scorn on those people, playing the keys quieter and quieter so the horrible, ugly, talking people would be exposed as the goblins they were, playing so quietly that I was eventually just lightly rubbing the tops of the keys while those people still rattled on about the latest episode of *The Bachelor*.

That was funny, right? My pain? My failure? That could be a book, right?

No, *The Bachelor* was too spot-on, too obvious a reference. But it was true. That really happened. And they *were* talking about *The Bachelor*.

Should I make it less true to make it more true?

I thought about how I learned from Robert a better way to write the number 8. I used to do it in one motion, starting at the top, carving an s down to the bottom, then mirroring that up to the top again. These always ended up looking like squeezed-out tubes of toothpaste.

I loved the way Robert wrote his 8s: first the top circle and then the bottom one. It was like he was building a snowman from the top down.

I sat at my desk drawing a series of beautiful, fat 8s in my notebook and was able to write absolutely nothing else.

2.
The Cemetery

"We are looking for the elusive blewit," Dennis said. He let that word linger on his lips.

He saw the confused look on my face.

"Blewit," he said again. "Like, *boy, you really blew it.* Yes, they are out there under the fallen leaves. We just need to find the right spot. They are the loveliest lavender-white color you've ever seen. And they smell like orange juice."

I kept my car in neutral and rolled behind him, listening to the classical music station as he wobbled down the pathway of the cemetery. He looked like a Muppet the way he spasmed one way or the other in search of mushrooms, in this case the blewit.

Dennis's hair was straight and white, and it poked out at all angles like he had been raised in a culture that didn't believe in combs. He wore a windbreaker at all times, even inside, the plastic whooshing offering a soundtrack to his erratic movements. When his body slowed down, the whooshes slowed down as well, still like a soundtrack, but the part that becomes quiet and reverent when all hope dies out with our protagonist.

"Yes, the blewit," he said as the string quartet swelled around him.

He pronounced the word like he was saying the name of a rival pirate at sea. "We will find you, little blewit, in the one place that isn't overrun with people."

A Dvořák quartet swelled as he swooped down to reach for one. He straightened up with nothing in his hands. He insisted mushrooms were out there in the cemeteries of New York. I wanted to believe him.

We had gone all the way up to Woodlawn in the Bronx looking for blewits. He kept cursing the secretary of the New York Mycological Society, which gave me the impression that Dennis was a rogue mushroom hunter, unsanctioned, off the grid. As he jerked this way and that, I was worried he might fall right into an open grave.

I thought about all the places Robert could have wandered off to, the happy reasons that would explain everything. I felt my thigh tense up as I waited for my phone to buzz with some good news from Melissa. I kept pulling it out of my pocket to make sure it was still working.

I parked the car and got out as Dennis sifted through some grass.

"I'm gonna have a look around," I said. "Is that alright?"

He waved me off.

There was no agreed-upon amount of help I was supposed to offer Dennis. I was always worried I wasn't doing enough and the free rent would be rescinded. I should have been writing, but now I was too preoccupied with thoughts about Robert to find any joy in my words, and I let myself get carried along on every request Dennis made.

The gravestones poked out of the grass, advertising the one bit of information they knew, the simple details of when someone lived and died. Around one corner of the cemetery I stumbled upon Herman Melville's grave. Before I left Indiana, Robert had given me a copy of *Moby-Dick* that I still hadn't started.

"It's not what you think," Robert told me. "They *love* the whale, you see. They just don't know how to express that love."

Carved into Melville's gravestone was the image of a scroll of paper with a vine running behind it and a feather quill pen. The scroll was very prominent, unspooling in front of us, but, curiously, it was blank. Below it was written, "Herman Melville: Born August 1, 1819, Died September 28, 1891."

I took a picture of the grave and sent it to Robert. I looked at my phone expecting a response.

I thought, *I can touch a satellite that touches someone. How did we ever let the satellites come between us?*

On the grave were trinkets of affection well-wishers had left, mostly plastic whales. Next to his grave was his wife Elizabeth's, marked with a big stone cross. On top of her cross someone had left a red jar of salt, the La Baleine brand, which has a prominent whale in the logo.

I couldn't decide if this was sweet or tacky. It seems a shame everyone always tells the dead to rest in peace and then never gives them a moment alone. And I wondered how Elizabeth would feel about her grave being another mantle for her husband's trash.

I realized I hadn't seen Dennis in a few minutes. I walked around the corner to find him frozen in place.

"Fucking *cunt*," he sputtered, using his last bit of energy. I wasn't sure if that was directed at me or at his own body.

"I'm sorry," I said. "I got distracted."

"You *can't*."

"I'm sorry."

Whatever I did after that, I at least learned not to get too distracted by Melville, and not to leave this poor old man unattended in a cemetery, should he become just another statue on which people left trinkets.

3.
The Diner

The waitresses at the diner down the street wore pink uniforms with their names sewn into them in cursive script. The whole diner seemed like it had been grandfathered into the modern age. A handwritten piece of paper above the counter said, "No, we do not have 'WIFI.'"

I leafed through a copy of the *New York Times* someone had left behind.

Astronomers announced on Monday that they had seen and heard a pair of dead stars collide. Such explosions, astronomers have long suspected, produced many of the heavier elements in the universe, including precious metals like gold, silver and uranium.

All the atoms in your wedding band, in the pharaoh's treasures and the bombs that destroyed Hiroshima and still threaten us all, so the story goes, have been formed in cosmic gong shows that reverberated across the heavens.

Big things are always exploding. I pictured that science writer at the *Times* feeling gleeful at having a chance to bust out with a gorgeous line of poetry in the midst of a story about dead stars.

I looked at my phone and saw one photo of Robert through all of social media. A glitch in the system, I thought, or rather a perfection of the system. The algorithm was finally able to read my thoughts and spit up what it tfigured I wanted to see: Robert, alive and well.

But no, his photo was there because it was now public knowledge that Robert was missing.

The whole affair felt cheapened. To have his picture next to posts of people talking about their new baby and their perfect brunch felt wrong. Dying stars were colliding while people arranged the blueberries on their French toast. I wanted to protect Robert from this display. He was like Han Solo frozen in carbonite. Even as he was in the midst of being dashing and brave, he was stuck in time. All of us frittered about around him, putting our jars of salt on his slab of rock. It felt *irreverent*, if I had to choose a word for it.

And still, what could I even communicate to him, if I were able to get to him before he was frozen?

"I love you, Robert."

"I know."

I felt sure that he was in the woods somewhere. If any of us wanted to connect with him, all we needed to do was walk into the woods. Unfortunately, I was in the middle of Brooklyn and there weren't any woods nearby. Instead I drew lodgepole pines and 8s in my journal.

It was the people who had no deep connection with Robert who annoyed me. They were talking about him like they had drunk chartreuse together and discussed time travel on the porch as six fireflies all managed to blink at the same moment.

No. *I* had done that.

I heard clattering from the diner's kitchen. There was always a well-timed fire bursting out of a pan whenever someone took a tentative step in the direction of the galley, as though it marked a circle of Hades they were not authorized to enter. The ruckus was from a man who would later end up pulling me on an adventure. I had a vague foreboding something was shaking out on the horizon, that gods were remodeling their summer homes, and herds of cattle were fleeing the territory.

In this clamoring of a furnace lived the cook, a Mexican man with a round belly that protruded around corners. I could hear this man's smile before I ever got a square look at him, because it cut through grease fires and tufts of flour hanging in the air. He rallied everyone who passed through the kitchen into believing that this current crop of omelets and hash browns was important to keep the cog-works of the world running. I could hear his spirit whirring before I ever got caught up in it, and I had a ridiculous thought that he would be the one to bring Robert back into my life, even if I didn't see how that would possibly be true.

4.
The Last Time I Saw Robert

"LET'S PLAY A GAME," Robert said.

Always a game. I tried to resist.

"I'll take that as a 'hell yes,'" he said. "Okay. Your race car driver name is your favorite pasta plus your favorite espresso drink."

"Hmm," I said. "So, like . . . Spaghetti Americano?"

"Come on, really?" he said.

"What? Did I do it wrong?"

"It's just the two most obvious answers."

We were in a thrift store the day of the wedding. We were looking for a gift, but I don't know what kind of gift I was hoping to find at the last minute.

"We're bad wedding guests," I said.

"We're busy, complicated, fascinating people," he said.

At one point we stood in front of a mirror with a Miller High Life logo in the middle of it, Robert and I on each side of that red and gold crest. Robert: tall, with a kind face. A kind, ruddy face. That chin. What an expressive, complicated chin. I always pictured a sculptor trying to carve it into a statue and spending the rest of his life never getting it right.

And then me: shorter, pinprick eyes, a face that people constantly misread as sour. I wanted to live the High Life. Could you really find it in a bottle of domestic pilsner?

We moved on to the appliances.

"What do people give for wedding gifts?" I asked.

"Domestic items," Robert said.

"I don't want to give her a coffee maker," I said. "Everyone is going to give her a coffee maker. She already *has* a coffee maker."

"But does she have"—he picked up one next to him—"a vintage 1980s coffee maker that . . ." He looked at the tag. "Works!"

I felt lucky to be near him, like at any moment he could just walk away and find a better group of people to hang out with.

"Rigatoni Affogato!" Robert said, like he had just solved an equation.

"Wow!" I said. "That's good. That's so good."

We walked over to a piano at the back of the store and fiddled with the keys. They were yellow and dusty. How do the kind-faced people ever befriend the sour-faced ones, after all? Is it part of some community service? Or are they just there to torture us?

"There's gonna be one of these in the apartment in New York," I said. "But in better shape, I hope."

"So many keys," Robert said with a smile over my shoulder.

"Yeah," I said. "Eighty-eight."

"The super low ones don't ever sound very good," he said.

"Yeah," I said.

I mean, clearly, but what was he getting at?

"Do you know what they're for?" he asked.

"Um. The low keys? So you can play them?"

"No," he said. "They are *not* for that."

He was toying with me. This was another game. I turned around. "What do you mean?"

"I mean," he said. "Some of those keys are there for a different reason. Do you know what it is?"

"I think so," I said.

Robert walked away. I turned back toward the keys. Above the piano was an old painting of silver moonlight on a lake. The frame looked like it was more valuable than the painting itself.

"Is it for head room?" I asked Robert, who was now on the far side of the room. "Just in case?"

He put a finger behind his earlobe pretending he couldn't hear me.

"Just in case?" I said louder.

He shook his head no.

5.
The Pass

"It takes so much to make you have flavor, and still you resist it," Dennis said to his oatmeal. "What do I have to do? I've already given you two spoonfuls of honey."

He was a playful man. My only regret was meeting him at the tail end of his life. He showed me pictures of his days producing television in Seoul during the Olympics, and a short film in which he appeared while he was living in Greece. Old age and disease can cloak a person in such a way that the youthful around them can't believe someone ever had any kind of exciting life at all. Instead they were born old, always old, right out of the womb asking for a sweater and bifocals so they could read the *Daily Shouts*.

I woke up every morning to the sound of him turning on talk radio. My stomach instinctively turned sour. The chatter of radio voices in the morning reminded me of listening to conservative talk show host Gordo Messing in the car with my dad. At the time I thought Gordo was funny because my dad thought he was funny.

Dennis listened to NPR instead of Gordo, thank God, but still I had trouble finding a connection with him. What was the oldest thing I could think of?

"Have you ever read *Moby-Dick*?" I asked.

"I did, back in school," he said. "My teacher was an actual dinosaur. I remember liking Queequeg, the—what did he call him? Cannibal? But that book spends a lot of effort just to paraphrase the Bible and Shakespeare, doesn't it?"

"I mean, I just started," I said.

Dennis had a membership card to the Museum of Modern Art that dangled from a hook next to the front door.

"Do you think I could ever borrow that?" I asked.

He didn't even look at it or me.

"Don't lose it or I'll never get a replacement," he said. "First let me read you something better than Melville."

"I wasn't going to go right now," I said.

He pulled out an old book and turned to a page with great delight. He sat back in his chair and read it.

> down a threaded and tethered way
> I backed down a scarlet purpose
> without a worry or posture misplaced
> my unwisdom was overtaken
> for I was a wholesome gent
> I can't believe my bravery now
> that I sit in echoing chambers

It wasn't my kind of verse, but Dennis gave an extra whistle to every word that started with a w. His voice was full when he read, where it would otherwise tremble with fright at the coming darkness whenever he was in the scriptless waters in which we all swim.

I went into the bathroom and looked in the mirror. I pictured a Miller High Life logo in the middle, dividing me and Robert.

"The *fuck*, man?" I said quietly. "There are so few of us out here in the world. You can't just disappear."

Farfle scratched at the door and whined.
"Just a minute," I said.
Like he could tell time.

6.
The Painting

I MEANDERED THROUGH MoMA looking for one painting that really meant something to me. On the second floor, tucked near the elevator, I found that painting. It was not where anyone would ever think to put a work of art. It was almost like they were throwing it away, and before the garbage men came to pick it up the museum staff propped it up at the end of the hall by itself.

It was *Christina's World* by Andrew Wyeth. I had seen an image of it somewhere before, but I couldn't remember where. It is of a woman in a pink dress. We are looking at her from behind as she sits in a field. She is looking at a farmhouse on the horizon.

It looked like a picnic. But something was off. There was no food. No blanket.

I thought first of the waitresses at the diner, how jarring the pink was out there in all that green and brown. But this woman wasn't a waitress. I didn't know what she was.

The next day the man in the kitchen of the diner, that tamer of flames, left his post and came to talk to me.

He had colorful patchworks of tattoos down his arms. His hair was black and thin and long, and it cascaded down to his shoulders. Like the fabric of the dancer's skirt, it showed gravity, and therefore showed strength.

"You play music, right?" he asked, as though stepping straight into my thoughts.

"Sort of," I said. "I play piano."

"That's music, right? I saw you play in a band a while ago at 190 North."

"Oh. Yes."

The show with the people chattering about *The Bachelor.*

"You guys were great. I'm in this band and we're looking for a bass player. I thought maybe you'd know someone? We're leaving in two weeks to tour the country. Our singer is badass, man."

Okay, maybe someone was listening at that show after all. His name was Daveed, and as he typed his number into my phone I saw that, yes, that was how he spelled it. And, though he was a year late, at least he finally showed up.

I went back to see *Christina's World* over and over again.

Some days I'd only spend five minutes with her. Some days I'd spend an hour. I pretended I was recording a radio show for blind people, and this would be the one way they would ever experience this painting in their lives, listening to me describe it.

I cleared my throat and pretended to hold a microphone. I looked over at a father as he shielded his daughter from me.

What details to include for the blind?

"Ladies and gentlemen, this is *Christina's World*, a painting by Andrew Wyeth. It is about as tall as your waist, and as long as a sleeping Labrador stretching himself. Her dress is pink. Pink, if you don't know, is the color of bubble gum and piglets. Pink is the color of blankets they give to girl babies at hospitals. Pink is like a red turned soft. A soft fire truck. A soft anger. A soft apple.

"Her hair is pinned up. It is dark brown, like rich soil in a garden. But there are these thin silver threads in it. The smallest things hold their center.

"The field is so many colors. The field is all of us gathered together during the fall.

"There is a house and a barn on the horizon. Oh. Do you know what the horizon is? It's where the sky meets the ground. The horizon is not something you can ever touch, or hold, or put a fence around.

"The house and the barn are separate. There is a ladder leaning against the house. The ladder's shadow is slanted down the front of the house. Oh right, shadows. Shadows are something else you can't touch. They happen when something gets in front of the sun and casts a flat, dark shape of itself on the ground.

"I want to say that Christina is a beautiful woman, but she is turned away so you can't see her face. So, if she is beautiful, it is because I want her to be. I suppose if you don't have any other information, you have to fill it in with something. And that something tells you about yourself.

"But also—why does a person's beauty depend entirely on their face?

"Anyway. Thank you for your attention, dear listeners. It is an honor to describe this painting to you, perhaps my favorite painting in the world."

When I returned to Dennis's apartment, there was Farfle yapping.

"Oh hush," Dennis said. "The armies are storming the beaches. You'll be free any minute now."

I took Farfle down the street, and as we waited at the corner for the light to change, he lay on my feet and stared up at me, pulling his lips back to show his teeth in an imitation of a smile.

Such devotion. Such love.

"I want to tell you about a painting," I said to him.

He looked up with that dumb smile.

"It's of a woman in a field."

He pricked up an ear, like he was trying.

"She has a clean pink dress on."

Still he smiled.

"*Why is it so clean?* you might wonder."

The light changed.

"Never mind, let's go."

He sprinted into the intersection, almost pulling the leash out of my hands.

7.
The Video Store

"CAN YOU GO TO THE GROCERY and get a few of those Hungry Man dinners?" Dennis asked me. "Hungry *Men*? What would the plural of that be? Get some with the cranberry sauce but not the corn. I hate the way the corn gets."

The next time I went out, he amended his order.

"Try to see if they have a Hungry Man with the—I think it's something like a bread pudding?"

Poor man. Poor hungry man. Dennis was in search of something that maybe only *he* imagined was out there, out on the horizon like a farmhouse. He had seen it in a commercial thirty years ago and assumed the promise of bread pudding still stood. The pain of this searching knitted his brow, and the glow of the television cast its spell, stirring other desires. I wanted to shake his frail body and tell him he wasn't going to find satisfaction in goddamned bread pudding.

I would also go to the pharmacy to pick up his medication for him. I'd give his credit card and driver's license to the pharmacist and quietly imply that maybe I was an eighty-year-old man with Parkinson's.

The tired woman in the pale fluorescent light would glance at the photo and at me and fill the bottle with little green pellets that did release Dennis for a brief moment, only to lock him up again.

The only two things I wasn't trusted to handle getting for him were his mushrooms and his porn. I understood the tactical expertise needed for the first one, though he never seemed to find any mushrooms.

As regards the porn, of course he knew about the internet, but to him, using it a couple of times a week was an obligation he felt to his son rather than something that could make his life easier. I imagined he saw the internet as being powered by a machine housed somewhere near the post office, a steam-powered device with a magnifying glass and a laser hovering over a copy of the yellow pages. Somewhere nearby a cat would be doing something cute.

He insisted his fetishes would only be satisfied by a trip to the video store. And so there we walked, five blocks with his perilous machine of a body that could close up shop at any moment, Farfle weaving in between us like a worried tugboat, not sure whom to assist. Dennis walked straight and slow, unable to take anything other than the most direct and efficient route to his destination.

Down through Brooklyn we went, the three of us, looking as determined as all the delivery men, couriers, and one-legged pigeons around us, though I hoped that everyone else was doing something more important with their afternoon than we were.

The video store was just a normal video store with a curtained-off section in the back for adult videos. I stood in the comedy section, looking at the covers of movies where famous actors pretended to be in love with—but charmingly frustrated by—each other. Farfle stood outside breathing fog on the glass door.

Dennis stumbled around in the adult section like a magician doing a quick change in slow motion, tripping over the doves and saws he had hidden from the audience.

He did *not* want my assistance in this. A man's porn choices are private and mysterious. I wondered, as I waited back in comedy, if he would come out holding a video that was really shocking, something that would make me say, "Well, *that* looks worth all this trouble."

Instead he kicked his foot through the curtain and stumbled out with the spoils of his searching. And why did we risk a frozen embarrassment on a street corner in Brooklyn when his medication and disease could have hit a lull and stopped his body from working? What was it all for?

Naked Yoga and *Swedish Babes Ahoy*.

I said nothing at all as we walked back to the apartment.

8.
The Singer

AT FIRST I WAS UPSET that I hadn't gotten a letter from Robert, and then I was happy, because that meant he wasn't gone. Then I was sad again, because maybe he was really gone.

I pictured him wandering around outside, but maybe he wasn't in a survival situation. He could be in someone's house, safe and warm, eating soup, dabbing his chin with a napkin, inquiring whether they wouldn't mind putting the soccer match on, and—for some reason that left this entire equation an aching, unsolved mess in my head—not letting anyone who cared about him know where he was and that he was okay.

The social media flurry died down. I wanted to call Melissa again, but I didn't want to talk any more about MISSING signs, and I'm sure she didn't either.

I thought about calling Robert's number, but I was afraid he would answer and nonchalantly say, "Yeah, what's up?"

That would be a relief, I guess. But why would he have gone so long without getting back to me, or anyone? That potential embarrassment kept me from calling.

Instead I looked at maps. I tried to think where he would've wandered off to. I called campgrounds around the Midwest, asking if they'd seen someone like Robert recently.

"A guy with a beautiful chin," I'd say.

"I don't know," they'd say. "You have to be more specific."

"A dreamer," I'd say.

He wouldn't have checked in using his own name.

"Anyone check in under the name 'Herman Melville'?" I started asking.

I made posts on Craigslist under different categories in different cities, as ambiguous as he would've wanted it, should he have wanted to be found. I figured if he was missing because he didn't think anyone cared, then he would want to know that someone really *got* him.

Dennis was listening to the radio, as he always was. He rattled the kibble in Farfle's bowl.

"Yes, yes, eat up, my pretty," he said. "We attack the castle at noon."

I took Farfle out for a walk and found the text Daveed had sent me with a link to his band's music.

Tashtego. That was the band's name.

You can tell a lot about a band from its name, and this was an unfortunate one. I pictured a jam band with bouzouki and a drum pad.

"Sounded good, man," I'd have to say. I rehearsed this phrase in my head before I even pushed play on the music. *Sounded good.* I had found that phrase to be the default comment I could manage when I had nothing better to say about someone's band. The subtext was *There is technically nothing wrong with the sound waves that emanate from your musical project.*

"Sounded good, man," I said to Farfle, who looked unimpressed.

Sounded good, man: a sentiment that is a mixture of nice and necessary.

Nicessary.

I try not to judge a band too quickly—and I'm not looking for a trophy here—but I usually am able to give them at least five seconds before I make up my mind, but it all depends on the singer. Either someone has a voice that pulls the flaws out of diamonds or they are wasting our time.

I have to believe them, their voice, and what they are saying. I have to believe that, for them, it's either singing or immolation. Otherwise, what are we doing? Trying to get our music into commercials?

I should know. I wrote a song that went on to sell air fresheners. They stripped the words out and used only the music, like they had removed the pearls from a necklace and used the string. At first, I thought the money they gave me was too much, considering I didn't have to do any actual work for it. Then, the more I thought about it, I realized that the money was not nearly enough. There couldn't be enough money that would make it worth co-opting a song I wrote about loving an avalanche of a woman to turn it into a song to sell plastic and chemicals that make people sadder.

I put in my earbuds and pressed play on Tashtego.

The first few seconds of the first song were fine enough. No bouzouki, thank God. It started with a long, slow instrumental introduction, nice enough to listen to while walking through the city.

Then the singer's voice came in. I had forgotten I was waiting for a singer. Her voice was strong and husky, like she had swallowed a piece of burning cinder, like I had done once at a campfire when I was young.

But.

I.

Could.

Not.

Sing.

Like.

That.

Her voice was a train running off the tracks, but in just the right amount of control. It terrified and comforted me. She sang like it tore her apart to sing, and like she couldn't stop.

There was no way I could go on tour with Tashtego. I *could* play bass in a pinch—I mean, everyone can—but I was in New York to write and I still hadn't written one word in my journal. Maybe I could meet this singer, though. Maybe I could pretend to audition.

I kept listening to the music. I looked around and dreamed Manhattan was at the bottom of the ocean. All the balustrades and intricate carvings were now coral reefs. The faces of demons high above the street were now shaded by algae, sitting under fathoms of ocean. A school of hammerhead sharks turned the corner onto Broadway instead of a sea of taxi cabs.

I walked down, as Ilya Kaminsky called it, "the street of money in the city of money in the country of money, our great country of money." I walked through the bejeweled canyons of that city with Farfle and was in awe of all those angels and demons perched above. Around every corner there was another beautiful, tall building with proud archways and some carving way up high. I was the only one who stood and looked at these faces as everyone else streamed past me, annoyed that I was blocking their path. Did that mean I was the only one who saw them?

Farfle looked up at me annoyed as well. We carried on.

That singer, though. I felt like she was walking there with me. We walked through Prospect Park. The leaves were starting to tremble and let go for the season. It was as though the Pantone swatch factory exploded and shot out colored cards of cardamom and verdigris. The swans in the lake were biting at each other. Farfle looked on with envy.

They get to have friends, he seemed to think.

I took out my earbuds and stopped the music.

"Yeah, but look at how much they fight," I said.

He stared at me in the quiet center of the city.

"I mean," I said. "Never mind."

The next day at the diner I leaned into the kitchen to talk to Daveed.

"Your band—" I said.

"Yeah, man!" he said.

"—is great. That singer. Wow. She sounds like she's burning up."

"I know! She is, man. That's the way to put it, yeah."

Shooom. Another flame shot up. He was shepherding several pans at once. His apron was lashed to him like you would tie down a sail during a storm.

"Yeah," I said. "It's great. But. I appreciate the offer to join the band. That would be fun. But there's no way I could go on tour. I'm sorry. I came back to the city to write, and I just got here, and I can't leave this old man I take care of."

"I was just asking if you knew anyone who played bass, really," he said. "But we just found someone already. Sorry I didn't mention that."

"Oh."

"Yeah, so, no worries." And then, as though he really had no worries, "I'm having a party at my place tonight. You should come."

"Yes. Of course," I said.

Of course what?

9.
Afraid of Grief

I AM AFRAID THAT IF I GRIEVE FOR ROBERT, he will pop back up over my shoulder and say, "Got you!" I'm afraid that he will actually be there in the flesh, that face I missed, that body I pictured floating in a ravine, and instead of being happy, I will be upset that he exists again and that I have grieved unnecessarily.

I am afraid that I have poured too much emotion into him already. If he can just disappear, how can I stay tied to him?

How did Schrödinger handle it, with his cat? Did the not knowing tear him up?

I know it was a hypothetical cat. But what a brilliant marketing gimmick to put a cat in the equation, to scare us all into caring about quantum mechanics.

What was Robert's disappearance scaring me into caring about? Oh right, oh right, that whale book.

10.
The Dispute

I RETURNED TO AN APARTMENT FULL OF SMOKE. Curtains of smoke.

Which was funny, because I had just been wondering at what point was it too late. When do you switch from purposeful nonchalance to absolute devastation? Do you have to have a trigger point?

A few people had responded to my Craigslist posts about Robert, which made my heart leap, but they were the wrong people. They had no information about Robert. Somewhere in Indiana there was a file folder in a police station with a number on it. Where someone could put all the pertinent information about his whereabouts. I imagined it was completely empty, and someone put a cup of coffee on it and it left a ring, and the fluorescent lights pounded it with the most unearthly colors.

Anyway, Dennis's apartment was full of smoke. Sharp chirps from some electronic bird. Dennis had finally done it. He had ignited all that paper—every *National Geographic* and *Parade Magazine*, every photograph of King Tut's gold and Queen Elizabeth's silver, all of it was surely burning now because Dennis loved the authenticity of a Hungry Man cooked in the oven instead of a microwave.

My honest first impression was that this was a tangible crisis that

I could solve instead of some frustrating equation like Robert's disappearance: find what was burning and put it out.

Farfle was barking at the smoke alarm, and the smoke alarm was barking back at him. They were having a conversation about how dire and desperate and wrong this whole situation was, and how neither of them had any thumbs or problem-solving brains to rectify the situation.

Then I walked in, full of thumbs and brains, but what exactly was happening? Dog and alarm shouted at me without any specifics. Was it intentional self-immolation, or an over-cooked turkey with bread pudding? (I *had* found the right dinner at the store after all.) The smoke was sharp white and smelled terrible. Not that you should waste time critiquing smoke at a moment like that, but certainly something was burning that never wanted to burn.

I walked past a sleeping (I hoped) Dennis into the kitchen where there was a pan on the stove. Whatever food-like substance was in it had long been transformed into a horror film version of itself. The fire was well contained. No magazines had in fact been involved. I turned the stove off and put the sizzling pan in the sink. I grabbed a nearby *New Yorker* and waved the smoke away from the detector to try to get it to calm down.

Dennis sensed my arrival and woke up.

"What happened?" I asked.

"Those bastards. They shot me," he said.

He wasn't delusional. He had a childish—or let's say childlike—will to imagine different surroundings, different causes for his suffering. It was his one escape. For once I wasn't willing to play along.

"You left the stove on," I said, still waving smoke away from the alarm so it could catch its breath.

"What does it matter?"

"It matters if you burn the building down. It matters to people who care about you, who don't want you to just disappear forever—"

You selfish prick, I wanted to say. *You selfish fucking prick.* That would have been too much.

I looked at Farfle, who was beside himself with stress. I should've mentioned the poor dog to Dennis as an example of an innocent victim of this negligence. The alarm finally stopped.

I set the magazine down.

"What do we—" I started and then gathered myself. "Can I do anything for you?"

"No."

He said this as firmly as you could say it. He said it so that it resonated on more levels than whether I could pick his body up and move him somewhere. The word went up and down the elevator of my soul.

I looked at Farfle like, *Sorry, bud.*

"Okay," I said, and I walked out the door.

11.
Blue

"WHAT'S YOUR FAVORITE ALBUM?" Robert asked me.

We were both sitting on the dirty linoleum floor of his mother's kitchen.

"I think a better question would be—"

"Wait, you're correcting my question?" he asked.

"I just think there's a better way to ask it," I said.

"Okay, what is it?"

"I would ask, 'What was your first favorite album, as an adult?' Or, 'What's the first album you remember really getting you?'"

"Hm. I suppose it would be—"

"No, you're supposed to ask me that question. I was reframing the question for you."

"Oh," he said. "Thank you. What was it again? What album first got you?"

"Yeah. Good question. I think it would be *The White Album*."

"*The White Album* really got you? 'Rocky Raccoon' really spoke to you?"

"No. It's the accumulation of all that whimsy. It just sounds so fun to be a part of."

"You realize they were having a miserable time when they were making that, right?"

"I don't know. Were they?"

"Yeah. You ever hear the outtakes? They'll play this masterpiece of popular song and then call each other cunts."

"Well, that's what art is about, right? Turning pain into something beautiful?"

"Is it?" Robert asked.

"I don't know," I said. "What's the first album that really got you?"

"*Blue*. Definitely."

"Joni Mitchell?"

"Yeah."

"I never really got into her," I said. "Her voice is just so high, it's like I can't relate to it."

"It sure came down a couple of octaves as she got older, if that helps you relate to her. I love that she has this way of writing songs asymmetrically. Her words and her chord progressions feel like they're always spilling over the edges. In a good way."

"That's what I like about John Lennon."

"Then you should give Joni a try. She's like John Lennon without all the rage and entitlement. Well, maybe some of the entitlement. A lot of the rage, too."

12.
The Party

THERE IS A FLOWER CALLED THE QUEEN OF THE NIGHT that only blooms one night of the year. Separate individuals of this species all bloom on the same night, and nobody knows how they all communicate. They probably send out some incredible scent that rides the wind. It's like they all have their own internet and they're organizing a potluck. They do it without any discernible action. Then *BAM*, one night they all bloom, and every human goes out in the desert with their camera and treats them like starlets on the red carpet, and by morning the flowers are withered and dead.

I had only been back in New York for a week. A week of cemeteries and porn stores and *Christina's World*. That's what people do in New York, right?

Daveed's party felt like the desert before the blooming. I sat there watching the room as it wanted to turn into a dance floor. It takes one beautiful soul to go to the center of the room with solid intention to start a dance party, and we were just waiting for that soul.

And then *BAM*. The Queen of the Night walked in. She wore leopard-print pants and bunny slippers. She danced like she was doing us a favor, like she had come downstairs from a cooler party and would return to it in a minute, but for our sake, for a few minutes, she would show us how it was supposed to be done.

She had silver threads in her dark hair, which was cut into bangs. She had tattoos all down her arms. She was taller than any woman I had seen in weeks. Taller in purpose. Taller in self-realization.

Part of my reaction was "Haven't I seen this face before?" and part of it was *"Here we go."* And part of it was "How." With no question mark. Just. How.

She twirled in the center of the room in those bunny slippers. She looked over at me on the couch, me with the red journal that was so blank, embarrassingly blank for how much it meant to me. And I felt like its utter blankness was visible to all, that everybody in that party knew there was a boy sitting on a couch in the hallway with a journal he had made himself that was completely blank, and how sad was *that*.

But either way, I walked over to her. In the public record, if I were to look at the video tape of that night, I would probably see five other sad, pale writers in the room who thought she was their dream girl, too.

But I got there first.

We danced, and in that dancing everything was alright. Robert would find his way back home. We would dance on the head of this pin while giant machines ate our childhood homes. Athletes would practice their butterfly stroke; birthday cakes would flatten in the fridge.

I had forgotten how much I liked to dance. How long had I been asleep? How long had I kept all the mirrors covered, afraid I would be exposed as a vampire? I shook it out of my ankles, out of my hips, the pain of adolescence, the spirit that creeps into your body and freezes you.

Then the song ended and I went to the bathroom to collect my thoughts.

I came back to the couch and my red journal. The Queen of the Night was sitting there, smiling.

"What are you doing here?" she asked.

"I was invited," I said.

"No, not this party," she said. "What are you doing in *New York?*"

I wanted to say again, *I was invited.*

"I don't know," I said.

"Well, welcome," she said.

"Thank you."

"Not *you're welcome*. I meant, welcome to the city."

"Oh. Thank you."

Did I look like I had just moved there? I checked my shirt to see if patches of Indiana were still sticking to me.

She said, "I had a dream last night."

I smiled and sat down.

"I was on a boat on a smooth lake," she said.

She paused, collecting her memory.

"But at the edge there was smoke. I thought maybe there was a dragon over there. My boat was drifting toward the edge. I didn't have oars. The water was spilling over a waterfall and there was nothing I could do to stop it."

"Were you scared?" I asked.

"No. I wanted to see if there was a dragon over the edge."

"Was there?"

"I kept getting closer and closer. And the smoke surrounded me. I couldn't see anything anymore. Then I woke up."

I sat there for a second. Were we married now?

"Anyway," she said, and she got up to go to the kitchen without us exchanging names.

[Exit Queen of the Night, she of leopard pants and bunny slippers. We all knew she only bloomed but briefly.]

I opened my journal and wrote something without even thinking about it. Let's call it a poem. Then I closed the cover of the book.

I wanted to get out of there. I didn't want to have a conversation with someone where they asked me, "What do you do?" And I'd have to tell some sad story about moving into my dad's friend's apartment and taking care of him and his dog and trying to write a book but getting almost nowhere with it.

What do I do? I walk an old man to a store so he can rent porn. I drive behind him in cemeteries so he can pick mushrooms. I listen to him cough at night while the radio is on and I hide in my room. That's what I do.

I saw Daveed for the first time and realized I had to have the awkward moment of saying *hello* and *goodbye* at the same time.

"So soon?" he asked.

"I wrote something," I said, holding up my notebook.

"Great!"

I stood there smiling and then realized it didn't explain anything about why I had to go.

"I'm just excited to write more," I said.

"Okay, I feel you," he said. *"MAURICE!"*

A big man in a flannel shirt apparently named Maurice had walked into the kitchen. Daveed didn't even take off his oven mitt before embracing him. I took one step back, thinking this could be my time to leave.

"Have you met Maurice yet?" Daveed asked me.

"Hi, nice to meet you," Maurice said to me. "What do you do?"

13.
The Sign

When I finally slipped out the door, I walked to my car and started to drive off, but then decided to go to a park across the street. I sat on a bench and looked deep into the sky, disappointed that it wasn't black, and I couldn't see that subtle layer of stars lurking behind the layer of stars that everyone knows, something I loved in Indiana.

Above the stone angels and demons of the city are wooden water towers on the rooftops, more objects to admire. They're built with loose slats of wood, and when filled the wood soaks up the water and swells, creating a seal. Until that seal is made, though, you have to let all the water spill out of the vessel. I looked at those towers, silently holding on to all that water.

I closed my eyes and heard the city around me clatter. Flashing yellow lights fell across my face. I could feel them moving at an angle, and then they stopped moving, still flashing, still yellow.

I sat up. I couldn't tell if I had fallen asleep. I walked to my parking spot and saw it was empty. My car, my tired old Civic, was gone. It was so clean on the pavement—no broken glass or fresh skid marks—I could tell it hadn't been stolen, it had been towed. She wouldn't have been coaxed into some thief's arms without putting up a fight.

I went to the nearest parking sign and gave it a thorough interrogation, something I had neglected to do at first. I was sure before that it had said, "No Parking Tuesday & Thursday" and the times, but no, the sign said, "No Parking Tuesday–Thursday," the whole meaning of the sign hinging on the placement of a dash instead of an ampersand.

Too much of a burden put on that poor dash, I thought. An entire *day* rested in there.

I thought to myself, *Do I want the car back?* It was just a stupid Civic that was almost dead anyway. They might have been saving me the cost of a tow. I could just let it go.

But then I realized: that journal. Damn it. Caring gets you into so much trouble. I called the number on the sign and asked if they had my car. They said yes, it just came in.

"Great," I said. "I'll be right there."

As if they cared how soon I got there.

14.
The Lot

I PUT MY DRIVER'S LICENSE ON THE COUNTER.

"Hi. You have my Honda Civic. Silver. That one."

The man behind the window was tall, and his skin looked the same color as the great sequoias on the West Coast, those trees that live so long they might as well be immortal.

Behind him I could see the car lot, and in a prominent place in the lot I could see my Civic sitting right there, a bad kid stuck in detention. He didn't look where I was pointing.

"That'll be 487 dollars plus a service fee—"

"I don't have that much money," I said.

"If you don't pick the car up now, there will be a storage fee of fifty dollars a day."

"Look," I said. "Fuck."

The man gave me a direct look.

"I'm sorry," I said. "I don't have the money. But—"

I looked at the man's face.

"There's something in my car—"

"I can't let you in there," he said.

"It's a notebook. I just—want to see *one* poem."

"I can't give it to you, man, I'm sorry."

The "man" in that sentence struck me as a tender gesture. He was trying to be kind.

"Is there a way," I said, stretching out the tension in my fingers, "that you could just . . . get the notebook and hold it up to the glass—"

The man shook his head.

"Why?" I asked.

"That's the policy. I'm sorry."

"There's nothing you can do? That notebook . . . I don't care about anything else in the car. I don't even care about the car itself. It's right there! Isn't there something you can do?"

Nothing.

"Please?"

Stillness. I bowed my head. I resigned myself to starting over. I stayed there for maybe too long.

"God damn it," the man behind the counter said.

I looked up as he stepped away from the window and went to the back of the office to talk to a woman. She started laughing, and he laughed too. I figured they had moved on from my situation and were talking about what they were going to do later.

I got ready to walk away.

He finished talking with the woman and walked out to my car, found my notebook, leafed through it for a second and got out. *Ignore the pages full of 8s,* I wanted to say. He held his finger on one page of the notebook as he stepped up to the window. He looked at me with a raised eyebrow and cleared his throat.

I could not believe what was about to happen. He was going to read my poem in front of me. I reached into my pocket for my phone and it almost jumped out of my hands. I turned on the voice recorder.

The woman sitting in the office laughed and hid her face in her hands. Then she composed herself and looked intently at the man.

"You are not crazy," he started.

I wasn't sure if this was the poem or him talking to me.

"You are a wild animal who has been domesticated."

This was the poem.

"You know what happens to animals when they are put in zoos."

He took his time with the words. His voice was deep and broad.

"They pace, they worry, they fall asleep to themselves. Those who encourage you to stay put are afraid, too. They fall asleep to themselves. You know what happens to animals when they are put in zoos. They fall asleep to themselves, they worry, they pace. You are a wild animal who has been domesticated. You are not crazy."

That last line floated through the garage. I didn't know if he was finished or pausing for effect.

I didn't want to move. I was holding my phone in the air as I heard the footsteps of someone come up behind me. I stood there staring at the beautiful man behind the window. He closed my notebook and put it somewhere below the counter.

"Yes, sir," he said to the man behind me. "Can I help you?"

I turned and walked away, and only hundreds of steps later, after I had left the building and was back in the open night air, did I have the thought that maybe the man behind the counter, that impossibly tall and still man, had made it all up on the spot. It didn't sound like anything I would write.

15. The Note

I RETURNED TO THE APARTMENT around two in the morning. Farfle was silent. No TVs or radios were humming. I went into my room and sat there. I opened my copy of *Moby-Dick* and started reading. It took me a while to get through each page because I kept drifting off in my thoughts about the Queen of the Night, how she was so determined in her actions, like she had rehearsed this all before and was going through it a second time, while we were still on our first read of the script.

But every thought of her was followed by the sting of realizing that my car was gone. And then that thought was filled with a flood of panic about Robert. I tried to focus back on the book.

The first chapter was about how we are all pulled to water, water runs through us, we are skipping and tromping on water all the time. I knew there was an encounter with a whale at the end of the book. I felt impatient about getting there. I set the book down.

I thought of a time when I sat on the roof of my Civic with Robert.

"Where do you think we go when we die?" I asked him.

"Well," he said. "Maybe there is something else that remains, and it's not our body and it's not our ego. That's possible. It might be wonderful to escape all this."

New York was unusually quiet, like it was some holiday I didn't know about. It was like all the garbage and delivery trucks were waiting, anticipating, sitting on the side of the road having a hot chocolate before they started their crashing.

I also didn't hear any stirring in the house. I was used to the sound of Dennis switching on the radio, hearing the sounds of those strings playing on NPR, the host of *Morning Edition* talking in his calm voice about the readiness of nuclear warheads in a foreign country.

And then there would be the rattling of kibbles in a metal bowl, and Farfle whining about how they weren't coming out of the bag fast enough, then the sound of Dennis quieting him, "There, there, my liege, we must assemble our forces. We must be patient."

But there was nothing. I looked at my phone to see that it was indeed the morning, and that the illumination slanting through the window wasn't the blaring lights of some film shooting its edgy romantic confession scene in our industrial neighborhood.

No, it was morning. And it was silent. It was the silence I had so dearly wanted, but now it was unnerving.

I opened my bedroom door slowly, quietly, afraid I might be stepping out into Day One of a zombie invasion. I looked to the left down the hall at the put-upon piano. If it was indeed a regiment of soldiers as I often thought, it was a lost regiment, abandoned by their own country, considered an acceptable loss, interred in a mass grave without even a stone cross on top.

I walked to the kitchen. No one was there. I was afraid now that in any crevice of the house I was going to find Dennis's dead body, and Farfle cowering in fear next to him. But that wouldn't be what Farfle would do. He would, with all respect, chew off a bit of Dennis's face, get bored of that, and find a way to get down the fire escape.

Dennis's bedroom door was open a crack. I tried to push it open more, but it wouldn't budge.

I gathered my voice for an announcement.

"Dennis?" I called. "Hello?"

I pushed the door harder and it skidded open on the carpet. His room, which I had never looked in before, was exactly as I imagined it would be. Magazines and tissues and old mugs stacked all around. But he wasn't in there.

Now I was confused. I couldn't imagine what scenario would bring Dennis and dog out of the apartment with no notice. Was this my fault? How much had been towed away the night before?

I walked back to my bedroom to find a pink Post-it note stuck on the door that I hadn't noticed before.

Hello, this is Dennis's son George. Dennis had a heart failure last night and we took him to the hospital where he passed away at 12:30. I came back to take the dog to be with us. If you have questions please call me. We'll have to clean out and transfer the apartment, but you'll likely be able to stay until the end of the month if you need.

The morning broke over the river. Now, suddenly, the garbage trucks had woken up and were battling in the streets. People were honking their horns in a recitation of Brahms. I sat down on my bed and thought about all the gold rushing toward us from supernova explosions.

Small things. Small things. Keep it small.

16.
The Bell

THE DINER EARLY THE NEXT MORNING was brighter than it had any right to be. Someone had polished every corner of every chrome object, and now that I noticed it, everything in the diner was chrome.

All the waitresses looked different. It was like they had all been replaced by stunt doubles, as if a supernova explosion were about to hit the diner.

I started to think I was causing destruction all around me. As I danced with the Queen of the Night—maybe at that exact moment—Dennis's heart had stopped. I was being punished for reaching out for beauty. Maybe if someone else had stood up at that party to dance with her first I would have gone straight home and saved a life.

The bell over the door rang.

I opened my eyes.

Somehow *she* stepped in. The Queen of the Night. The girl with the leopard pants and bunny slippers.

Except now she was in a nice overcoat, with a red dress poking out of it. I could tell that she, like me, had stayed up through the night. She brought with her a whirlwind of laughter and dancing and music. As soon as she saw me, she quieted it all.

I stood up and faced her. She walked up to me and didn't say a word.

This would have been the time to ask me what I was doing there. In New York, in that diner, on the same physical plane. I suppose I should have asked her what she was doing there, but I didn't want to ruin the secret.

The bell above the door rang again and a man in an unbuttoned white collared shirt walked in. He was holding something wrapped in foil, in the shape of a swan. He looked at the room all around him before he turned his attention to the Queen of the Night.

"Hey," she said to this companion of hers with whom she had just shared a much more exciting evening than I had experienced. Then, with a thumb in my direction like we were old friends, "This guy was at the party last night."

The man reached out his hand for mine.

"James," he said.

I didn't know what to say. What even was my name? I took a stab at something.

"Ian," I said.

Yes. That was it.

This man James stood like he was pulled skyward by some American approximation of nobility. His chestnut hair was ruffled, and it looked like you could keep ruffling it for ages and it would always be charming in its dishevelment. He was a good-looking man in a way that made me suspicious. What kind of rejection had he ever faced in his life? My heart (not that we're going to start comparing hearts) was a canyon shaped by the pain of people saying no to me. What canyons did the heart of someone like *that* contain? Was there a canyon in there? If not, how could anyone else have any room to get inside it?

"Hitomi," James said, turning to her. "Sweetheart. The city is full of wild horses. We have to be careful."

"Or," she said, "we can saddle them up and ride them."

"We can't ride them all," he said.

Daveed came out of the kitchen and greeted his friends. Somehow I was surprised to see him, even though this was where he worked. There we were, the four of us. The unslept, the Ones Who Walk Straight Through the Night.

"Hey, homies," Daveed said.

"Hey," James said. "How are you?"

"Rough morning," Daveed said. "But I'm all good with Sal for getting the time off."

"Oh good," James said. "Well, we're kind of screwed. Andrew can't do the tour."

"What?"

"Yeah. He just told me. Do you know anyone else we can ask who plays bass?"

Daveed looked at me, and so did Hitomi and James. I looked at everyone like I was a raccoon caught rummaging through garbage cans. Suddenly the random dots of ink formed a picture. Hitomi, the Queen of the Night, was the singer in Daveed's band. The voice I had listened to on that long walk through Central Park was the same person I danced with at the party, was the same person standing in front of me right then. But.

"Ian plays keyboard," Daveed said. "I think he'd be great."

"Okay, but," said James, "what are we now, the Doors?"

"Maybe it could open things up if we didn't have bass and added some Wurly," Daveed said. "Maybe he could handle some of the bass lines with his left hand. If he's willing. But he says he has to stay in New York and write."

They were talking about me like we were at a parent-teacher conference and I had bitten a girl on the playground.

"Write?" asked James. Suddenly he had been sold on my participation in the band and was angry I wasn't already in the group photos. "What are you going to write? A novel or something? Who's going to read that? You want to be on a stage playing music. Don't you know that there's no future in writing?"

"Man, leave him alone," Daveed said.

"You have to live a life first," James said. "They say it takes twenty-one days of experience for every page you end up writing. You should consider it an investment in your future. And a gift from us to you."

I wanted to tell these people that a man had just died in my apartment last night. That he stepped through a prism and turned into a beam of light. That my car was swept up by a misunderstood dash. That a little dog who wanted nothing more than to walk the streets of Brooklyn was fretting in a lonely tower somewhere.

And where would I even start with Robert?

The bell above the door rang again. We all turned to look at who walked in, as though it would be some *deus* who would *machina* this situation into a resolution.

Instead it was a sweet lady with white hair and a soft smile who looked overwhelmed to see four strangers confronting her at the door. One of the stunt double waitresses intervened to hand her a menu and usher her to a booth.

"Look, I'm sorry I brought it up," Daveed said. "Not everyone loves to go on tour."

"You don't want to come on tour with us?" Hitomi asked. Here she turned her head and raised her voice in a way that I'm sure she was aware could get an ocean liner to take a perfect right angle turn. "This city is on fire. Come with us! See the frontier before it's gone!"

I hadn't said anything to any of these people so far except for my name, which now for the first time in my life felt like the wrong name for me, something I'd have to change right away. I'd have to petition a judge to give me some other name that fit me better. I'd have to give away my books and throw that stupid clay pot in the garbage. A week after returning to the city, I would go on tour with a band, back into the furnace of music. For what? To do what exactly? To try to get closer to a woman who appeared to already have a boyfriend? That would be the most irresponsible thing I could ever do.

None of that mattered. I don't know if I said anything at all. I don't know if there was anything to say, but of course I would have to go on tour. Of course.

17.
The Ship

"HITOMI IS QUITE A SINGER," I said to James as we drove up to Yonkers. At rehearsal that day, Hitomi told us to play like we were on fire.

"She can sing, yes," James said. "That's what brings us together and brings us to Yonkers. The lengths that we will go to . . ."

The Bronx Zoo blurred past us at highway speeds, zebras and lions all blended in a menagerie.

"Are you—" I started. "Are you guys . . . ?"

"What?" He knew, but he wanted me to ask.

"Are you guys a couple?"

"A couple of what?"

I sighed.

"Jesus," he said. "I didn't mean to upset you. We've been together almost two years. She is—"

Here I felt like he could say almost anything. *She is a lighthouse. She is the first snowfall. She is a ringing bell. She is a split cedar. She is a hem of a satin sheet, smoothed out by the warm press of an iron.*

"She is quite a singer," he said.

In Yonkers we knocked on a door where a man answered while a small dog yapped behind him. What portal had I slipped through, ending up back at such a place again?

The man's name was Bill. He seemed neither happy nor upset to see us, but he definitely wanted it known that he was a musician.

"Here, I'll show you *Cassandra,*" he said.

Cassandra was the name of a Chevy conversion van, and in those five words he displayed a captivating Long Island accent, one of those accents that turns the word into "Cassandrer," with that extra er on the end. You'd think regional accents would dry up as we all try to emulate neutral diction, but then you open a door in Yonkers and find *this*.

Something about the name he gave the van told me Bill didn't want to part with her. So much harder to let go of something once you've gendered and named her.

Bill took us outside, showed us the trick to opening the side door: push in first and then pull. It was as big as a gymnasium in there, enough room to house five people and still play a good game of hide-and-go-seek.

"Can we take her for a ride?" James asked.

Adopting that pronoun showed Bill we would take care of his girl. The three of us jumped in. James looked so proud to be in the driver's seat. He adjusted the mirror and eased her out of her spot.

"Hoo!" he said as he coaxed *Cassandra* down the tree-lined streets of Yonkers.

"She's never had any major problems," Bill said. "I have all the paperwork here in the glove compartment. I've gotten her oil changed before the 3,000 mile mark every single time, and I always replace everything they recommend."

He wasn't quite saying this like he was selling us on the van. He was saying it like he was presenting a litany of reasons why he should be allowed to keep her.

"The gas mileage isn't great. There's a lot of play in that steering wheel, so be careful."

"I've driven big commercial trucks before," said James.

We circled the block and arrived back at the parking spot. James gave a baffled look when he put it in reverse and tried to figure out how to tell where the back end of the van was and how close it was to hitting the Peugeot behind us.

"She's not as big as you think," Bill said. "You'll be surprised what kind of spaces she can fit into."

"A miracle of science," James said. He hit the curb with the back tire, and we were all glad he hadn't just crushed a Peugeot and initiated a complicated insurance claim.

He managed to right the vessel and put it into park.

"Well," James said, "I think this'll do. You said $3,200, right?"

Bill was in shock. "Um, yeah. But if you have cash . . ."

"I've got it right here," James said, not one to negotiate at such an auspicious time. He pulled an envelope out of his jacket pocket. "Should be all there."

"Okay," Bill said.

He took a full minute counting it, poor Bill, and I could tell his mind was only half-focused on the currency moving through his fingers.

"Okay, seems right," Bill said, putting the money back in the envelope.

"You'll just need to sign the title and then that should be that," Bill said. He was searching for some way to stall.

"You mind if I use your restroom?" James said. "It's going to be a bit of time before we get home again."

He looked at me in the backseat.

"Yeah, me too," I said.

This was one small gesture of kindness on James's part, giving Bill some time alone with his love.

"Door's unlocked," Bill said. "Don't mind the dog. Go right in. I'll wait here with my girl."

18.
What Am I Thinking?

I LOOKED UP A PRIVATE DETECTIVE IN CHICAGO. Was that the way forward? I called the number, and as it rang I pictured an old phone in an office in a brick building in Chicago. No, it was probably a cell phone in a strip mall. One of those cellphones in a holster on a belt, an old flip phone so that the detective could flip it open and give a really curt answer like, "Hawthorne here. Talk to me."

Instead it rang and there was a robotic voice saying the voice mailbox was full, and then it clicked off.

What was it Robert had said about the low keys on the piano? They had some secret purpose I still couldn't find. When you are a piano player and you join a rock band, you have to accept you will almost never get to play your actual instrument onstage. You have to find something that approximates a piano but doesn't weigh so much.

Digital keyboards are an understandable attempt, but they are problematic in how perfectly in tune they are. You never get a little wobble in the air when you play octaves that are a few cents shy, you can never coax out weird growls and grumbles by manipulating the hammers and strings in ways that are impossible to notate. It is not something you can play wrong in a pleasing way. If you beat on it, it can only provide the maximum volume an engineer in Japan programmed it to have. You don't want to be at the apex of a song, filled with joy and frustration as you bang out a chord, the audience pulsing with energy, and find that your heights of expression have been circumscribed by an *engineer*. Fortunately, James had a Wurlitzer electric piano I could use on tour.

"Fucking pound on it!" was Daveed's exhortation at the first rehearsal, and I admit I had to start imagining the Wurlitzer as something different from a piano so that I could start beating on it. I thought of it as Robert, dressed in black and white. I punched him in the shoulder for being so stupid as to leave us without saying anything.

"Yeah, man!" Daveed said in agreement.

"Have you ever played What Am I Thinking?" I asked Hitomi after rehearsal.

"No," she said. "Sounds . . . *intrusive.*"

We were on the front steps of a warehouse in Bushwick where the band had a rehearsal space. She had a paper bag with a beer in it.

"It's not intrusive," I said. "Just . . . think of something. Anything. Can be anything at all. And I'll think of something. And, just keep it to yourself. Do you have something?"

"Okay," she said. "Wait . . . okay."

"Okay. Now. Just think of that and I'll think of something and we both count down from three and then say them out loud at the same time. Okay?"

"Okay."

"Ready? Three . . . Count out loud with me . . . Three . . ."

"Three . . ."

"Two . . ." "Two . . ."

"One . . ." "One . . ."

"Ocean!" "Chicken!"

"Okay, great! So I said 'ocean' and you said 'chicken.' Now . . ."

"Did I do it wrong?" she asked.

"No, there's no wrong. The only wrong is if you don't say anything at all. So now, try to think of the thing that's in the middle of 'chicken' and 'ocean.' Like, in whatever way you interpret that. Okay?"

"Okay."

"So, we count down again from three and then both say what we think is in between 'chicken' and 'ocean.' Okay? Three . . ."

"Three . . ."

"Two . . ." "Two . . ."

"One . . ." "One . . ."

"Seagull!" "Seagull!"

We both froze and looked at each other with wide eyes. Then we burst out laughing.

"It usually takes a lot more steps to get to that point," I said. "That's never happened to me before."

"Don't worry," she said. "I won't tell anyone."

Afterward, I texted Robert.

I met someone who reminds me of you.

I know that sounds funny.

It's a woman. She has a boyfriend.

What am I thinking?

I called Melissa and told her that I had somehow joined a band and was on my way back to Valparaiso, or at least Chicago, in a couple of weeks. She said that she would come to the show.

"Robert, too," I said. "If he wants to make himself known again."

She didn't think that was funny.

I wasn't trying to be funny.

19.
Back to the Painting

THE LAST TIME I LOOKED AT *CHRISTINA'S WORLD* I tried to give a name to every shade of green and brown in the field. There was *straw* and *army tent* and *potato sack* and *discarded cocoon*. There were so many colors sprawled out in that field, like a kid was running with a box of crayons and tripped and spilled them everywhere.

I looked at her in that field and thought about how it wasn't beauty that I wanted. At least not in the way most men want beauty. I didn't want the destruction of it. I didn't know what the men in Christina's life had done to her, but they didn't seem to be helping her. Were they just watching her while she struggled?

In beauty I wanted freedom. Beauty seems like a permanent pass to all the rides. A guarantee that you will always be the center of excitement. To be with beauty, to dance with it, to be smiled at by it, to have its approval, would be like merging with the center point of a circle. It is a permanent hug, to dance with beauty. It would solve all the aching and insecurity and wondering why.

Except.

Except that for all the beautiful people I had ever talked to, none of them had ever accepted the premise that they were actually beautiful. And, to the extent that they would allow that they were beautiful in some way, they claimed that it only brought as much trouble, misunderstanding, and danger as anything.

I don't know how Christina would have felt. Or if she would even have considered herself beautiful.

I was about to leave the painting for the last time when five nuns walked up chattering. They were head-to-toe dressed in their habits, but about them was the energy of being off the clock, at play in the great halls of New York.

They all stopped in front of the painting, *my* painting, and enveloped me. They were like a cloud of mist that settles on the glen in the morning, silently, respectfully settling into a dip in the environment. They ceased their talking as soon as they got in position and I felt us all standing there wondering together at the glory of creation. Thirty or forty seconds went by, and I let my focus go soft, and I sank into the painting with them. I saw what they saw, without them even explaining what they saw. For the first time Christina wasn't a tragic soul. She wasn't tossed around by chance. Her longing toward the barn wasn't envy. It was acceptance. She was proud of her struggle. It carved her into a better form of human. It made her a spirit to behold. As she looked at the house and the barn, the nuns and I stood behind her, admiring the torque in her back. We were there with her and we weren't. We *were* Christina after all.

I thought of something I read Andrew Wyeth say in a big book in the gift shop: "I get literally hundreds of letters a year from people saying that it's a portrait of themselves. And they rarely mention the crippled quality. They don't see that."

But I never thought that. I didn't think I was her. I felt like I was standing behind her. The looming angle gives you such a direct feeling that you are there, and you are standing up while she is on the ground. It is such a silent condemnation of the viewer's complicity in the cruelty of the able-bodied.

That woman, the actual woman Christina Olson, dragged herself around the fields because she couldn't use a wheelchair out there. She wouldn't have had a clean dress unless it was new and she had just put it on, if it was a special occasion like her birthday.

So maybe that's why I liked the painting. Maybe it was a little celebration in a field in Maine, and in the midst of that, she was looking with hope up at the farmhouse because no matter what, she still had to crawl along that entire field, negotiate the divots and the burrs, try to hold onto some dignity in her pink dress.

All the hours I spent looking at that painting I had never looked at it with such hope. I wanted to thank the nuns for seeing the painting this way, but I didn't want to break the holy silence. I tried to hold it as long as I could.

Then one of them gathered herself, turned to the others, and said, "So. Where's the cafeteria?"

20.
The Launch

OMINOUS CLOUDS HUNG OVERHEAD as we prepared to leave New York. The late September air held on to summer for one more day, for us.

I wished I could have scratched Farfle's head once more and told him it would be okay, but I hoped he would understand. I walked over to Hitomi and James's place and passed the video store with the curtained-off porn section that Dennis so loved.

Hitomi's face had a Japanese touch to it, but in certain shades of light or shadow that quality would disappear. I couldn't tell if her name made me see that in her more.

Hit-oh-me. I liked to hold her name in my head, three syllables with the tip of the tongue on the teeth in the middle. I liked that it started with *hit* and ended with *me*.

I got to their apartment to find James in the midst of packing. Everyone's instruments were out on the sidewalk like they were being catalogued.

"This isn't as bad as it looks," James said. "All we have to do is get all of *this* in *there*."

I stood there wearing my backpack and holding my copy of *Moby-Dick* close to my chest, with the title sticking out, like I was some proud schoolboy on the first day.

"Ah," James said. "You have the band textbook, I see. Extra credit for you."

I looked at the book, having forgotten I was holding it.

"Does the band like this book?" I asked.

"Uh," James said. "Isn't it obvious?"

He opened up his hand, but I didn't get his meaning.

He dropped his hand.

"Have you not read it yet?" he asked.

"No," I said. "I'm just starting."

"What a coincidence, then."

"What do you mean?"

Hitomi stepped up to the van, holding a cup of coffee. As the sunlight hit her I could see that she had cut off all her hair. Every black strand with the silver threads running through it, all gone. I thought of a meadow near my house where I used to play capture the flag that had long ago been turned into the Rolling Meadows Housing Subdivision or something.

"Di-*saster,*" she said as she looked at all the instruments on the ground.

"No, no," James said. "Disasters are when something blows up. This is going the opposite direction."

Hitomi set her coffee on the sidewalk and stretched her back and we both watched as James pieced together the puzzle. All of Daveed's drums, the amps, the guitars, the keyboards, he managed to fit them all in the van in a five-minute spree of spatial navigation.

"This is the Wurlitzer," he said as he put the last piece in place. "I put it in a soft case to save some room. Be careful with it."

There was maybe three quarters of an inch left for him to close the doors.

"There!" he said and then ran around to the driver's seat. "Shall we pick up Daveed?"

"Did you leave the spare key?" Hitomi asked as he put the van into drive.

"Pretty sure," he said as he stopped to think. "Yes. Maybe. Let me go check."

He put the van back into park and jumped out. Hitomi looked back at me, nestled in the middle seat, still with New York all over me.

"Whatcha reading?" she asked.

I showed her the cover.

"Oh God," she said, turning away from me.

"What?"

"Nothing. You don't *have* to read that, you know."

"What?" I asked. "Are *you* reading something?"

"Yeah," she said. "It's a book about the color blue. It's the kind of book you can jump in and read anywhere, which, even though I've probably read it seven times, I still come across new parts."

James burst out of the apartment in a joyous exaggerated run that was maybe half for our benefit, and he almost ran into an old man walking his dog. James stopped on a dime and gave a bow as the man shuffled past.

"Are you sure you want to do this with us?" Hitomi asked as she turned back to look at me.

The answer was *no, I am not sure*. I looked at her face. She looked like she had been up all night, like she was always up all night. I couldn't picture her ever sleeping quietly. But there was nowhere else for me to go. I had no car and no apartment.

"I am committed to being your keyboardist," I said as I put my hand on my heart, thinking that had a noble, military sound to it.

"So inspiring," she said as she turned forward.

James jumped in and we drove to Daveed's apartment and sat there double-parked, waiting for him to emerge. James stood on the running board and leaned out, surveying the day in Brooklyn. He held his cup of coffee in his hand. The light all around him was a pale yellow.

"The fool brings nothing," James said. "And the more we learn, the more we think we need. Isn't that something."

Hitomi closed her eyes and whispered to herself, "Don't say it."

"We forget there are plenty of provisions out there in the world," James said. "All the same things we have at home. We don't have to cross every t and get every bag of every kind of chip. They have toothpaste in Pennsylvania. They have earbuds in Ohio."

The van's hazard lights flashed, as though they provided some permanent "Get Out of Jail Free" card for any traffic violation we could incur.

"But it's hard to remember," he said as he looked back at me. "There is more abundance here than any other place in the history of Earth."

I nodded the most imperceptible nod.

Now he pitched his words to the random people walking down the sidewalk.

"There is nothing to worry about. Trust in that abundance. Strangers will be so kind to us every day. They will say, 'Here. We don't know what to do with all this stuff. Please use it.'"

Daveed came out of his apartment with a big black duffel bag so overstuffed he couldn't even close the zippers. He placed the bag at the foot of the van, right there in the street, and held his finger up, letting us know he either needed one more minute or he had to get one more toothbrush.

James continued.

"One day I'll pack nothing but a pair of socks and a knife, and feel satisfied I didn't overburden myself."

Daveed came back with something in a plastic bag. He tried to shove that in his duffel bag, which wasn't having it, and then he picked up everything and brought it into the van.

"Let's do this!" he said as James revved the engine to take off.

I looked at the back of Hitomi's head as it bobbled with every bump of Brooklyn's streets. I opened my new store-bought notebook and wrote down one line:

We are all looking to find the water because we are all on fire.

I felt carsick already and closed the book. I looked in the rearview mirror and saw Hitomi writing in her spiral-bound notebook. I suppose she didn't have the same weakness as me.

I was grateful for the stunning views of our escape from the city. Every garbage truck pulled back its mandibles to let us through. Every old woman pulled her cart onto the sidewalk as we came trundling past.

Crowds of kids ran up to an ice cream truck in front of us, and for a minute they ran in stride with our van. It was like they knew we had something sweet to offer. We had joy, too. We had wonder. I watched one boy as his head turned toward us. He locked eyes with me, though what he really must have seen was his own reflection in our tinted windows. He looked timeless, like he knew everything there was to know, like from that moment on he'd only be told to forget the important things. I wanted to say something to him but figured it would be too shocking if I slid open the lower part of the window and shouted to him, "Trust yourself!"

We peeled off from them and slipped under the stream of a fire truck's hose. I was glad we were headed out into the world, where Robert was. It gave me something to look for along the way. You never knew where he could be. Maybe he would be on the New Jersey Turnpike, on the side of the road near Cheyenne, or out on the edge of the California coast.

We climbed over the Verrazano-Narrows Bridge, up and up to the mysterious outlands.

PART TWO

21.
Edison Township

"WE HAVE AN ANNOUNCEMENT TO MAKE," James said. "Me and Hitomi. Hitomi and I."

We were standing outside the Edison Museum, a house in New Jersey with an exhibit of phonograph and wax cylinder players, the beginnings of recorded sound and—when you think about it—the whole record industry that roped people like us onto its cascading seas, which maybe wasn't the miracle everyone made it out to be. Maybe it was a bit of devilry that inevitably led to selling out your love songs for air fresheners.

Hitomi looked at James, not with love, not with the beaming face of someone who had just gotten engaged. She looked at him like she was watching a kid apologize to the neighbors for breaking their window.

"We have ended our relationship," James said.

Everyone stood still.

"Look," he said. "I know you're probably worried this band has gone from the Doors to Fleetwood Mac. But this is all very amicable. We won't let it affect the tour. It was a long time coming."

Hitomi kept looking at him.

"I mean, not *that* long," he said. "I'm just saying, we considered it, and last night we decided we should just make a clean break before the tour."

Daveed and I looked down at our feet.

"You are both free to hate us," he said. "I just. Come on, let's just get to the first fucking show."

22.
Delaware

It was already like New York had never happened. Slanted, flaming-bright New York was not a place. Christina was a dream. Every pivot of every dancer with noble arms practicing in every walk-up apartment was a cloud that would change shape in a minute. Even Hitomi and James as a single entity was now erased. It was a relief to leave it all behind, but then I remembered that I didn't really have anything in New York I was leaving behind. Everything had been whisked away or had died.

See the frontier before it's gone, indeed.

Before you get to the frontier, though, you have to cross through Delaware. They don't tell you that in the movies.

We didn't intend to go through Delaware. It didn't come up on our maps. It wasn't any sort of consideration, some group decision, "Hey, let's make a stop in Delaware." We thought we were on a bridge that was going to take us to Philadelphia, a great arcing rainbow of a bridge that would touch us down on the other side. But as we got to the toll booth at the end of it, the man there said, in complete earnestness, but almost like he was taunting us, "Welcome to Delaware."

"Aw, Christ," James said. "How did we fuck this up?"

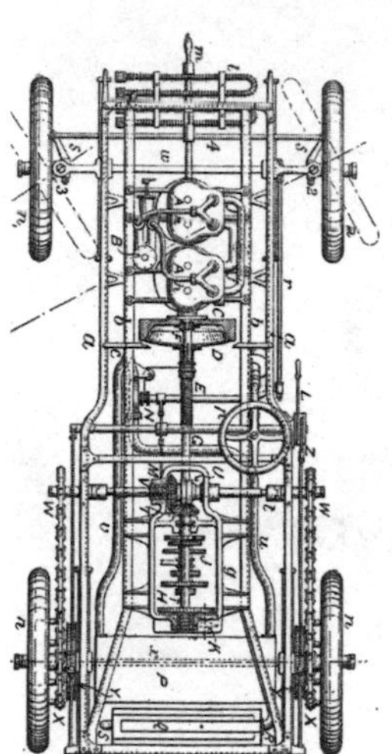

23. Philadelphia

"THERE'S A DEAD BODY IN THE BATHROOM."

I wasn't trying to be dramatic.

The rest of the band were looking at their phones in the green room. Not a green room, really. More of a green storage closet. A tiny room that stored bottles of chemicals and a dirty mop. A room you could also squeeze a band into while they were waiting to play on a tiny stage in a tiny bar in Philadelphia called The Fire. All over the walls were stickers of past bands, scraped off and stickered over again, like the bones of the explorers who came through there and didn't make it.

"What?" James asked, looking up from his phone.

"I mean. I *think*. I think there's a dead guy in the bathroom," I said.

They did not look alarmed. They looked at me like they were looking at a farm boy from Indiana who had never been on tour, who had never been to a real city where real things happen, and just because some stranger in the bathroom wasn't smiling at me and saying "Howdy," *I* thought it meant he must be dead.

"Let's go see!" Daveed said as he jumped up.

"Report back," James said as he went back to his phone. Hitomi kept writing in her journal.

Instead of band stickers, the walls of the bathroom were covered in crude, ignorant phrases, and rebuttals of those phrases. It was a true palimpsest, a living document that changes as the current prominent figures of the culture change.

I pointed to the stall and whispered to Daveed, "He's in there," like I was trying not to wake up a dead guy.

Daveed surveyed the scene: a motionless leg in black denim poking out of the stall. Through the crack in the door you could see the guy sitting on the toilet, head slumped over.

"You alright in there, man?" Daveed asked as he knocked on the door.

No response.

"Should we poke him with a mop?" I asked.

"Nah," he said. "Give me a sec."

Daveed scrambled to get on top of the sink. This poor sink that already had such a sad life now had to support the weight of Detective Daveed as he got an aerial look at the scene. He somehow balanced himself on it as I put my arms out to maybe catch him or the sink if it all came tumbling down. I pictured broken ceramic and water gushing everywhere as I cradled him in my arms and said, "I got you."

Above his head in white on the black bathroom wall was a drawing of a big dick with dotted lines coming out of it. A petroglyph speaking to us through the veil of time. What was it trying to tell us? Was it a symbol of fertility? Did it speak of the enduring life flowing through humanity's phallus? I peered closer and saw just this one word written next to it:

HILARY

Daveed stood up and looked over the top of the stall, then back at me and then back in the stall.

"Yo, dude!" he said as he rattled the door. "Stop being dead, okay?!"

Stop being dead. That's what he said. This champion of the fires of DUMBO shouted through the heavy curtain of death and into the Dream Land. It startled me so much that I jumped back, but, remembering the state of the walls, I kept my body a quarter of an inch away from any surface.

The man in the stall moved slightly, ever so gently roused from his opiate dream.

"He's alive," Daveed said as he jumped down. "Did you need to crap, or—"

"No, I'm fine," I said.

"Well good, he might take a while to get out of there."

We all gathered onstage in that bar, a Tashtego for the first time in the wild. After my inability to determine whether someone was dead or in an opiate dream, my confidence was teetering. I used to think the distinction between the living and dead was so clear.

We had moments in the Bushwick rehearsal space where the band seemed we might be able to, as Hitomi requested, play like we were on fire, but I didn't know if we could do that at will, even in a bar that was named The Fire.

Hitomi took a shot of tequila and told us she wanted us to play something sad and blue. "But not *the* blues," she said. "Just sad and sexy."

I looked at James. James looked back at me. "You heard her," he said. "Five-dollar fine if you play the blues."

The idea was that we'd start every show with something improvised while Hitomi read a new poem, but there's the idea of something and then the actual doing of it. How did it actually, you know, *work?*

We looked at Daveed to start. He closed his eyes and clicked off a tempo. We joined in.

I noticed that on the side of the stage was an old curtain printed with lilies. Hitomi held out her journal and read a page. Thank God I remembered to set my phone to record it. In transcribing it now, I'll have to guess at the punctuation and line breaks based off the pauses she left.

a body
is a collection of habits
the muscles, the knots, the scars
I am only the average of
what I have done
my body is a history of failures
which were not accepted

And then we moved on to the songs. I looked into the audience and saw one guy staring at Hitomi, staring at her the way *I* probably stared at her, except that he looked pale and sad and from a separate dimension, whereas I surely looked noble and brave in my admiration of her.

We are all humbled by our desires, feeling ourselves suddenly lacking this thing we never knew existed. It cuts us and we want more.

It did make me realize that I wasn't going to be scrutinized by the audience while playing in this band. Everyone would be entirely focused on Hitomi. Looking at the guy in the audience, I wondered if he was the dead guy from the bathroom, woken from his eternal peace by Daveed.

Then, before I knew it, a resolution to the set, applause, and a curtain that would have closed triumphantly were it not pinned to the wall.

"Ian, this is Tom," Hitomi shouted at me over the metal band that was playing after us, destroying our little tea party. "He fought in the Gulf War."

The man blushed and looked down. This was not the dude in the crowd who had looked enraptured, nor the dead dude from the bathroom, just to keep tally of the dudes who were numerous this night and every night.

"Well, you did!" she yelled.

Hitomi leaned in to listen to him for a few seconds. On the bar for some reason was a corsage of pink carnations, the stems wrapped like a ballerina's feet. Hitomi turned back to me to relay what Tom had told her. She leaned into my ear so close I could feel her lips touch it.

"Tom says," she said. I could feel her smile on my ear as she realized how close she was, and then she gathered herself for the subject matter. "This guy's name is Tom, by the way. Tom says he wishes he could forget some things he's seen. Or he wishes his eyes could forget. But really. Don't we all feel that way?"

I smiled and nodded, thinking if I shouted even one word I wouldn't have a voice the next day. Hitomi went back to talk to Tom. James was now standing next to me, and he leaned in to my other ear.

"I miss her already," James said. "What did she say to you?"

I looked at Hitomi, three feet away.

"She says," I said. "She says she misses you, too."

"Liar."

"She says she forgets who you are."

"Shut up."

"She says it's gonna be okay."

"Really?"

And then, I heard a laugh.

A familiar laugh from across the room. A proud, knowing, warm, generous laugh. It cut through the metal music and bashful war heroes and everything else swirling in The Fire. I cocked my head and looked around for the source. Surely Robert was there. Surely he had come to surprise me at the first show of tour.

I stepped away from the bar. All around me were a bunch of non-Roberts, inelegant and unintelligent. But that laugh.

It was a laugh at six fireflies all turning off at once. It was a laugh at silly race car drivers' names. It was a laugh with a chin. A chinny laugh, comforting and confident in its every utterance.

I walked around, looking for the person laughing this laugh. I found a corner booth where a man was sitting and holding a glass of beer. He was smiling and his cheeks were red, but he had a sloping, mediocre chin. He laughed again and now I heard that his laugh was quite different. Somehow it had gotten distorted in the din of the bar into something that I desperately wanted to hear. Now his conversation and laughing stopped. This was not Robert.

This is the pain of missing those who are gone: They are not fully gone. They are nipping at the edge of your awareness. They are coyotes looking for scraps. Their laughter is bouncing off the stickered, black walls of depressing bars in Philadelphia. Every bad thing you come across in your day, every sleeping opiate user, every dead animal on the side of the turnpike is something you want to tell them about to relieve your sadness. But every good thing, every successful first show, every celebration is something you want to share with them, too. And then, cruelest of all, a mixture of frequencies creates the exact sound and rhythm of a laugh that you would exchange every word in *Moby-Dick* and all the other books in existence to see fully embodied by the actual person.

I slipped outside into the alley, caught my breath, and texted Robert:

Stop being dead, okay?

24. Fettuccine Cortado

"What if I told you," James half whispered to me as I was carrying an amp while stepping over a baby gate, "that we can only really afford one hotel room for the band this whole tour? Like, one night, one room, that's it. Where would you think that hotel should be?"

I had cleared the baby gate with the first leg and now had to find a way to set my second foot down without stepping on a plastic castle.

"Um," I said. "I guess, the desert?"

"Exactly!" James said. "*You* get it. Explain that to Hitomi."

We were in the tenement apartment of someone James knew from college who was already asleep and would leave the next morning before we woke up.

"We'll take the bedroom," James said to me and Daveed as we got into the living room.

They were both gone in a swirl of wind, and it was just Daveed and me, alone in a strange apartment.

"Didn't they just break up today?" Daveed asked.

Around us were framed photos of happy people. People we didn't know and would never know. I thought of the gravestones in the Woodlawn Cemetery.

"It's funny how much you can do in a day and not be tired," I said to him as we prepared our humble beds on the floor, "and then other days you do nothing and you're exhausted."

From the other room I heard Hitomi and James arguing. I couldn't understand most of the words.

"Bah-bah, bah-bah, RIGHT THERE!"

And then:

"Buh-buh BAH BAH BAH BAH, I KNOW!"

This might become unbearable. To lie there in the Philadelphia darkness, hearing them arguing on the other side of the wall. I don't know why I thought the tour would be a good idea.

"Are you still awake?" I asked.

"Yup," Daveed said.

"Let's play a game."

"Okay."

"Okay," I said. "Your race car driver name is, um . . . a noodle. And an espresso drink."

"Wow. Okay. How about—" He laughed. "Fettuccine Cortado?" he said.

"That's good!" I said. "That's so good. Okay, mine is . . . Linguine Breve."

The muffled conversation in the next room died down. And then, like a rising drawbridge letting in a parade of boats, Hitomi laughed. It was a melodic laugh going up and down the scale, dancing around and tickling the ribs of a curious creature.

Then a silence.

"I lost my best friend," I said to Daveed. I had never said it like that before.

"What do you mean?" he asked.

"He disappeared a couple of weeks ago, and I don't know where he is."

"What?" He sat up. "Were there any warning signs?"

"No. He would drink. But. No, lots of people drink. I guess he was emotional. Emotionally volatile. But, who isn't? He was also sweet. I've just felt frozen since it happened."

"I can't even imagine what that would be like. Are the police helping?"

"I wish there was someone other than police who could help," I said. "They're always looking for bad people. Robert wasn't a bad person."

"Private detective?"

"Isn't that the same thing? I wish there was someone in a white robe who could just walk through the forest with their arms stretched out and gather him up and bring him back."

"Yeah. Maybe Google that?"

I laughed.

Daveed turned over and I saw his hands illuminated by the streetlight outside. They had wild designs on them, like a language I didn't understand.

"What do you have tattooed on your hands?" I asked.

"Protections."

"What do you mean?"

"They're just symbols I made up to feel safe. I never felt safe as a kid. Do you have any tattoos?"

"Just one," I said.

That story would have led to a discussion of Robert, which I wasn't ready for. He sensed my hesitance and left it there.

"It's funny," Daveed said. "I was talking to this priest tonight."

"There was a priest at the bar tonight?"

"Outside, yeah. And I told him what I was interested in doing with my life and how I like listening to people's problems and he told me I should go to divinity school."

"Yeah, but," I said, "a priest *would* say that, wouldn't he?"

"Yeah, I guess."

It was all quiet in this weird apartment, except for a struggle in the kitchen that sounded like maybe the ice machine was working on its thesis paper.

"What if . . ." I started.

". . . What?" Daveed said.

"What if . . ."

Silence from the next room.

"I don't know if I can finish that sentence," I said. "Just: What if."

"Good question," he said. "You can leave it at that."

"Thank you, Fettuccine."

He laughed.

"What were you?" he asked. "Scungille?"

"No. But maybe I should be."

I pulled out my phone and texted Robert.

Thank you for all the games.

I'm sorry if I ever resisted them.

25. The Mütter

The Mütter Museum of Medical Oddities was waiting for us the next morning, an old building in downtown Philadelphia full of specimens of human deformities.

"Are we gonna do, like, a museum a day?" Daveed asked.

"We're just getting them out of the way while we still have energy," James said. "This time next week we won't care about anything."

Inside there were rows of skulls hanging in wood and glass cases all down the walls.

"This place is making me have my period," Hitomi said.

I thought this was a metaphor at first.

"There's just so much suffering in here," she said. "It really opens the floodgates."

Not a metaphor.

"Do you need to leave?" I asked.

"No, let's keep going."

We stared at a display of Madame Dimanche, a.k.a. the Widow Sunday, a French woman from the 19th century who had a horn growing out of her head. The horn was not centered or graceful like a unicorn's horn. It was ten inches long, black and brown, and—I'm sorry for this description—it looked like a demon had roosted inside Madame Dimanche's skull, turned around, and started taking a shit.

Hitomi whispered to me, "God, that looks like—"

"I know," I said.

"Where the fuck is the bathroom?" Hitomi asked. "Do they have a bathroom? Or are we supposed to suffer too?"

She asked an attendant and he pointed her to go downstairs. I watched her descend slowly, holding her purse close to her as though one of the skeletons might reach out and grab it.

I thought of Dennis, his hunched-over body, his straight white hair. I thought of his wit, his sharpness, his desire to turn something into a joke even as he could barely move his body. I looked around for a suggestion box, a place to nominate skeletons for the display.

After a few minutes I walked down the stairs and ran into Hitomi again.

"The bathrooms are normal here," she whispered.

"What were you expecting?" I asked.

"I don't know," she said. "It's just so weird to walk in there and see a hand dryer and a soap dispenser. I expected them to be full of blood and skin."

"Did it feel safe?"

"I don't know."

"Listen," I said. "I wonder if you can help me with something."

"What is it?"

"I don't even know how to say it."

"What is it?"

"I just. I lost someone."

"Oh," she said. "Right, your housemate died, right?"

"Yes. But not him."

"There's more?"

"It's not like that. It's not someone who's dead. I just. I know this will sound strange, but—"

We had walked down to the basement. At the very back there was a large jar filled with formaldehyde, and inside of it was the fetus of a two-headed boy. A single light illuminated it with a yellow glow.

"My friend Robert," I said. "He disappeared a few days before I met you. And—"

The eyes of the fetus were closed so tightly, like it was still trying to shut out the cruel daylight and have one more minute of sleep in the womb.

"You kind of remind me of him," I said.

Hitomi looked at the jar, the two heads sharing one body. Then she looked up at me.

"Are you about to propose to me?" she asked.

"What? No!"

"I was kidding," she said. "I'm sorry. It just occurred to me that this would be a terrible place to propose to someone."

I realized I had no idea what I was asking. Was I asking her to put on a blazer and talk about Joni Mitchell? What did I want from her?

"I just wanted you to know that, I guess," I said.

"Thank you for telling me," she said. "It'll be okay. Let's—Jesus, let's get out of here."

26.
Entwined

A TEXT FROM HITOMI IN THE FRONT SEAT OF THE VAN as we rolled through Pennsylvania:

Sorry about your friend. I didn't mean to be callous. Just all the fetuses in jars, you know.

I stared at the back of her head. She made no indication she was texting me, like we had a little secret. James was explaining how GPS worked and why it could never truly locate everyone, because of Heisenberg.

And then another text from Hitomi: *Or is it fetii?*

I texted back: *We can go back there if you want?*

No! she texted. *Just. Shh.*

"You can't expect technology to solve every miracle," James said.

"What are you talking about?" Hitomi asked as she put down her phone.

"I think you're asking too much of our robot friends."

"You're telling *me* this?"

"You're always looking at that thing like it's going to solve some riddle for you."

"I think you're thinking of yourself."

"Which one am I again?"

"Look. Can we just have a detente?" Hitomi asked.

"What's a detente?" he asked.

"Like a peace agreement," she said. "A truce. Let's hold it together until Austin."

Daveed and I said from the back seat, almost in unison, "What happens in Austin?"

"There's—nothing," James said, looking back at us. "Look. Alright. Mary Cornish said she'd come to our show."

"Who's Mary Cornish?" we asked, again in unison.

"She's a booking agent," James said. "She books bands. Bands you've heard of. Don't make me name them."

"She's willing to watch our show," Hitomi said, "and if she likes us, she'll book us. And if she books us, then we can have real tours. No offense, James. But. We can have real tours and we won't have to go play shitty shows. Or the shitty shows we play won't be the fault of someone in the van I can yell at."

James looked at Hitomi. The idea of Mary Cornish, savior of our band, now hung above the hood of our Chevy, an ever-receding image we would drive toward until our glorious communion in Austin. Mary Cornish, who could no doubt send one email and get us gigs without metal bands and dead bodies in the bathroom, who could get us on a tour with *that* band, whoever that was. She could do it all, if we just got to Austin. But we couldn't just drive straight down to Texas right then, because we needed to loop around the whole country, because even Ulysses had to meet a bunch of seductresses and homunculuses before he could return to see his dog die and his wife move on to other suitors.

Or was it *homunculi?*

"Hey, can you plug my phone in?" I asked Hitomi.

"Sure," she said.

She went back to writing in her notebook. I looked at my phone as it now sat on top of Hitomi's in the center console, bumping along together with the bumps in the Pennsylvania Turnpike. They were having quite a conjugal moment. If I were touching Hitomi right then the way my phone was touching hers—

Hitomi whipped around and interrupted my gaze.

"Guess what?" she said.

"What?"

"You're now in the band," she said.

"What was I before?"

"You were *theoretically* in the band, but until we played our first show, it wasn't really for sure. But now Philadelphia happened and it's done. You're in the band."

"Might I still screw it up?" I asked.

"I guess you could."

Hitomi looked over at our phones for the first time and saw what I had seen, that this electronic copulation was almost pornographic. They were protected by hard plastic, but they were still entwined. She looked at them in their writhing and seemed to consider the propriety of it, out there in the daylight of the turnpike. Should she let these creatures have their perverted copulation? She could've intervened, a great, judgmental god looking at her creation and cracking down with a lightning bolt of shame as punishment for their rumbling profanity in a cup holder. Maybe she thought about moving my phone off of hers, but with great generosity she left it there.

"You're just in the band," she said. "I thought you'd like to know."

"Thank you," I said.

The van hit a bump, and the phones jostled into a new position, and my stomach almost dropped out of my body.

27. Pittsburgh

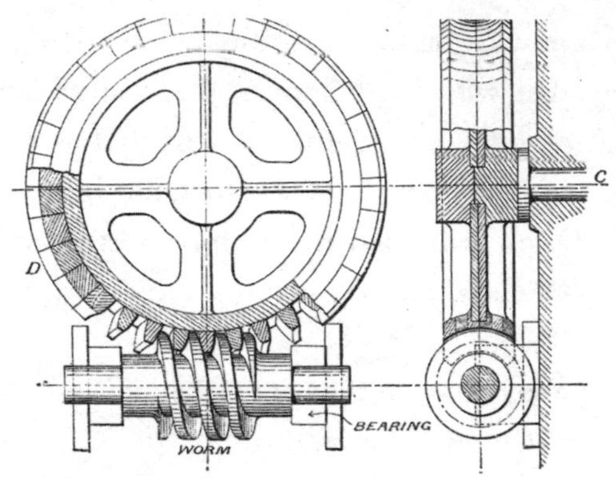

"Do you know what the earth is here for?"

There is never enough time alone on the road. You have to fight for every bit of space, and sometimes that space is only existential, the ability of your imagination to float off in wonderment.

"It's here for *us*."

The music playing on the van's stereo could offer that escape, but James and I had different ideas of how to soundtrack our days. My main intention was to find music that had some connection to the land we were moving through. Some places were hard to find appropriate music for. "Pittsburgh"? It's not a name that sings well.

Regardless, James put on talk radio, which ate away at my soul.

"We are meant to take what is here on Earth and use it for whatever we want. This is what God created us for."

"Well," James said, "he knows how to deliver an argument."

Hitomi stared at James.

"You gotta admit he's a good showman," he said.

"I don't actually have to admit that," she said.

This was the same radio host from when I was young, Gordo Messing. Except now, instead of my father listening to him, it was

James.

I looked out the window and tried to think of a way that "Pittsburgh" could carry a melody. What rhymes with *-burgh*?

"Do you feel like you're holding your breath?" Hitomi asked me.

"What?" I said.

"About Robert."

"Oh. Yes," I said. "I do. I was always a terrible swimmer, too."

"Well," she said, "even when you're good at holding your breath, there's a point where it starts to burn, and you feel like you can't hold it anymore. I used to be able to stay underwater for two and a half laps in the pool when I was a kid."

"Two and a half? That sounds like a lot."

"Well, it was a non-regulation pool," she said. "Unreliable form of measurement."

Pittsburgh has so many bridges, which are all the same color yellow, and the impression they give is that a really good door-to-door bridge salesman came to town one day and made a killing. When the bridges glint in the fading sunlight as you enter the city, you feel like you're being admitted to a special club, a club the actual citizens of Pittsburgh aren't even a part of. You are a traveling spirit, barely there at all, but acutely aware of every dent on every bridge.

I am the flood
 the banks of the shore
  the water they couldn't hold back
   I am the flood
tearing down your playgrounds
    swelling your homes

The stage in Pittsburgh had a backdrop of stars, everything implying to us that there was more of the story outside the frame, off in the distance.

You never know what could be back there. Maybe . . . Robert?

After our set, another band started playing. A young man sat at a keyboard singing songs. Not exactly like me and my songs, but if you were new to music and you squinted, you might think we were similar.

Except now I was the one in the audience. I sat in a booth tearing a napkin as a man named Darrell talked to me. Behind me I kept hearing pieces of a conversation, but I couldn't get the context.

"She's a seven," someone said. "And she wants me to be a seven, but I think I'm a four."

I couldn't tell if they were talking about enneagrams or hotness, but Darrell didn't let me dwell too long on the subtleties of it.

"You get a lot of pussy on the road?" he asked.

"Tons," I said.

"Yeah, that's what it was like when I was out with my band," he said. He continued on with a recollection of his band's conquests as I tore that napkin and started on another one.

Hitomi was across the way, two men on either side of her. I thought about what Hitomi had in common with Robert. You could call it a curse they both carried, eating the pomegranate seeds and never being able to uneat them. Forever after it meant they had to spend a certain amount of their lives in shadow, with clouds covering parts of them. *What's under there?* I always wanted to know. Everyone wanted to know. We all flocked to the people who we thought might understand the shadows.

"I don't write poems," Hitomi said after our first rehearsal. "I just write what I feel. And I feel in fragments. And if you pause enough when you read them to people, they call it poetry. It's just because they're scared of their own feelings."

I thought of that as she rebuffed the vampires around her.

"Mad pussy in Denver," Darrell continued. "You been there yet?"

"Next week," I said.

"Get ready," he said.

The man onstage with the keyboard seemed to glare at me and say, *How could you?*

We stayed that night with another old friend of James. How did he get so many friends?

As we all sat in their living room, I traced the patterns on the couch with my finger without even thinking about it, up and down the petals of blue lotus leaves arrayed in straight rows, lined up for an interrogation.

James's friend held a glass of scotch that was almost as old as our van. There was a pause in the conversation when the light caught the brown liquid and seemed to wink at us through the years.

The effects of the medication are the same as the symptoms of the disease.

"So you guys tour around the world?" our host asked.

"Well," James said, also with a scotch, leaning back in an imitation of a rich person. "Right now it's been just Pennsylvania and a mistaken visit to Delaware. But yes, we'll eventually get around to the world."

"How does that work?"

"How does what work?"

"Like, how do you set up a tour? Do you just show up?"

"Well, no, we email places months before and say, 'Can we please have a corner of your bar for an hour, and can you turn off the Steelers game?'"

James's friends laughed and James took a sip.

I caught Hitomi's eye as she smiled. We had found a brief moment to talk after the show. I told her my favorite things about Robert, and she closed her eyes and took them in like she was making a rubbing of a leaf in her mind.

James continued, "And they say, 'We're going to leave the Steelers game on, but you can play in the other room.' And we say, 'Hooray, our art has been respected!'"

Daveed returned from the bathroom.

"I have an announcement to make," he said.

We all looked at him.

"I've decided to grow a horn."

"That's a bold decision," James said.

"Don't talk me out of it. It's something I've been thinking about all day. I just—I think it's time."

"We support you," Hitomi said.

"Now, that's a big commitment," James said. "Make sure you get enough calcium."

"It'll take a while," Daveed said. "But you'll see. I'll make you proud-slash-horrified."

I thought of the two-headed boy, which we had stood in front of earlier that same day. Everyone's whiskey glasses had that same unsettling glow of embalming fluid.

"You sure you don't want something to drink?" someone asked me.

"I can't. I mean, no. I'm good."

28.
Something Too Small to Mention

WHEN YOU GATHER YOURSELF WITH AN *AHEM*. A little clearing of the throat. I can see your mother. I can see your grandmother. Even as you are young and loose-limbed and dangerous, I can see the stillness, the composure. I love the space between the two syllables of your throat-clearing. The first is more of a ***huh***. It is slightly louder, like it is asserting itself. The second syllable is more of a ***hum***. It is quieter. It is like the little sister of the first.

Both sounds are quiet and personal. They are not trying to get attention. They are not gathering us all together at the beginning of a speech, signaling that we should listen (like some people tend to do). They are a change in scene. They are a resetting of our clocks to some universal time. We had only gotten off by a second, but still.

It is like you are saying those syllables, but since your mouth is closed, they don't come out that way.

Hmm-mmm. Maybe that's more like it. *Hmm-mmm.* I see you as a dove collecting her feathers and settling in. I see you as a cat gathering herself. The space in there, the ***hmm***, drawing up in pitch a little bit, giving some optimism, making it seem like something more is beginning. That space. I wish I could live in that space. It is like a rainshadow. It is like the lee of the mountain, the side that protects us from the wind.

Then the lowering, quieter *mmm*. If I pointed it out, any of this, you would think I was making too much of it.

When you clear your throat, you seem both young and old. You seem outside of time. I feel reset by it, too.

29.
Columbus

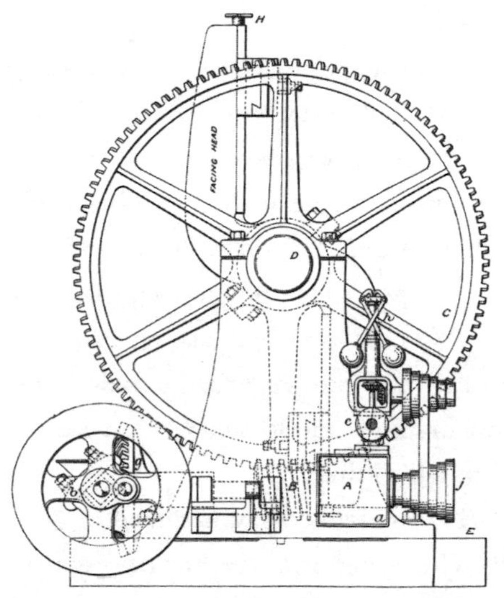

I COULD LEARN TO LOVE MY FATE, stuck in a chaste world where a glimpse of an ankle would launch and/or sink a dozen ships. I could adjust the aperture of my expectations, if I needed to, to the most minimal degree. I could be the world's foremost expert on the smallest things. Big things are always exploding. Small things hold their center.

Hitomi was in the front seat, holding a cup of coffee and singing a song to the tune of "Mr. Sandman."

"Bom-bom-bom-bom-bom-bom-bom-bom, bom-bom-bom-bom-bommmm . . . *Coffee!*"

She looked around at the silent car.

"Sorry, I'm just excited to have coffee," she said.

We rolled into Columbus. The idea of a college town should rightly send a shiver up and down anyone's spine. Collecting a slice of people who happen to be between the ages of 18 and 22, and setting them up in a pretend town inside a real city—well, you can't expect that to lead to anything productive.

Hitomi tapped her pen on the window of the van as she thought about what to write, and I imagined this was a Morse code message to me. But not Morse code, because that would be too obvious. Something smaller, more obsolete. A message encoded so many times that no one could ever hope to break it and you'd just have to know you got it right. A language only used by moths in captivity.

Hitomi wrote in her notebook big scribbly words with a blue ballpoint pen. She dove through the pages as though the words she wrote, upon their completion, would liberate prison camps.

"We only leave home so we can return home again and see it with fresh eyes," James said as he pulled into the parking lot of the venue in Columbus and looked over at Hitomi. "Remember that, as we go through all this."

Hitomi looked unconvinced.

We walked into the bar to see a tree growing inside it. An actual, living tree, like the bar had captured one of the last vestiges of the frontier and was holding on. It was a silver maple that pushed through a hole in the ceiling.

"I love you," Hitomi said as she pressed her face against the trunk and tried to wrap her arms around it.

you turn my compass
toward a terrifying new north
while on the sidewalk today
an old man
had his keys out
and I knew just what he'd say
before he said it:
"you're grieving for something that you never even had"

Sometimes Hitomi would sing the lines. Sometimes she would speak them. She seemed to test them out herself as she read them. You could easily say about her that she could read the back of a Lucky

Charms box and make it sound good, but in actuality both words and voice seemed to rise from the same cauldron, and you could never separate them into different entities.

I felt her words were about me, which is exactly the illusion I laughed at back in Philadelphia.

But still. *Were* they about me?

Regardless, somehow our set that night in Columbus did not ignite anything in the audience. No recognition, no wonder, no discovery. We started with new tricks and fell back on old tricks. They all failed. We looked at each other in confusion.

"You guys should get into this," Hitomi said into the microphone, in between songs. "This is good shit."

She scratched at her stomach.

I thought of the last time I played my own show. I hunched down behind my keyboard.

After the set I sat with Hitomi in a booth.

"So," I said.

"Yeah," she said. "So."

"That was . . . rough, huh?"

"Yeah."

"What happened?"

"I don't know."

"Was it just—was it *them?*"

"I think so?" she said. "But. What does it matter? It sucked."

"Yeah. Are you able to brush it off, or?"

"No," she said. "It sucks. I hate it. It's like. I feel like I'm a kid."

"Yeah."

A burst of cheers came from the next room. Someone in a bachelor or bachelorette party had done something bold and unexpected, like drink an entire pint of Hefeweizen in one gulp.

James was over by the suitcase of Tashtego records, trying to sell our music to one of the wayward partygoers who probably hadn't even watched us. Meanwhile, on the stage with the tree was now a ska band. A *ska* band. I'm sure James had no control over whether we'd be paired with a ska band, but still, I wished he would have thrown down his body to prevent it from happening.

On the other hand, he was very minimally doing the Running Man while he stood there by the records. I mean, like a 5 percent version of it, but I could see it.

"I remember this time when I was six," Hitomi said as she scratched the stubble on her head. "I set up a lemonade stand, and no one came. I sold zero lemonade. I was in this nice purple dress for the occasion. I felt so stupid."

She paused for a second to take a drink.

"And that night I was in bed crying and my dad tried to console me, and he brought in this old guitar he had, and he tried to play me a song. But he didn't know how to play guitar. I guess he thought he could just fake it."

She considered this.

"*That's* how I feel when I play a show and nobody listens," she said.

"Wow," I said.

"Also," she said. "It's hard. These songs. They're about my love with James. They're about our story. Falling in love. Finding each other. Gaining strength. And to keep singing them while that love is falling apart. It's just so fucking sad."

The other room burst with cheers again at some heroic act.

"But," Hitomi continued. "I want to believe they can be more than that. I wrote them at a time when I was strong, and I had all this power to lift these songs up and put these beautiful messages out in the air, and then they boomerang around and whack me in the face and they seem syrupy and stupid. But I want to believe I can learn from them. Like when you have kids and they end up teaching you something."

She took a drink and the bar quieted down for a second.

"I *want* to believe that," she said. "At the moment it's just annoying."

Another pause as she drank again and seemed to reset her mood.

"Thank you for listening," she said and smiled.

"Sure. Well, it's my band, too."

"Is it now?"

"Yes," I said as I took a drink to conceal my smile. "And I'm thinking of making some revisions."

"Oh?"

"Yeah. I think, you know, it's cute, this whole thing you guys have going. But I think we could add some more *relevant* material. Something where the beat keeps increasing until it feels like we're going to explode, and then it drops and the whole dance floor is like, *whoaaa!*"

"Yeah, we should do that. Anything else?"

"Just. Yeah. Maybe cut the poetry."

"Okay. Right. I'll get on that."

Another burst of loud applause from the other room. We both looked over, expecting to see an elephant standing on his hind legs.

"Honestly?" Hitomi said, turning back around. "The poetry is the only thing saving me."

Then a ritual chanting from the other room. A steady beat that started speeding up, like someone had dared someone to do something.

"It's hard to start caring," Hitomi said. "Because you open yourself up to so much pain. Like with Robert." I blushed at hearing his name come out of her mouth, like she knew my imaginary friend. "I think, whenever I've lost someone, I think of the parts of those people that are inside me. And maybe I can live up to the way they made me feel. Like, the best they made me feel. The heights they pushed me to."

The chanting overtook Hitomi's voice and she gave up.

"Sorry," she mouthed as the crowd of people came out of the room, all with flushed faces stretched with laughter. I looked at them and they didn't notice me at all, like I was just watching them on a movie screen and they literally couldn't even see me.

"Zombie movies tell us it's too late for some people," Robert said once. "Because some people are already dead. There might come a time when you see someone who has my face, but it isn't me, because I've been bitten. And you have to be willing to shoot me in the head."

"No," I said. "What a horrible lesson."

"I'm just speaking to the subtext," he said. "*I* didn't come up with it."

"I just prefer movies where everyone hangs out," I said. "And no one has to shoot anyone."

I thought of this as I fell asleep in the back of the van in Columbus. The rest of the band squeezed into a tiny apartment. Outside it felt like a zombie village was stumbling around, a collection of college kids desperately carving out their own brains to fill their skulls with something, anything else.

I was almost completely adrift when I heard the sound of someone fumbling with the handle on the side door.

Zombie! I thought, and sat up straight, trying to figure if I needed pants or a phone or a crowbar or what. I tried to wake myself up a bit and listen closer. Thank God there was a trick to opening the door.

"Iaaannnn," came a voice. "Ian, you bastard."

It indeed sounded like a zombie, but a zombie with a very personal grudge.

"Ian, open the door."

I opened the door to see James standing there. He was drunk and lit by a very unflattering streetlight that chose right then to flicker in a disturbing way. I thought of the Widow Sunday.

"Are you okay?" I asked.

"Do you like her?" James asked.

"I don't even know her," I said.

"Yeah, but do you think you're going to like her?" James asked.

"I don't know how to answer that."

"I just loved her," James said. "Love her. And I want her to be happy." He started to turn away and then stopped. "But. Equally. And just as important. Paaaarrrrt of me wants her to never talk to another man again. Or woman. How do I reconcile that?"

I looked at the rear wheel of the van and just behind it on the ground were some pebbles arranged into two intersecting circles.

"Did you do that?" I asked him.

"What?"

"That."

"No."

"Well," I said. "I'm gonna go back to sleep?" Was that a question? I waited for him to say something. "I'm gonna go back to sleep." I shut the door.

I waited to hear him shuffle away. And then all he muttered was, "Son of a bitch."

30.
What I Really Want to Say

WHAT INHIBITS A PERSON FROM WRITING? It's not that he has nothing to say. It's that he's afraid what he has to say is so ugly and unacceptable that people will read it and recoil. "What a monster," they'll say. "Lock him in the dungeon. We can't have this monster among us."

What I want to say, what I really want to say:

Ninety-nine percent of people are mindless sacks of saltwater. They will not stop until they've consumed it all, photographed it all, wrapped everything up in plastic and sold off the naming rights to a company that literally produces hellfire.

Also:

I want to suck lemonade off Hitomi's legs.

Also:

I secretly hope that if Robert is really gone, he killed himself because he didn't want to live in a corrupt world that takes your humanity away from you and makes you beg to get a fraction of it back.

Also:

I wish James would apologize just once for something he did, see himself as the creator of all his and our problems, and then fuck right off into Lake Erie.

See? You're backing away. I am a monster. I can't say these things. So, the whole trick is to very delicately put into words the concept that I want to be king of the world and live in the boughs of an old oak tree, and that I want to know that I am truly beloved without ever actually having to listen to anyone say anything ever again.

31.
West of Cleveland

TWO DAYS LATER THE SKY WAS OVERCAST. James was driving as we headed out of Cleveland.

"Hey, Hitomi, what was the name of—"

"I don't know."

"Yes, you know. Let me explain who I'm talking about."

"I don't know."

"How do you know you don't know?"

"I don't want to talk, James."

"Because of last night?"

Indeed, Hitomi probably didn't want to talk because of the previous night. We were in a big house on Lake Erie, what we would've called a mansion back when we were kids.

We were having our requisite glasses of amber-colored liquors and explaining our lifestyle to these random acquaintances of James when the question came up about what Greg, the man of the house, did. He gave a long explanation about medical supplies and carriers and the confluence of this sector and that sector and we all sat there trying to understand the syntax of the bizarre language this man was speaking, but happy enough in our ignorance to assume we were just fools who didn't understand how the world really works.

But James, ever analyzing, always trying to find the angle or the scam of something, especially if he wasn't in on it, processed all this information and came to a conclusion.

"Wait a minute," James said. "Do you work for an HMO?"

"No," Greg said. "I *run* an HMO."

Greg nodded and sat back as he said this, like this was going to impress us all, like we were going to high-five him and run around whooping at his brilliance. His wife winced, like she knew what was coming.

"Holy fuck," James said, "It's you."

Suddenly James put together who this was, whose house we were staying in. Up until now, this sleeping spot was just what had come to us after casting out a wide net for places to stay in Cleveland, and someone had responded on social media with, "Hey remember Greg? He lives in Cleveland."

And apparently James didn't remember Greg, or not really. Assumed that maybe Greg had come about his money by teaching inner-city kids to read, instead of—

"You're fucking ruining the world," James said.

Everyone in the house froze. Even the hummus on the table in between us iced over. Daveed had a cracker in his mouth and was afraid to chew it, for now the sound of cracking crackers would be way too loud, here in this big, mansion-esque house after a show late at night in Cleveland.

"What?" Greg asked.

"You're gambling with people's lives. It's fucking sick. People are suffering because of you."

"Now, come on," Greg's wife said.

"We're leaving," James said, and stood up.

It was half past midnight. We were tired and ready to go to sleep. I was already half asleep, to be honest. This was not a pleasant declaration to hear. It hurt in my body when he said this, because my body didn't care about politics or proving a point about capitalism, it just wanted to sleep on the assuredly plush sheets in a dark, quiet room upstairs, very soft and clean-smelling sheets, but at that moment, fighting back against James would have meant standing up for the American health care system.

But, when I thought about those sheets—

"Okay," Hitomi said, getting to her feet. "Thank you for your hospitality."

Hitomi could have resisted, but now the exodus had more than enough momentum. We were really going to walk out of this house in the middle of the night.

"Dude," said Greg. "You don't even get it."

"I do though, *dude,*" James said. "I really do."

Daveed still hadn't bitten into his cracker, still held it in his mouth, and looked around at all this with big eyes. I set down the plate that was in my lap, put it on the table and shrugged. We grabbed our bags and loaded into the van, and the whole encounter from knocking on the door to driving away in mutual disgust totaled only thirty-five minutes.

"Where are we going to sleep now?" Hitomi asked.

"I don't know," James said, peeling out of the suburbs of Cleveland. "You guys have any ideas?" he asked back to me and Daveed. Of course, we did not. We didn't have the reach and breadth of acquaintances that James had.

At least it was for a noble reason. We could all agree on that. I looked over at Daveed for some mutual agreement, and he whispered to me, "What's an HMO?"

We slept at a rest stop outside of Cleveland as semi trucks idled all around us. We were a little raft lapping up against their container ships. It wasn't a comfortable way to sleep, but I suppose it was principled and purposeful. Do principled people sleep better? That's what they say, but in practice it was fitful and uncomfortable, which led to the next morning when we were so tired our minds were breaking, except for James, who seemed to have no trouble at all in the world now that he had rebuffed corruption in the health care industry.

"Just," Hitomi said the next morning as we drove on, "no questions today, please."

"Okay," James said and turned on the radio.

I heard that old familiar voice of Gordo Messing. It was like a taunt, though there was no way James would've known this. In fact, I don't know why James wouldn't tolerate staying in the house of someone who worked in a business he didn't agree with, and then be okay with listening to this voice on the radio and not want to change the station.

"Socialists want to put you in an egg carton," Gordo said. "And stamp you with a number and make you all the same size and shape, and tell you that if you're good little eggs, you can have your place, but you can never have any more than that. But guess what? They still want to make an omelette out of you."

Okay, well, he was funnier when I was ten.

I sat in the back and looked at James's face in the rearview mirror. I admired his decisiveness, that he wouldn't let us sleep in the house of someone profiting off of misery. That it only took him the few seconds to put all that together, to decide we would not sully our humanist heads by laying them on plush pillowcases paid for by the blood of the poor and sickly. Plush, cool, clean pillowcases covering multiple pillows of all levels of firmness. I imagined it was the kind of decisiveness that originally brought him and Hitomi together. Even though she had her own searing vision and resolute way of moving diagonally through the world, there was probably a day when James looked at Hitomi and said, "You. Me. Let's do this."

I admired all of that, even admired that he didn't apologize for the zombie encounter in Columbus, as much as I feared there would be a moment down the road when I would punch him, not because I especially wanted to or we were even that different fundamentally, just because one day my fist would rise as though pulled by a puppeteer's wires and swing toward his beautiful face and smash into it, and maybe he would even be able to appreciate the righteousness of my action and see me as having made a bold point by punching him.

Or maybe I was too tired because I had barely slept at all in that rest stop the night before.

32. Detroit

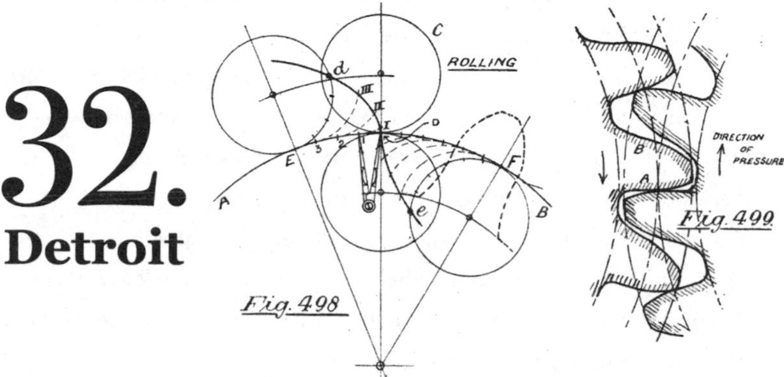

To Detroit, then.

Curl around Lake Erie. Turn right at Toledo. Scurry up into the thumb of Michigan.

The show in Detroit was deep in the city, past empty field after empty field in an art gallery. I thought about how all the space in the city left so much room for music to express itself. If you picture a sound wave as a big piece of rope that you shake, you could have enormous pieces of rope in Detroit. One person on each end, whapping those ropes to create music, moving them in concert and in contrast to other pieces of rope next to you.

I'm not saying we were successful at all of that, of unifying humanity's vibrations. But we at least tried.

Hitomi wore a baby blue baby doll dress she had bought at a thrift store that day. Before our set she stood outside in the adjoining yard with a bottle of beer in her hand, talking while five guys circled around her. I walked up while she was in the middle of what she was saying. The sun streamed through the trees.

"When I was fifteen, I went to this horrible place called Pathway," she said. She looked at me for a second as she gathered her thoughts.

"It was so horrible. It's like rehab, but your parents take you there, and if you're under eighteen you can't leave. It's really fucked up."

A drink from her beer. She pulled off her hat.

"It was this dingy building, and they treated you like you were insane prisoners. If you ever talked back to them, they would wrestle you to the ground, and this one fat orderly would sit on me, and when he did I could feel his hard-on. It was so disgusting."

Another drink as the five guys around her were speechless.

"But my friend Jean, man. She was there for over two years. I don't know what I would've done without her. I still have nightmares about that place, but thank God I got out."

The group of men still had no idea what to say.

"How is Jean doing now?" someone asked tentatively, trying to turn the story to a bright ending.

"Um," Hitomi said. "Well. She killed herself."

Everyone froze.

"I don't know how to say it any nicer than that," she said.

She took another drink and turned to me.

"Shall we?" she asked.

Onstage, Hitomi asked us to play something slower than we had ever played before.

"Slower than the continents," she said. "Slower than the gears of justice."

That was enough for us. I got to set the key. My hands fell on a C-sharp minor chord. Daveed pulsed behind me as subtle as a jar collecting rainwater.

while you are unstoppable
sometimes I wish
  you would just stop
   and see me   I am standing here
    waiting for you to touch me
even a powerful touch
       so I know
      for sure that you see me
       even a push
  even (don't make me go further)
    even a slap
so I know that I'm something
        even
     (don't make me)
          even
         (don't make me)
           even
       while you stop
       sometimes I wish
          you were
          un
            stop
             a
                ble

I was not unstoppable. I did not offer a powerful touch. Tears pooled in my eyes thinking of Hitomi under the weight of a fat orderly.

After our set I walked up to a bonfire in the backyard where James was holding a bottle of beer and talking with a young woman.

"Ian, this is Kylie," James said.

"Hi, Kylie," I said.

Kylie touched the side of her head and smiled. She pulled a purple cardigan sweater tightly around her shoulders.

"Kylie goes to the university, and we're going to give her a ride home."

This young woman, what were James's designs on her? She didn't seem his type.

"Alright," I said. "We have plenty of room."

Not kidnapping room. Was it too late to say that?

"Yes," James said. "Kylie, can you wait a minute while I pack up the van? Talk to Ian. He sometimes says interesting things."

James slipped out behind us. That was the scam: distract my attention from Hitomi with some college-going young lady named—

"Kylie was it?" I asked.

"Yeah," Kylie said, smiling. "Were you the drummer?"

"Piano player," I said.

"Right. That's what I meant. Have you always played keyboard?"

"I wouldn't say always. Since at least—"

"I took lessons when I was twelve, but I hated it. It was just so boring."

"Yes. Lessons are usually boring," I said.

"Sorry. What were you saying?"

"Nothing. I just. I never cared much for lessons either."

"So then how did you learn?"

"I guess I just always thought that—this is going to sound privileged, but I just always felt like a piano player, even before my hands knew what to do."

"What do you mean?"

"I don't know."

We loaded up the van as Kylie, unsure how to help, stood around. I got in my usual seat in the center, giving Kylie the backseat. That seemed like a nice gesture at first, because it was such a long and spacious seat, but then I realized that you should probably offer guests the most frontward seat that is not the driver's seat. It was too late to change the situation, though, once we started driving.

"How are you guys doing back there?" James asked, looking in the rearview mirror at us.

"Just fine," Kylie said.

"So, what are you studying?" I asked.

"Well, actually, I'm studying business."

"What does that entail?" I asked.

"Well, actually, I'm taking precalculus currently."

"You need to know calculus to start a business?" I asked.

"Oh. I didn't say I was going to start a business."

"You're just going to run one."

"No. I don't know. I might not do that either. Maybe I'll do the books for a business."

"And that requires calculus?"

"Well, I'm just taking *precalculus* at the moment, actually."

"Where does that lead, though, precalculus? If not calculus."

"Ian?" James interrupted. "Can you pass this drink back to Kylie?"

He handed me a tumbler. I don't know how he managed to make a drink while he was packing and then driving the van, but he somehow did it. Obviously, he was not as concerned with seeming to Kylie like a non-kidnapper as I was, in my battle to define what exactly precalculus entailed.

"What's in it?" Kylie asked, and rightly so.

"It's gin and tonic," James said.

"I can't drink gin," Kylie said. "I'll start sneezing and then fall asleep."

"Ah, we don't want that," James said. "Daveed?"

"Gin, man? What the hell?"

"Okay, pass it back up, then."

"So. Kylie," I continued. "I know geometry is concerned with shapes and areas and stuff. What is calculus concerned with?"

"Well. I'm not sure, actually. I mean, I just started the class this week."

"I'll look it up," I said and pulled out my phone. Suddenly I was obsessed with the knowability of this one fact. "Ah, okay. It says that calculus originally referred to counting on an abacus. Is that what you guys are doing?"

"No, actually. We have calculators."

"Of course. Maybe this is out of date, then," I shook my phone like it was broken and looked at Kylie. She gave no sign of levity. "Calculators. Maybe that's where that word came from."

"Calculus came from calculators?" Kylie asked.

"Well, probably the other way around," I said.

"This town is so enormous," James said. "Do all these streets circle back to the center? Kylie, that was a question for you."

"Oh. I don't know, actually. I mean, I've only been here a week."

"It's on such a grand scale," James said. "I don't know how to tackle it."

"How did you get to the show in the first place?" I asked Kylie.

"I came with my friends, you know, but they left in the middle of it."

"So they're big fans?" I teased.

"No, they left in the middle of it."

"Right."

"Ian," James said, "I don't know where we're all sleeping tonight. It might be in a field."

"That's great. I like fields."

"I mean the field might be dangerous."

"Will it be?" asked Hitomi.

"No, not that dangerous," James said.

"I can handle it," I said.

"I mean, it *is* Detroit," James said. "I heard police response times are as slow as an hour."

"I heard that too!" Kylie said.

"Really?" Hitomi asked, turning around.

"We won't need to call the police for anything," James said to Hitomi.

"No, it's true," Kylie said, leaning forward. "Actually, it's really fucked up. It's definitely worse for black people, too. If you're in certain neighborhoods the police just never come. But we have the campus police and that's a different thing."

"Different thing entirely," James said. "Very safe there."

"I mean," Kylie said. "I've only been there a week, actually."

We dropped Kylie off and I didn't dare get out of the car to give her a hug for fear that James would drive off without me.

We did all end up sleeping in a field of wild sage and mallow, with the beautiful downtown buildings visible right over the crowns of trees. The field took up an entire city block, and it had an old driveway into which we pulled our van. I rolled out my sleeping bag and lay down to look up at the constellations above Detroit. Cassiopeia, lounging on her throne, smiled down at us. I streamed Joni Mitchell's *Blue* on my phone.

I texted Robert.

You were right about Blue. All the details in the lyrics.

Her songs are so crooked.

You know what I mean.

33. What Is Sleep?

WHAT IS SLEEP?

Why do we have to do it?

Why do we go crazy if we don't?

Is it our brain's way of returning to the ground? Are the neurons like roots that want to sink into the dirt and soak up something real?

Is it a bath for our ego, a time when it can chill out and not have to worry? Is it a playground for our id, a cutting of the leash that ties it to sanity, a ticket on a roller coaster that constantly runs off the tracks?

Is it a time-out from figuring things out? A pause in the constant calculations? A moment apart from knowledge and rules and customs?

Is it a dive into the ocean of the subconscious, where whales who are invisible from the surface are now so big and present and obvious that we have to deal with them somehow?

Is it cracking the ice, reaching into our reflection, abandoning reason?

Is it a temporary form of suicide?

Is it an embrace with a lover who will always let us go back home every morning, until the one time he doesn't?

Is it personal to you?

Is it anything like mine?

Could we ever meet in our dreams, away from judging eyes, and play games in peace?

Will we ever figure it out, get enough of it, grow tired of it?

What would it even mean to get tired of sleep?

If I could have a journal of everything I've ever seen in my dreams, would it look like some insane person's confiscated writings, found in a Honda Civic in a junkyard in New York somewhere?

If I can fly in my dreams, why doesn't it work when I'm awake? Is gravity different in dreamland?

Why do we sleep? Thank God we get to, but really, why?

34.
Detroit Morning

WE WOKE UP TO A DAWN CHORUS OF BIRDS. The kind of chorus that is fighting over the solos, fighting over who was supposed to bring doughnuts, fighting over which hymn to sing next.

I lay in that field and read *Moby-Dick* in the early morning light while waiting for the others to get up. Melville was listing the crew, and he mentioned a familiar name: Tashtego, a harpoonist.

"Tashtego!" I shouted out loud to the band, who were all splayed out on the ground, sleeping. Then I realized how confusing it would have been to be in a band, tour for a week with a new keyboardist, sleep in a field in Detroit with him, and wake up in the morning to him shouting the name of your own band at you.

But James got it. Without opening his eyes or lifting his head, he raised up his arm and gave me a thumbs-up.

We meandered out of the city, admiring the layers of design, neglect, and restoration. Daveed, in his hoodie with string ties flung this way and that, looked up at the buildings, and I pictured him floating down the Colorado River and looking up at the walls of the Grand Canyon.

I drove the van, so we had J Dilla beats on the stereo. The drums bounced through those canyons, showing us the purpose of such a large scale.

On the side of one brick building was a painting of a bright orange marigold. It was like a gorgeous sun bursting with life. But when I looked closer, I could see in the painting there was a glass jar around the flower. In the script on the side of it was painted this phrase:

the lacquered bloom,
once alive
now entomb'd

Sort of rhymes, I thought.

35.
Defiance

AT A REST STOP IN DEFIANCE, INDIANA, a small gang of motorcyclists were revving their engines. On the way to the bathroom, I talked to Hitomi.

"That was sad, about your friend Jean," I said.

"Yeah," she said.

RANNNNNGGG

"I didn't know about that," I said.

"How would you?"

"I don't know," I said. "You told it to someone you had just met last night."

"Well, he asked."

RANNGGGGGG-Guh-Guh-Guh-Guh

I felt stupid for saying something. I wanted to pull the words back into my mouth. And the stupid motorcycles took away all subtlety.

"She slipped away," she continued. "Drug addiction. It was just a few years ago, but. You know, it was already like I didn't know her anymore. Drugs will make you miss someone before they're even gone."

"I know what you mean," I said.

"Robert did drugs?" she asked.

"No. I don't know. Maybe."

"Also, no offense, but you don't know if he's actually dead, right?"

Then we were back to the van and the conversation was over.

I pulled out my phone and texted Robert.

adfhhdfhfsadhdashasdhashdhdahdh

Gordo's voice come on the radio as soon as James started the van.

"Feminists are just angry because they're so unattractive and they didn't get invited to the prom in high school. So they're taking it all out on us. They're furious about it. They didn't even get invited to the father-daughter dance!"

Hitomi and Daveed had both already put in their ear buds.

"Jesus, really?" I said as I slammed the dashboard.

James looked over at me and turned the volume down.

"Not Jesus so much as the cherrypicked parts of what Jesus said," he said.

"You like listening to this?"

"It's good to know what's out there."

"Why?"

"You never know," he said.

36. Indianapolis

"THERE IS NO GETTING LOST," a woman in a quilted vest said with a smile. She was standing in a church in Indianapolis in front of an enormous vinyl mat that had a labyrinth printed on it, patterned after one in an old church in France.

Hitomi, Daveed, and I had come inside while waiting for the venue next door to be ready for us. We took our shoes off and gathered at the start of the labyrinth, and I saw a piano in the corner. Above it was a framed drawing of a minotaur pulling against his chains while a man struggled to corral him.

There is no getting lost.

I went to the piano and started to improvise something Bach-esque, if that were possible. Hitomi strode through the labyrinth first. Daveed went slower and looked like he was having trouble balancing.

I looked at the carvings on the soundboard of the piano, beautiful flowers cut into the rosewood. The piano had been made in Boston over a hundred years before, and I imagined it had been carried to Indianapolis by horses. Now I got to spend time with it. Every piano is another node on a great river, and it carries songs within it, and whenever I get a chance to connect, I am playing *the* piano, the only piano that matters at that moment.

I had been reading about Joni Mitchell in the van all day, so it reminded me of her song "River," in that the piano was something I could skate away on when Christmas was coming and people were putting up reindeer and cutting down trees.

It helps to feel that continuity, so that when Joni starts writing that song in the back of a bar in Santa Monica, echoing the rhythm of "Jingle Bells," chewing the ice cubes in her glass as she figures out where the river goes, she can pick it up again a week later in James Taylor's living room in the Valley. As she works out the ascending melody of the chorus and tries to figure out if she can teach her feet to fly, the song is—where? Not on vinyl yet. It is in her brain, yes, but what even is the brain? The song is somewhere between her hands and the piano, between the first piano and the second, between the cigarette and the ice, between Santa Monica and the Valley. It's there after breakfast, and it's there at midnight.

Where does the love between two lovers live? Not in either one of them. It must be somewhere in between.

Earlier that day we had driven past Marion, Indiana, the place where, in 1930, two young black men were lynched by a mob. Someone saw a photograph of the bodies and was so moved by it that he wrote a poem. He compared the twisted dead bodies to a "strange fruit" hanging from the poplar trees.

That turned into a song that Billie Holiday sang with a kind of curiosity and subversion that had more grace and understanding than you could imagine summoning for such a situation.

Every piano has wounds. There are keys that have swollen so much they get stuck. There are keys that have trouble repeating if you play them too fast. There are keys that are out of tune, but tunable, and keys that are out of tune and forever untunable.

There are keys that are never meant to be played, as Robert said.

I looked back at my bandmates walking on different paths. Hitomi was far ahead of Daveed, but at certain points she passed next to him. Then James stuck his head in the door of the church.

"They want us now," he said. "We're late."

Our little play was prematurely closed. Hitomi was at the end of the labyrinth anyway and put on her shoes. Daveed was still a ways from finishing and walked quicker around the corners. I finished up my piece of music and went to put on my shoes, having missed the labyrinth entirely.

Before the show a storm raged in the next room. Gods tearing down their summer homes. Some horrible argument between Hitomi and James, mercilessly muffled from our ears.

We were at the Kurt Vonnegut Memorial Library, a small, white-walled space devoted to the life and words of that great author from my home state of Indiana.

We are what we pretend to be, read a quote on the wall, black letters against white. *So we must be careful what we pretend to be.*

James came out of the other room looking like he had drowned a kitten, saw the quote on the wall, and then looked back at me and saw I was looking at it and made a face of recognition, like, *remember this.*

There was no bar in the venue, since it was essentially a bookstore that only hosted a show a few times a month. This made the drinkers in the band nervous. James had a flask he passed back and forth with Hitomi during the set.

Hitomi had her shoes off before we started. She looked at me as she rubbed her socks into the carpet. She smiled as she said my name.

"Come over here."

I walked up to her, wondering at her sly smile. She reached out her hand softly for mine. What was this? I looked over at James setting up his guitar.

"It's okay," she said, and then she touched my hand, and there was a big spark from the static electricity. I leapt back, wondering at this strange power. I think the intensity of it surprised both of us. She just stood there, mouth open in surprise.

"Indianapolis," Hitomi said at the top of the show. "What. Is up." It wasn't a question. "Okay. Let's do this."

She took a drink from the flask and we started playing. Instead of waiting for us to build up the vibe, she was anxious to start reading over it, but she seemed to have nothing more than a couple of words written down in her book. She looked at the page, and then she put the book down. She started singing the first line of a song, one of our actual songs, and we all stopped the improvisation so we could back her up.

"Sorry," she said, letting us catch up. "I mean. I'm not sorry."

We were disjointed like that for a while, all our boxcars banging into each other. I looked at her face during one song and it seemed like she was going to burn up, start crying, or boil over.

"You are all so well-lit tonight," Hitomi said to the audience. "Usually we're in dingy bars and I can't see anyone. But now there's nowhere for you to hide from my . . . from my everything."

The crowd chuckled. I saw the men in the audience become enamored and look around at their good fortune. She took another swig from the flask and held it there as she teetered on the edge of a great show and a disaster.

I jumped the gun and played a chord. I tried to pull it back, but it had already happened. Hitomi shot me a look like I had spilled the royal jewels across the marble palace floor. She sighed and hung her head.

Had I broken her? One chord at the wrong moment?

Then we broke into a slow love ballad and hit our stride. The boxcars clicked into formation and stopped undermining each other. I suppose to the audience it seemed predetermined, like it was going to happen all along. But inside such a contraption, it never feels secure. There is always the possibility the whole delicate device might just fall apart.

I wonder sometimes what makes it worth getting in a van and traveling around the country, when so much of it is so unnatural, so punishing to the body. There are at least three small moments that pay dividends:

(1) When people are dancing to the music you make. There is nothing better than this. You have provided inspiration or excuse for dancing, and people are never happier in their lives than when they dance. Not just happy, but free. Free in the wilderness of their bodies.

(2) When someone makes a sound of delight after you finish a song. Something like "Ah," or "Wow," or—if you're lucky—"Yes!" This is rare, and it only comes from a certain kind of person, a person who feels comfortable talking back to the screen, as it were. Someone who, at times, loses control of their words, and accidentally lets one slip out.

(3) The forearm grab. This is even rarer. Partly because it is so subtle you might just not see it happen. Someone touches their lover gently and says, "Hey. This. I feel like *this* about *you.*"

You might say that it's like shooting fish in a barrel to get two lovers to sigh in reverence to their own love, that they might as easily find that resonance in a postcard or a Sandra Bullock movie. But that doesn't diminish the value of it.

The forearm grab happened on that love ballad. Right there in the first row, a couple grabbed forearms. Behind them I saw on the wall, *We must be careful what we pretend to be.*

37.
A Case of You

We ended up at a bar after the show. There was a tiny dance floor that wasn't really a dance floor but a narrow strip of the room where people could dance if they were so determined. That's where I found James, holder of the van keys, bobbing next to a young lady.

"Ian, this is Megan," James said.

"Hi, Megan. James, can I have the keys?"

"Dance with us for a minute."

"Uh."

"No, it's okay, right, Megan?"

The lights were flickering around us, a great plaid parade. James grabbed one of my hands and invited me to take one of Megan's. She was not excited about the situation.

"Let me go get a drink," James said suddenly. "You guys dance for a second."

We both started to protest, but he disappeared into the crowd too fast. I pulled back my hand from Megan's, and she had a disappointed look at James being out of her life.

She had a face that looked like it was always one second away from saying either "I love you" or "fuck you." She had wintry eyes, and her hair was the blackest of blacks. I reached out one hand for her shoulder and then grabbed her other hand. She slowly fell into my arms and I felt her hair brush up against my cheek.

We spun slowly around the dance floor. Did anything need to be said?

"I wonder if he's really getting a drink," I said.

"What do you mean?" she said as she looked up with concern.

"Oh," I said. "Just that, it's a long story, but he keeps trying to set me up with girls."

"Is that what happened?"

"It seems like it, yeah."

"Oh. I really liked him."

"Well. He's not dead," I said as I looked around. "He'll probably come back."

"Well, who cares?" she said as she let her head flop on my chest. "Spin me around."

I spun her around, the two of us somehow now dancing in a style that was decades older than any of the others around us. Someone bumped into us and Megan got annoyed.

"Hey. Just. Come on," she said.

We spun around some more and then landed in a booth, still as close to each other as we were on the dance floor. On the other end of the room I could see Daveed. I couldn't see Hitomi or James.

"How much have you had to drink?" she asked me.

"Nothing," I said.

"Would you be willing to drive me home in my car?"

"Yes."

"Okay."

"Now?"

"Yes."

I looked over to Daveed again. I pointed to Megan and made the sign of a steering wheel. Daveed smiled and gave a thumbs-up. I shook my head and tried to convey the charity of the act I was doing. He kept smiling and put another thumb up.

I followed her as she led me to her car. As we walked past the van, there were those overlapping circles near the rear wheel again, as though they were tied to us like a bridal train.

"Hold on a sec," I said to Megan, and hopped over to it.

I crouched down and went through my pockets and didn't find anything to add.

"What are you doing?" she asked.

"Nothing," I said.

I stood up, and for some reason I kicked all the pebbles, spreading them around so they didn't look like anything anymore.

I drove her home and she leaned her head against the window.

"Turn left," she said.

"Here?"

I swerved and barely got the car over in time.

We got to her house and I turned off the car and gave her the keys.

"Walk me in?" she asked.

She got to the door and looked at her keys, baffled as she tried to figure out how to open the front door. Then she picked one key at random that clicked open the lock. She pushed through the door, dropped her purse on the couch, and stumbled into her dark bedroom, leaving the door open, not turning the light on, not looking back at me.

I stood there in her living room, looking at the decorations on the wall. There were some show posters. In the kitchen was a cat standing over a knocked-over orchid.

"Hey," she said from the blackness of her room.

"Yes?" I said, having just noticed her record collection.

"What's your name again?"

"Ian."

"Ian, come in here."

In my head I saw James's face, shaking his head, doubting. What was he doubting? That a girl would take me home with her? That she would want to spend the night with me? I could identify the ridiculousness of that feeling, as I stood there thinking of James. His being, his totality consumed me more than any thoughts of the girl in the dark. I felt like I had to prove something to him. Even if he would never know what really happened. Even if it was just for a story to tell him. A story I could just make up anyway.

"What's taking you so long?" she asked.

"I'm just seeing if you have *Blue*."

"Why?"

"It's just comforting to be able to look through a record collection and find that record. It's like home base."

Silence.

"Do you have it?" I asked to the blackness.

"What was it again?"

Now I started to doubt this encounter. I felt like this was a threshold to cross. Maybe it would be okay if she hadn't yet found a used copy of *Blue* or had one that she loaned out to someone. But if she had never *heard* of it before?

"Uh," I said. "Joni Mitchell's *Blue?*"

My words hung in the room for a second.

"Yeah, of course," she said. "I think it's already on the turntable."

I looked and indeed it was. I put the needle on "A Case of You" and took off my jacket. I stepped into the dark room.

"I just . . . I wasn't sure," I said.

"Shut up," she said.

I thought of Robert and me sitting at a bar and discussing the line about drawing a map of Canada on the back of a cartoon coaster, the awkward specificity of it. I stepped through the dark bedroom, lay down on the bed next to this woman, and we immediately started kissing. I already couldn't remember what her face looked like, and now it was too dark to see. I also couldn't remember her name, but it was too late to ask that now.

I pulled away for a second.

"Isn't it funny," I said, "how this song is about how her lover is intoxicating, but then she says she can drink a whole case of him and still be on her feet? I guess she's saying she's strong, but you could also interpret it as she thinks he's weak sauce."

I couldn't see her face, but I could sense her sitting there trying to process that.

"What?"

"Nothing."

She was soft and her sheets were clean. She unbuttoned the top of my shirt and put her hand on my bare shoulder and I leaned my head back. Was it easy enough to just receive the touch of a random person in—where was this, Indianapolis? Had I even shut the front door behind me? Was my phone charged enough to make it through the night? Where was the band going to be staying? Would I ever find them again?

Jesus Christ, had we never actually left that labyrinth?

"Hey," she said as she looked at me in the darkness. "Would you be a little rough with me?"

". . . What?"

"I mean, don't leave bruises. But. Can you spank me?"

"Um."

"Come on, don't be a pussy."

She rolled over on her stomach and invited me to slap her. I suddenly lost all my nerve and affection and suspension of disbelief about what I was doing. This was not what I wanted from a stranger in Indianapolis at all.

"Come on!" she said.

Now what? My heart and my soul and my body were not into this.

In what way could I get through this? I gave her a light slap.

"More!" she said as she giggled.

I tried again.

"Come on!"

I stood up and buttoned my shirt.

"Um," I said. "I'm sorry, I just. I'm really tired."

"No, don't!"

"I really just wanted to make sure you got home . . ."

"Goddamn it. Just lie down next to me."

I did and I could feel the squirming in her body as she wanted something in a way I couldn't give to her. Maybe she should've just gone home with James. Not that he even necessarily wanted that. But I'm sure he would have been willing to carry through with whatever she wanted. It wasn't that I was judging her, or that I was prudish or anything. Or. Maybe this is what prudishness looked like. But really, I just wanted the softness.

"Could we go back to the softness?" I asked.

"What?"

"I just mean the kissing part."

"No, it's fine," she said.

Did that mean no? I didn't mean that as a compromise. I just thought that was the good part. There was already enough conflict in the world.

We lay next to each other in the darkness, and suddenly everything felt weird. Where even was I? Somewhere in Indianapolis with someone who was maybe named Megan? The brief burst of excitement was gone and now we were just two strangers lying in a bed together.

She reached for my hand and pulled it close to her chest. She held it in a way that didn't let me do anything with it. She put it on her breast and I cupped it awkwardly.

I thought about the band loading into a house across town somewhere. I thought about us all getting up in the morning and driving past Valparaiso.

I released my hand from her grip and touched the bottom of her bra, tracing that arc with my finger. I thought about Hitomi's lips. How it would feel to be lying next to her, touching her back, her long legs.

I sat up suddenly and said, "I should get back to my band."

"What?"

"Yeah, we have to leave early in the morning."

"No, that's crazy."

"It is crazy. But it's also true."

"Shit."

"It's okay. Just. It's okay. I'm sorry. This is nice but."

I tried to think of something to say. This was a person I could spend the night with, or I could spend ten more seconds with and never see again in my life.

"I'm sorry," I said.

I got up and went to the living room and put on my jacket. Joni was singing about the last time she saw Richard and he put a quarter in the Wurlitzer and the thing began to whirr.

I hadn't realized that the Wurlitzer company made jukeboxes in addition to electric keyboards. I called for a ride and walked out on the porch in the Indianapolis night. One firefly, perhaps the last one of the season, flashed for a second. I guess it doesn't matter to the electronics makers whether they make devices on which people create music, or if they make devices that just play recorded music. To me that was such a strange combination, like if Kellogg's also sold strip steaks.

But then again, what the hell do I even know?

38.
What I Am in Love With

I AM IN LOVE WITH A GHOST. A person who is always disappearing. It is in the smile, the same smile, the same corner of a smile, in a flip of the hair, in catching someone looking, looking at them and looking away.

I am in love with the breeze behind a curtain, mistaking it for a love of the curtain itself, going online and searching for more of those curtains to buy, forgetting about them, receiving them in the mail three days later, opening up the box and saying, "What the fuck is this?" Not even opening the box all the way before kicking it into the corner of the room, kicking it down the stairs, never looking at it again.

I am in love with a whisper of a voice, and when the voice is full, it loses me. Or I am in love with a shouting voice, but not normal conversation. Or I am in love with your handwriting but not your typing.

39.
Indianapolis Morning

I WOKE UP ON THE COUCH OF A STRANGE HOUSE the next morning. Daveed had let me in the front door late at night, and I stayed up writing. As I rubbed my eyes, James and Hitomi were in the kitchen making eggs.

"Did I ever show you how to make eggs?" James asked Hitomi.

"Oh. *Please* tell me how to make eggs. I have *no* idea," Hitomi said.

"I know everyone can make an egg. It's just. I have a different approach."

"How has this never come up?"

"Well, you were vegan."

"I still am."

"What are eggs, then, 'Tome? Fruits of the chicken?"

"I'll eat eggs if I know where they came from."

"You know where these came from?"

"Yeah, they got them at the farmer's market."

"Hey," I said to them.

They stopped what they were doing and looked over at me.

"Whose house is this?" I asked.

They looked at each other.

"We bought it for you last night," James said.

"No, really."

"A very nice person from last night offered to let us stay here."

"Was it a friend of that girl I was talking to?"

"What, you think everyone in Indianapolis knows each other?" James asked. "What happened with that girl, anyway?"

"Nothing. She asked me to drive her home because she was drunk."

"And?"

"I drove her home."

"And?"

"I came back here."

"It seemed to take you quite a while to get here. We didn't even see you come in."

I didn't respond.

"So, what's your technique?" Hitomi asked.

"Yeah, what's your technique?" James asked me.

"No, I'm asking *you*," Hitomi said. "What's your technique for eggs?"

"Oh, well, you have to go really slow," he said.

"Okay, but I mix them up first?"

"No! Just crack them in the pan and stir them really slow. Achingly slow. Gently. Here."

He stood behind her and held her hand with the spoon in it. He rested his chin on her shoulder.

I went back to the couch.

40.
Valparaiso

THERE WAS NO SHOW FOR US TO PLAY in my hometown of Valparaiso and not even any time to stop. Just the few seconds when we drove past the exit sign on the freeway.

Gordo Messing was originally from Valparaiso. Perhaps I should have mentioned that earlier. That's the reason I originally listened to him with my dad, because he was local. Later he went national and became famous, and I kept it to myself that I had known him from the beginning, and that my listenership was maybe one tiny peg on his climb up.

"The world is here for us to use as we see fit. We are so much smarter than any animal. Why are we wringing our hands about what they need? 'Oh no! The spotted salamander is endangered!' You've never seen a spotted salamander in your life. It's fashionable grief. It's show-off grief, and I don't buy it for one second."

Hitomi and Daveed both kept their earbuds in, but I couldn't turn away. It's like James was broadcasting recordings from my childhood.

Once when I was eight, my dad took me fishing, and we came back with three trout. I thought when we took them out of the water they would just die and that would be it, but they were still alive, flopping around in a cooler in the trunk of the car.

"Why are they still flopping?" I asked my dad.

"Because they're cold."

"Oh."

Of course they were cold. Of course that was why they were flopping. That was not what I was really asking. I didn't know how to ask the real questions at the time:

(1) Why are we okay with them suffering?

(2) Why didn't we kill them when we caught them?

(3) What are we even doing, on this Earth, with all this power, if we're not minimizing the suffering around us?

(4) Are we absolutely 100 percent sure we won't be trout next time around?

But I didn't say anything that day with my dad. Instead, Gordo talked about how the world exists for us to use as we want, us humans, us lucky, divine humans, what a playground we have in which to eat and play, and I guess that helped diminish the sting in my stomach a bit. It helped enough until the fish stopped flopping.

41. Chicago

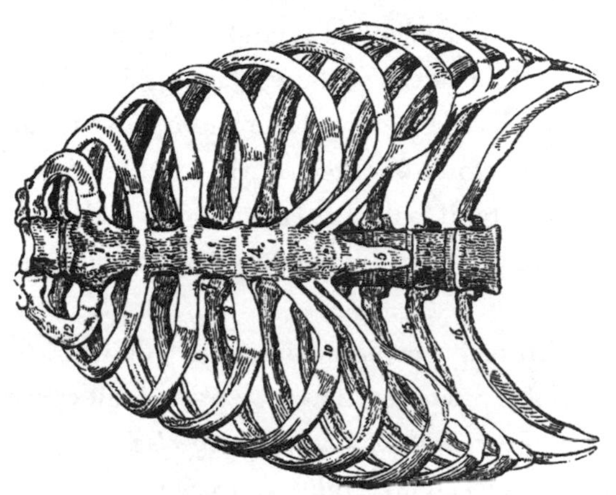

"I spent a summer here when I was eighteen," James said.

"I didn't know that," Hitomi said, looking up from her journal. "How close are we to the lake right now?"

"Lake Michigan?" James asked. "It's right over there."

"Right where?"

"Here. Put your left hand on the table."

James was now an authority on the geography of the area? I stared at a television showing the Cubs game in the bar where we were having lunch. One to nothing in the bottom of the third.

"No, palm down," James said. "Now, splay your thumb out so it is pointing at, like, two o'clock."

Such an expert, I thought. *I wonder who in the band might be more qualified to draw a goddamned map of Chicagoland on Hitomi's hand?*

"All of this here is Illinois," he said, and wrote "Ill." on it.

"And up here is Wisconsin. And here comes Chicago."

He drew a big sprawling dot and wrote *CHICAGO* above it.

"You'll have to get this checked out," he said.

She laughed.

I looked back at the game. Somehow it was now three to nothing, and yet nothing had happened. I looked over at Daveed to see his reaction. He looked as confused as me.

"The lake is up here," James said. "That summer I'd borrow my uncle's car and go up Lake Shore Drive to find something I had never seen before. *Woooooooop,* there I'd go, right up your index finger."

Hitomi looked at James and smiled. She kept smiling and left her hand on the bar, then picked up the pint glass and took a drink.

That night we played in a church downtown. A beautiful church with a large Steinway and a pipe organ built into the back of the stage.

Every miracle causes some suffering.

I picked up a Bible and saw those words written in pencil in the margins. I tried to figure if they were written in by a pastor, or a parishioner. Maybe it was a galley of the original copy of the Bible that God's editor had marked up.

Finding Robert was a miracle. Losing him was suffering. But was I actually just feeling fashionable grief? Show-off grief?

For once, I decided to indulge myself in a thought:

Fuck Robert.

Fuck someone walking away without saying goodbye. Right after a wedding, after me returning to New York, after ominously suggesting I should write a book. He just left. Like a coward. Like a fucking coward.

I needed him. You can't just cut all the strings tying you to the world and leap over a bluff and into the clouds.

That's a bullshit way to live. Write a letter. Explain yourself, you selfish fuck.

I took a seat at the Steinway. There was a vase on top of it with a single lotus flower floating in it. Somewhere in the audience were my parents. Melissa and Daniel, too. But not Robert.

There was a Steinway, though. I reveled in how fast my hands rolled along the piano, like they were wild horses finally unleashed to do what they had always dreamed of. That piano was a Ferrari compared to the Hondas I had known all my life.

I thought about Robert back in the thrift store.

"Do you know why those low keys are there? They're *not* so you can play them."

Fuck you!

I pounded on the lowest keys. Hitomi looked over at me like I was having a seizure. I *was* having a seizure. A seizure of liberation. I felt like those lower keys had been roped off with caution tape until I could finally figure out what they were for. *Fuck that.* They were for playing. End of riddle. Beers were for drinking. Whales were for hunting. Use the world that was provided to you, and enjoy thyself.

God, that's something Gordo would say.

stop saving us
we don't need it
let us split our heads open
let us get lost
in the archives
in the catacombs
let us get lost in the old growth
leave us alone
past the dusk
stop chasing after us
your pockets jingling with keys
stop calling the police
your head curled around the question of how
let us die
let us fall into the crushed leaves of autumn
let us be forgotten and ignored
leave our statues uncarved in the granite

let our words be untranslated, unheard, unheeded
stop letting out more rope
stop whistling echoes off of cliff sides
stop lighting candles for us
stop inking up paper with memories
let us be alone
and lose our shape and our form
give us the grace of being unwatched
unremarked upon, unfound
stop saving us
stop being a savior
stop

I thought of my parents in the audience listening to Hitomi's poem. I heard it through their ears, and it sounded so strange. I couldn't understand it. Why wouldn't someone want to be rescued from drowning? Why was she so dramatic? Why couldn't she just accept love? They would snicker. They would scratch their necks and look at their watches.

James wanted to play the Steinway on one song, so we traded, and I picked up his guitar. I didn't have a pick with me, and because I hadn't been playing much guitar to build up callouses, I cut my hand open on the very first chord I played. Right off the bat, bright red blood spilled out. All that rage over Robert was now covering the strings.

I felt like the blood was visible to all, and I wanted to let it hang out there. I kept playing despite the open wound, despite the stump of my hand flailing about. I pictured children in the first row gasping, *Mommy, why is he playing that guitar with a butchered ham hock?* I twisted and turned to give everyone in the church a view of my bleeding hand.

That was for Robert. That was the way I felt.

I gave James his guitar back, and he looked at the strings and then at me with a face that said, *What the fuck happened?*

After the show I saw my mom and dad standing backstage.

I thought of August 8, 1988. That was the first night game at Wrigley Field. Harry Caray had been all dressed up in a tuxedo like it was the Oscars. They had finally added lights to that baseball stadium, after only playing day games for decades, the last holdout in the league by far.

I looked at my parents across the back room of the church and I saw the three decades gone by. I hesitated before walking over to them. I pictured what my mom was going to say. Probably something like "I read there's a crime wave in New York City. Good thing you left."

Then my mom saw me and her face brightened. She had seen her harbor light, and she swam through the crowd to me. I held my arms across my chest.

My mom walked up to me, and I thought of her watching that game with me. She didn't care about baseball. She cared because I cared. She reached out her arms to me and she said, "I'm so sorry Robert couldn't be here."

And she hugged me. She hugged me before I could even unfurl my arms. She hugged me and I cried into her shoulder. My tears got her shirt wet and I kept crying. I didn't make a sound, but I poured out tears in the back room of that church in Chicago. My mom wouldn't let me go, and I couldn't stop crying.

42.
A Parking Lot

HITOMI, ON THE PHONE WITH JAMES in the parking lot of a Target: "Where. *Are.* You? Yes, we're all here. Ian and Daveed are playing some game. They're facing each other and trying to push each other over, I think. Yes, it's good to see they're getting along. I was so worried about that."

Daveed, to me, in that same parking lot: "I saw a great sadness in you back at the diner. And I like that in people. It's like, most people are just pretending to be so fucking happy, and, I don't know, I just don't believe it. I mean, sure, there's so much to be happy about, fields of green and clouds of white and all that shit. But also, it's like, what do *you* all have to be so happy about? Whoops. Watch it, now. I have a low center of gravity, so it's gonna take a lot to knock me over."

The streetlights had that strange multivalent glow, a color not from anything in nature. All the bugs gathered around them in reverence, or maybe protest.

Hitomi: "They're really intense. They're definitely competing. I know that. I don't think I should disturb them until they're done."

Daveed: "We used to always have crazy shit in my house growing up, and my mom and her sisters would talk to these objects. They had, like, Catholic shit, like beads and rosaries, and little altars to saints. But they talked to them so much that I think it carried over to them talking to everything around them. My mom would yell at a wooden spoon if the soup didn't turn out right. I thought it was funny, but now I'm like, whatever man. If it gets results even one percent of the time, I'll yell at a spoon."

Hitomi: "Are you coming back? How far away are you?"

Daveed: "It's cool to get out of New York sometimes. Even though, when you look at the valley and know that no flood of buffalo or lions or cheetahs—did you know there used to be cheetahs in North America?—knowing that there's nothing coming over that hill anytime soon. I really think that drove us all insane. Well. All of *you*. Mexicans aren't crazy at all. Whoa! You got too eager there. Let's play again."

43.
Your Voice

I LOVE YOUR VOICE. I always did, before I ever even heard it the first time. I heard echoes of it through my childhood. I felt it coming. I counted down the days. I love the way it rattles through you, like it has a troubled path. I love that it worries your face, as though your voice is not you, as though your voice is something that takes you over. I love that it is smoke. I love that it has no end. I love that I can hear melodies in your laughter.

The rainbow xylophone that kids have, with the wheels, with the mallet tied to it, every note a short ding. I love that you are that. Colorful and playful and here for the sake of wonder.

44.
Chicago Morning

"She has such a beautiful voice," Melissa said.

"I know, right?" I said.

It was nice to see Melissa in person after all the disembodied conversations on the phone.

"So, I don't know what else to do at this point," she said. "The police haven't given us anything."

"Fucking police," I said.

"And all the MISSING signs are now falling down and I don't have the heart to put them up again. There is an investigation, though. I mean, there's at least a case number. There's that."

I was at a table with Melissa at Cafe Mustache while across the way at another table Daveed stood up to demonstrate something to Daniel and the others. I couldn't tell which moment from our tour he was reenacting. Maybe it was something I hadn't been there for in person the first time, and now I was missing even the reenactment.

"What's her name?" Melissa asked.

"Hitomi," I said.

"How did you meet her?"

"I guess at a party," I said. "We just started dancing together."

"She's very captivating. Are you in love with her?" she asked.

"Agh, no," I said. "She has a boyfriend."

"That doesn't answer the question."

"No."

"I wish Robert could have seen the show," she said.

"Yeah. Me too."

"He would've loved taking photos of her. Of all of you."

"Yeah. I was secretly hoping he would show up."

"For some reason," she continued, and then paused. "This is kind of stupid. I thought about when I used to sing."

Daveed was now standing on his chair and getting more animated.

"You used to sing?" I asked Melissa.

"Only when I was a little girl. It's just. I can tell when people sing with their whole body, like they've done it their whole life. I used to love to sing. When I was five or six."

"I didn't know that," I said. "I've never heard you sing."

"Yeah, you wouldn't have. I haven't sung in years. But when I was a kid I'd always run around singing songs I made up, just to myself. Nobody ever told me how to sing, and I don't think I even listened to the radio. I only remember having one of those stupid rainbow xylophones with the little mallets."

"Yeah, I know those."

Daveed was lurching up and down. He looked like John Dunbar in *Dances with Wolves* when he was pantomiming a buffalo.

"But," she continued. "I just loved to sing. And one day my dad was on the phone in the kitchen and I was coloring in the living room, and I was singing this song. I still remember it for some reason. 'The rain kisses the lilies till they're blushing roses . . .' I remember because I was coloring flowers red. And I heard my dad say to my mom, he said, 'Can't you tell that kid to quit her caterwauling?'"

Melissa paused and held this memory in her body.

"I didn't even know what the fuck 'caterwauling' meant, but it sounded horrible, like the sound a cat makes when it's drowning. I cried so hard."

Melissa laughed at this and blushed at laughing about crying.

"I never thought anyone was listening to me sing," she said. "I wasn't doing it for anyone else. I sang like that for me. And to think, I was singing out loud and my dad thought it sounded bad . . . I really thought I was going to die. I don't know if I've sung out loud since then. God, that's so sad to say now."

She paused for a second, embarrassed she had told such a personal story out of nowhere.

"Any time since then that I've had the urge to sing," she said, "that word 'caterwauling' flashes in front of me, and my throat gets tight. What a horrible word. It's amazing the impact one word can have on you. I loved to sing so much."

She trailed off. And then added, "I sang like that for me."

We sat there with that silence. Daveed had finished his story and gotten off the chair, and everyone was recovering from laughing.

"Well," I said. "I wish there was a way to undo that."

45.
St. Louis

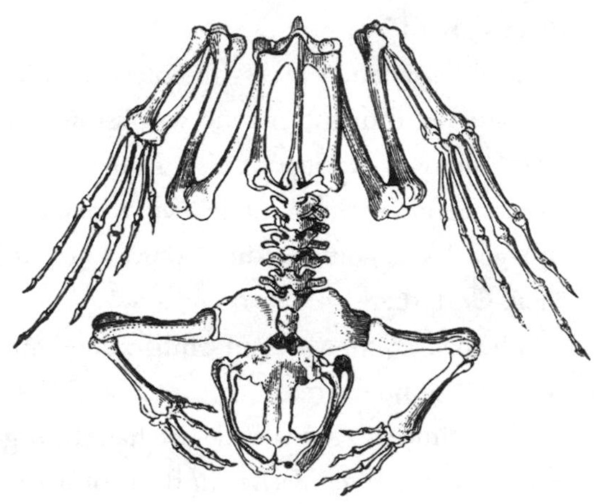

I WAS STILL READING *MOBY-DICK* and was now at the point where they were finally—*finally*—on the water.

What strange creatures, sperm whales. They were hunted so that men could put their oil in lamps to light the room while they read or cooked or whatever. I looked up what the sperm whale himself uses spermaceti oil for and found that scientists somehow still aren't totally sure, but they suspect it's used for echolocation. That means, in a way, that the sperm whale is a musician, bouncing vibrations off the world to figure out where to go. I instantly felt sorry for poor old Moby-Dick, singing his inscrutable songs in the dark seas.

But still, it reminded me what a precious thing it is to have a song in your head at all.

we converse
in a language
that has only two surviving speakers
a language that will be written about
in academic papers:

"how could they live so free
and love so wildly
and still be so misunderstood
by all the dumbasses
swirling around them?"

From line to line I would go back and forth, thinking the poems were about me or about James. This is the trap that poets set with their ambiguity: You walk right in and fall in love. You start planning where to put the baby's room, and then the light changes and it all falls down around you.

I became more fascinated with poetry because Hitomi was. I have always noticed that poetry, when it is presented in pop culture, often denotes to the audience that a character is some mix of pretentious and silly. If a character has written a poem, we laugh because it is a waste of their time, and if they are reading a poem out loud, we scratch at our necks because it is a waste of *our* time.

I'm sure I felt that way about poetry for a long time—that it was pointless, that it was annoying to have to endure even a few seconds of it. But somewhere quickly, possibly even in Pittsburgh, I understood the reason for it. I watched people in our audience as they felt uncomfortable when Hitomi got up and started reading. "No one told us we'd have to listen to *poetry*," I pictured them thinking. But by the time she was done, something in the room had changed. At the very least, she had directed people through a transformation, which is no small matter.

And so my appreciation for poetry became real, and my reasons for loving it were the same as the reasons I used to be indifferent to it: poetry is insignificant.

It is the opposite of talk radio. It is not offering policy proposals or critiquing some public person's verbal mistake. It is not doing anything so temporary. It is propaganda of the heart, and the heart changes its mind all the time, so poetry is contradictory in a way that constantly unveils the truth.

Writing a poem is like trying to halt a supertanker by holding a dandelion up to it. You can laugh at the frivolity of it. You can ridicule the person for doing such a thing. But—and I'm not saying this makes you one of them—when you laugh at poets, you laugh alongside tyrants. You are standing next to the powerful and the angry and the rich, and you might as well be a bully too, laughing at the weak person cutting snowflakes out of tissue paper. Yes, you are right. But is *right* everything you want to be?

So I loved poetry for its slightness, and I loved Hitomi for insisting on writing a new poem every day. When I first met her, she seemed taller and cooler than poetry. It seemed like she would have had better things to do. But for her to kneel down, to take an hour each day to try to arrange words in a pleasing order, to try to express something, *that* was really touching. I would hope people in our audiences saw poetry in a similar manner, as something so small and fragile it caused them to lose their breath. There are enough large machines that pound our breath out of us that it is a wonder to see something so small achieve something so profound. I would hope people were seeing that.

But you can't force anyone to do anything.

"I'm glad you're reading that book," James said to me at the bar after the show, "because I need your help with something. We need to find out what our whale is."

I remembered why I had avoided *Moby-Dick* for so long: every dude who reads it gets a hard-on for hunting his own whale. I thought about Robert, and how I was literally hunting him. Or I should have been, but I didn't know where to look. But to say this out loud would have sounded ridiculous.

"Is it Mary?" I asked. "Mary—what is it? Cornish? The booking agent?"

"No, no," James said. "We're not trying to *kill* her. Jesus."

"Oh. I guess I don't understand the metaphor."

"The thing that's keeping us going, the thing we are chasing. I guess ol' Mary could serve as our whale. It just seems like that's more a thing for Hitomi. I mean, what is there for *us?*"

I blanched at the suggestion that James and I had any mutual desires. Then I thought of Hitomi.

"Are you sure it's not fame?" I asked.

"It is," he said. "But we're never going to catch that, I'm sorry to say. We need a tangible, physical thing."

He looked around, like he would find it in that bar.

To sum up James's proposition: a metaphor for an unknown indie band's quest around the country should be physically manifested in their lives, the way Moby-Dick was a symbol of something and also actually a whale they wanted to kill. Daveed walked by us with his arm around someone. They were laughing like they had known each other for years, like they had gone to boarding school together and used to go to the woods to set off bottle rockets, but I knew Daveed had met this guy only ten minutes before and started a conversation about olives that had somehow led to this.

"Hey," I said to James, "you don't need to set me up with girls."

"I don't know what you mean."

"I mean. I know you're trying to find girls to distract me. Just. Don't. Please."

"They're coming up to me because they're too shy to talk to you. You don't offer a very welcoming facade. I'm an approachable, you know . . . what do you call it . . ."

"I don't—"

"Interloper!"

"I don't need you to—"

"No, that's not the word. *Consigliere* maybe."

"I don't need any help."

"Hitomi would know the word."

"It's just going to lead people to be disappointed."

"Alright then. I'll tell the stream of girls that come up to me after the show and ask about you—"

"There is not a stream—"

"I'll tell them you're not interested. That makes it easier on me." We both looked over at Hitomi, who was at the bar with an older man. They were rolling dice and laughing. A very put-together band was playing onstage, all dressed in suits and skinny ties and jumping around like they were trying to leap right into a record executive's arms.

"You know, it's hard sometimes," James said, "living with such a great writer like Hitomi. It's like she takes up all the inspiration in the room."

I nodded in agreement. Then I thought about it for a second, smiled as big as I had all week and said, "I don't feel that way at all."

That night, in a big, tall house in the suburbs, I saw *Christina's World* again. It was a framed print hanging in the foyer of the house we were staying at, and I wondered if maybe I should just take her off the wall and run away with her. Was she even still Christina, after enduring reproduction and framing?

I had thought my choice of favorite painting was so personal and subversive, that it was such a radical thing to like that painting, to like that famous painting hanging in the MoMA. Now that I saw it in St. Louis in the Edgebrook neighborhood or whatever, I felt embarrassed for ever having loved it. Of course it wasn't subversive. It was a painting of a pretty girl in a field. I felt like I had been tricked into liking it in the first place.

46.
Lawrence

SOME CITIES MIGHT HAVE SOMETHING WONDERFUL FOR YOU, but you only have an hour for them, and can you find that wonderful thing in just an hour? Some cities were home to great writers like Burroughs, and thousands of obscure writers too, but you don't have time to track them all down. In some cities, you only have time to stop at a Goodwill, where you might find a light gray blazer with a slim cut. A blazer that maybe belonged to some grandfather who just died, but as soon as you put it on it feels like it was tailored just for you, the shoulders perfect to the quarter inch.

And maybe you have the brief thought you've already been to this town. That you lived a whole life here. That you celebrated wedding anniversaries, buried your wife, carried on at the university for several years after her death until your hip was too stiff to allow you to make the walk. And even though you ate well and kept yourself trim, there came a day when you finally breathed your last breath and your children came and packed up your closets and put a particularly nice gray blazer at the top of a bag of stuff that went to Goodwill.

"Assembling the writer's uniform?" James asked as I looked at myself in the mirror.

"No."

"You never know. That might've belonged to Burroughs."

He walked away, and I put the jacket back on the hanger. I stepped away for a second and thought about it.

Hitomi tried on a big, floppy hat, and it swallowed her head whole. She waved her arms around like jellyfish tentacles.

I saw Daveed at a postcard rack. He selected what looked like the most boring one: a picture of a field, not even at sunset, with block letters that said KANSAS. He wrote on it right there on the counter, in big letters, "MISS YOU."

Hitomi pulled up her hat and saw this and looked over at me.

I picked up the jacket again and took it to the counter.

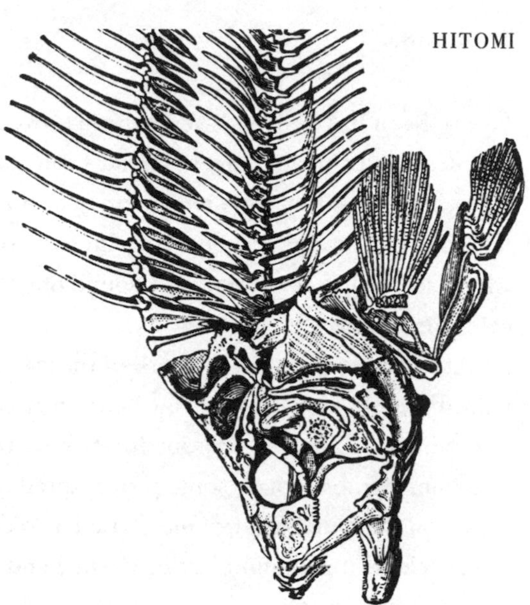

47.
Wichita

after all
we can read books
we can read the terrain
we can read tarot cards
even dogs can read,
our bodies, our intentions
ants can read the map to the spilled honey
I can't read sheet music
I can't read the ocean waves
I can't read German

but I can read your face
I know its hairpin turns
its dead ends
its church-free meadows
where no one has been

That was my face. I was sure of it. One thing I know about my face is that it has dead ends and hairpin turns. It has scared off enough people with its inexpressiveness that I can at least linger in the joy of believing it inspired a line in a poem once, in Kansas.

That night we played on a stage in front of a giant parabolic dish, which seemed to focus not only sound but also emotion into a concentrated point.

After the set, I sat in the dark of the warehouse with Hitomi and played the old piano. The front board had been taken off, revealing the hammers. Daveed was outside talking to the sound guy. James was rummaging through some props stored in the back room. Hitomi sat on the bench next to me. I tried to keep still so it didn't creak, didn't release a shotgun blast of longing and make Hitomi self-conscious about how close she was to me.

"A piano is always at your service," I said to her as I touched the keys. "It's like a regiment of soldiers, ready to spring into action whenever you need them."

"Why," Hitomi said as she rested her head on my shoulder, "does everything. Have to be. About war?"

James's heels clicked on the concrete floor as he walked through the shadows, holding his phone like a hermit's lantern. I tensed up.

"James?" I called into the darkness. I could hear him shuffling some metal around. Hitomi kept her head on my shoulder.

"Do I have a fever?" she asked.

I paused playing and put the back of my hand on her forehead.

"It's hot," I said. "But not feverish, I don't think."

I went back to playing.

"I feel like," she said, "every show I've ever played has been in such a tiny room, and it still hasn't been full, and there's always a couple people who leave in the middle. I don't want to dwell on the rejection. But there's just so much rejection."

James kept walking somewhere in the darkness.

"I think what you do is wonderful," I said as I pressed down one key slowly and watched the path of the hammer, amazed how when I looked at an odd angle I could convince myself it wasn't going to get there, that it would hit the wrong string.

"Thank you," she said as she reached out to touch a key in the same slow way as me. "But. It's just like. I'm just lighting paper on fire. It burns bright but it's not lasting."

James's heel clicking stopped.

"But," I said, trying to look around to see where James was, but not wanting to disturb Hitomi. "I think. Sometimes. A little ember catches on something else—"

"—and burns the whole forest down," she said.

"Yeah," I said. "Wait. What is the 'fire' in this metaphor?"

"I don't know," she said and stopped touching the piano and sat up. "I guess you're right. I light things on fire for a living. I can't complain about the burning."

A pause as we sat there.

"James?" I said.

"Yes, sir," he said.

"Whatcha doing?"

"Just looking at all this stuff lying around. I found a book about Wichita."

"That makes sense," Hitomi said. She got up and walked into the darkness, in a different direction from James's voice, and started her own rustling. "This is the exact place where you'd expect to find a book about Wichita."

I sat there and stared at the piano. All the patient soldiers, waiting for my order. No, no. They were midwives. They were Buddhists. So calm. So patient.

"James?" I said.

"Yesss?" he responded.

"What does the book say? About Wichita?"

"Just a bunch of stuff about a vortex. All the swirling winds of the continent all find their calm point. Right. Here."

"Hm," I said. "Do you think that Robert might have fallen into a vortex?"

"Perhaps. Maybe he's just looking for answers."

"Damn it."

"I just mean, people saying they need you isn't the same as them needing you. People say a lot of things. Sometimes you have to go where nobody's talking, where nobody's selling you on their importance in the world."

"Yeah. Okay."

His heels clicked again as he walked.

"Allen Ginsberg came here," James said. "Nobody ever talks about such a thing. That's probably why I booked the show here, now that I think about it. Do you think there are people following whims like that anymore? Following the ley lines of the world to track down a feeling? I don't know any."

"Well," I said, connecting the obvious dots. "There's Robert."

Those words bounced off the parabolic dish and rattled around the room. I felt good about saying it. I felt good about how I said it. Even if it was a trick he was leading me to, it still made me feel clever for getting it.

Or maybe James wanted me to say *he* was one of those people. It was too late to change my answer. I didn't hear him say anything, but I also didn't hear footsteps walking away. We sat there together, I guess, the three of us, in that room for several minutes, not saying a word. I think he and Hitomi were both still there.

Far off, way outside, we could hear Daveed laughing at something.

I turned to play the piano again. It didn't seem like the room needed much soundtracking at all. I pressed down a key slowly enough that the hammer rose up and never even made it to the string. The only sounds that filled the room were the tiny mechanical details of the machine.

48.
Wichita Morning

I SLEPT THAT NIGHT ON A WHITE, CIRCULAR VINYL COUCH with a backrest in the middle. I had to curl my body around it, which left me spinning around all night like the hands on a clock in a flashback.

In the morning I got up before anyone else and walked through the warehouse. It takes some real faith or stupidity to walk through a dark room whose layout you are not familiar with, especially when that room is full of jagged, expensive sculptures.

I got to the big front door and pushed on it. Warm sunlight poured in and washed over my face. I couldn't see anything for three seconds, but I imagined there would be a parade of white horses in front of me to pick me up and take me to a great celebration.

Instead it was an alley.

I called Melissa.

"Hey. I'm in Wichita. And. I just. I wish there was something more to say than just 'So' and 'Okay.'"

"We could share things we love about him."

"But that makes it seem like he's really gone."

"What if we shared things we loved about people before they were gone? Wouldn't that end up being wonderful?"

"Okay, but let's keep it in the present tense."

"Yes."

"Where do we start?"

"Start with the smallest thing."

I looked down and saw those overlapping pebble circles. I reached in my pocket and found a plastic ruby that a little girl in that house in St. Louis had given me. I crouched down and placed it in the middle.

"Okay," I said. "I loved the way he straightened his shoulders. It's not like he was ever slouchy, but sometimes I would see him center himself and pull back his shoulders."

"Yeah. I love that, too. You said that in the past tense though."

"Fuck."

"It's okay."

49.
The Waves

WE DROVE THROUGH WESTERN KANSAS and into eastern Colorado, up from the plains into the mountains. I looked out at the trees whooshing past: oak, poplar, and fig turning into fir and pine. I thought about the skulls at the Mütter Museum, how they were lined up to demonstrate how odd they were. But because they were *all* odd, they somehow blended together.

James asked if he could join me and Daveed in a game, and we said we could try, but after one minute of Many Long Ago we gave up, as James got frustrated because he couldn't figure out how to describe the Titanic sinking without using the letter *e*. He went back to listening to Gordo. I watched him as he did, knowing that James hated him, but was still obsessed with what he said. What he might say.

Here is the regret I feel over listening to Gordo as a child: I feel like I was tricked. His cadence was like a schoolyard taunting, and it was a rare opportunity for me to be on the side of the bully. My whole childhood I always felt like I was an alien, so it was tempting to belong to something.

It was like Gordo was in the truck with me and my dad. He was as real as pushing the boat across muddy reeds. He was as real as the tug on the fishing line. These were real, physical sensations, and the timbre of Gordo's voice was a part of that. He was angry. My dad was angry. I didn't want either of them to be angry. They weren't angry at me, but it didn't matter. It felt like I was running alongside a horse, a powerful animal who was almost unaware of me, and in that unawareness could trample me. But if I could run alongside the horse and keep him happy, I might be okay.

Hitomi looked out the window at the mountains and said in a soft voice, "They look like waves, don't they? They look like frozen waves. Petrified breakers. I just want to walk up and touch them."

Our van charted a course right through the break between those waves. I looked at them and saw what she saw. An ocean in the middle of the country. The trees were groups of surfers riding the biggest wave of their lives.

"But," she continued, "I would be afraid that if I went out there, at the exact moment I touched them, they would unfreeze. And I would be swallowed."

50.
Denver

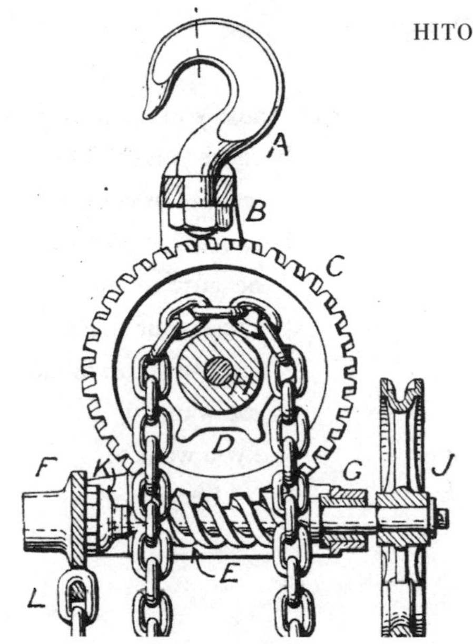

MOUNTAIN DWELLERS OFTEN DREAM OF THE OCEAN. The human brain is always thirsting for contrast. If you stare at a green square for a minute and then close your eyes, you will see a red square, and, likewise, those up in the mountains close their eyes and see only the ocean, even though the ocean is twelve hundred miles away.

If you want to lay with me
because you see me as a rainshadow
because I shield
if you want to know my sister's boyfriends
if you want to know my fourth-favorite animal
if you want every crumb
if you want to soak rags
and drape them on my fever
if you want my femaleness
if you want the spark of opposition
if you want to color in the block letters
on every brochure

it's because you drape your rags
because you shield from love
because of your fever
because the spark
because the block letters
because your sister
because your animal
if you want to
if you want to
because
because

After the set, I got to dance with Hitomi again.

"The eighties were insane!" Daveed said across a crowd of people. "What the hell happened to snare drums in the eighties?"

Don't ask me

INXS was on the sound system. I was aware I was just another man staring at a woman, like Wyeth staring at Christina, but was it sometimes okay? Was I supposed to shade my eyes every time? I wasn't hunting her, like Ahab was hunting the whale. I wasn't obsessed. Or maybe I was.

What you know is true

I was so starved for affection that earlier in the day I must admit I lingered on the symbol of a woman on the door of the women's restroom. I truly did that in a Cracker Barrel in eastern Colorado or western Kansas, and in the middle of doing so, an actual woman stepped out of the bathroom and gave me a real look of genuine upset, rightly so, because what kind of creep stares at a door?

Don't have to tell you

So, in the thin Colorado air after our show, I moved closer to Hitomi. Was it just the hypoxic air? Was it all those miles driven? What does it take to drive a tame creature wild? It's not as much as you would think. One drink at altitude, a little eighties music, a beautiful woman in the cascading lights of a dance floor.

What is civilization anyway? A handshake deal to try to get along? How many people break that deal, for jealousy, for revenge, just to survive? What did Robert say at the wedding? In the mason jar candlelight?

"We are all just trying to survive," or something like that.

I have lived quietly and patiently with moths inside my innards, my mummified organs wrapped and ready for removal. I don't want to be a zombie. Because there is no pill for zombies. There is no antidote. There is just a time when it is too late.

Too late.

There is a time when it is too late. Even though everyone says, "It's never too late," well, at some point it's too late.

I was now close enough to embrace Hitomi, or for her to embrace me. She looked to the side and then at me and smiled. She held her arms over her head. I held mine out to the sides. We slowly moved our arms to envelop each other, there at the still point of the dance floor.

Just a pinprick of daylight existed between our bodies.

Then I felt a sudden, dull force smashing into me. A solid, strong body had pushed its way through us. A mistake? Or a misunderstanding? It seemed intentional. It pushed us apart, forever changing the tenor of the night.

I laughed for a third of a second, thinking it was a joke, but then I saw James storming off the dance floor and out of the bar, a bowling ball who had done his work. Hitomi yelled after him and then chased him. I slumped my reaching arms down and stopped dancing in the middle of the room while everyone went back to their own dancing.

I rubbed my shoulder and thought, *Petrified breakers*.

I sat in a booth while Hitomi and James argued and I texted Robert:

I ruin everything by wanting it too badly.

And then, inexplicably:

I can't wait to see the ocean.

51.
Coleman

"THERE IS NO WAY," Gordo said on the radio, "no way that this *won't* be politicized."

James looked over at me with a conspiratorial glance.

He had apologized the following morning. Although it was the kind of apology that didn't include the words "I'm sorry" and consisted more of "Can we just move on?"

We were in a small town in Utah, and Gordo was talking about a mass shooting that happened that morning in some other small town in Utah. We pulled off to get gas. There seemed to be no one on the streets. Maybe someone was manning the store inside the station, but if we investigated closer, they also might turn out to be just a mummy wrapped in denim and handkerchiefs.

"Hitomi," James said as he pumped the gas. "Can you look up something for me?"

"Yeah, what?" she asked.

"Can you look up 'Gordo Messing' and tell me where he lives?"

"Why?"

"I would just like to know."

"That guy," she said. "What was he saying about feminists not getting invited to the prom?"

"Can you just see where he lives though?"

"Alright, I'll look it up." she said, pulling out her phone. "I bet he lives in Florida . . . Oh fuck! I'm right! St. Petersburg!"

"Ah. Interesting," James said as he kept looking at me. "We play there in a couple weeks."

"Look at this," Hitomi said. "Guess where Gordo got his start in radio? Valparaiso, Indiana. Hey, Ian, isn't that where you're from?"

"Um. Yes," I said.

"Um. Yes," James said, mocking my tone. "When were you going to tell us about this darkness in your past?"

"Well . . ." I said.

"Oh!" James said. "I was just kidding, but it sounds like you're actually troubled by this. What's the story? Did you know him?"

"No. It's just," I said. "When I was young I used to listen to him with my dad. And he was—funny."

"He *is* funny," James said.

"No, he's not," Hitomi said.

"Let him talk, please," James said.

"He was funny," I said. "I was eleven or whatever. He made me laugh. I was like, yeah, stick it to Hillary, or whatever. And I—he wrote a book. And I remember I asked for it for Christmas. And my dad got it for me."

"Oh dear," James said.

"I'm sorry on behalf of Valparaiso," I said. "And myself. We just thought he was funny. We didn't know it would get out of hand."

"Apology not accepted," James said. "I personally blame you for the rise of Gordo."

"Gah."

"And I expect you to do something about it."

"What do you mean?" I asked.

"When we get to St. Petersburg," he said.

"Oh. No."

"I think we've found our whale," James said.

"What whale?" Hitomi asked.

I left that scene and walked down the street. I saw a church with about eight million cars parked around it. They were parked in ditches, parked on lawns, parked so that surely not everyone could have gotten out. The church bowed under the weight of what seemed like the entire town gathered together. I listened for a hymn or some music. I heard nothing.

My phone buzzed in my pocket as I walked back to the van. Was it worth driving on farther? Should we just start living in—what was this town—Coleman? Join the church?

I pulled out my phone and looked at it.

It was a text message from Robert.

A text message.

From Robert.

Ian

That's what it said. My name.

Never had my name felt so personal and important. What it really said was *I'm alive*. Those three dots were flashing below it, showing that Robert—young, beautiful Robert—was typing another text message to me. It wasn't all over, the words between us. There were to be more. I was twenty feet from the van and my knees got wobbly. I wasn't sure I could make it the rest of the way. Why was he texting instead of calling?

I texted him back faster than anyone has ever texted anything:

!

Still those dots were there on his end. I looked up at the van and saw a bleary mirage of our vehicle with my bandmates gathered around it. And then, finally, another text from Robert:

Hello

Jesus. Way to spill the details, bud. Out with it, then! I quickly texted him again:

!!

Again the dots as he composed another text. Couldn't we just talk? I started to pull up his number to call him. My hand was shaking. God, I just wanted to hear his voice. Was he okay? Was he someplace loud where he couldn't talk? Was he in the hospital? It didn't matter. Nothing mattered. He was alive.

By now I had stumbled back to the van.

"Guys," I said in a trembling voice that barely registered.

Nobody heard me.

"Guys," I said again.

The dots bounced on my screen. I couldn't believe he was alive. I could now admit that I had really thought he was dead. I couldn't imagine a way that he would be gone this long and still be okay. I was ashamed to say I had almost given up. And there he was, texting the slowest messages anyone had ever texted.

"Guys!" I finally said loud enough to get their attention.

I held my phone up and smiled.

"He's . . ." I said. Tears were in my eyes. The phone buzzed in my hand. "Just a second . . ."

"What?" James asked.

I looked at the phone, still smiling. There was a message. It was a couple sentences. My excitement blurred the words. I had to calm down so I could make any sense of it at all.

Calm down. Calm down.

This is what it said:

This is Robert's mother. Can you please call me?

52.
What Is Grief?

GRIEF IS STRONGER THAN YOU. Because time is nothing. But when you fall for the trick of time, all your love feels wasted on those who are no longer present. Because sprinklers create rainbows. Because linoleum is not comfortable to sit on, but you never want to get up. Because all of life is a game and the little games remind us of this, even though they make us feel stupid. But feeling stupid is the point. Because Europe is a far-off place we never went to together, and now it's sitting there untouched by our feet. Because of your fever. Because the spark. Because the block letters.

53.
Salt Lake City

I QUELLED MY ANGER AND CALLED ROBERT'S MOTHER. God, all those stupid texts I wrote to Robert. She must have thought I was insane.

She told me she wanted to have a wake for him, even though there was no proof he was dead. She had found his phone in his house, which was not encouraging news, but still, it wasn't proof of death. She wanted to move on. I told her I thought a wake without a body was a terrible idea. She said she'd think about it.

At a small venue called Kilby Court, Hitomi read a poem I suppose was only half a dozen words long, but it lasted longer than the lifespan of some insects. Still, even when she was done, it seemed like we should have kept going. She said each utterance of each word like it had a new definition. She pivoted her head a bit each time she said something. I thought of an egret hunting in the grass.

because
because
because, because, because, because
because, because, because, because, because,
because, because, because I
I
I, I, I, I, I, I, I,
I, I, I, I, I, I, I, I, I, I, I, I, I, I, I
I
I still
still, still
still
still
still
still, still, still, still
still, still, still, still, still, still, still, still, still
still believe
believe
believe
believe, believe
believe, believe, believe, believe
believe, believe, believe, believe, believe, believe
believe in
in, in, in
in, in, in, in, in, in, in
in, in, in, in, in, in, in
in, in, in
in you
you
you, you, you
you, you, you, you, you, you, you
you, you, you, you, you, you, you, you, you

Was this poem for me? I asked this question every night. I think it was only in Salt Lake that I finally realized: *hell yes*, it was for me. If I could use it, it was for me. If I could find a way in, what did it matter what the intention of the creator was?

Like *Christina's World*, which maybe I had too hastily distanced myself from after seeing it in a suburban home in St. Louis. Maybe there was room enough for everyone to have their own view of something grand.

After the set, a couple of dudes descended on Hitomi like they had drawn up a football play to chat with her. They were two of a very small number of people at the show. The small crowd gave a desperate tinge to Hitomi's performance. I could see her taking it personally, like she might quit right in the middle of the show, though from where I sat we were the same band we had been when things were great in Pittsburgh or Chicago. We didn't suddenly forget how to play music.

Kilby Court had no bar, which stressed out James. He stood next to me around the bonfire outside, holding a can of soda. Hitomi was across the patio, laughing with one of the dudes.

"Well," James said. "I guess we've reached our—what was it? *Détente*."

The music over the sound system was from the eighties, like it was taunting us to revisit Denver. And what better music than eighties music to say, *Remember me?*

Daveed walked up and stood in between us.

"Hey, man," he said as he put his arm around me. "How are you?"

He had his big, cozy hoodie on. I laughed at first at this expression of concern for some reason. Then I instantly almost felt like crying.

"I'm—" I said. "I feel like a cinder block. And someone just took a hammer to me. And I'm trying to hold the pieces together. But. Why?"

Hitomi was now playing a game with the dude. Something about balancing different objects on their noses, which seemed rather intimate.

"It's a world full of hammers," James said. "And don't forget, we're holding them, too."

I tried to think whether this actually meant something.

"Tomorrow is a day off," Daveed said. "We can get stoned and play games."

"Okay," I said. "Yeah. I'd like that."

The dude next to Hitomi had a log. A dirty log on his chin. And his arms were spread out wide as he contorted his body to balance it.

"Do you know why the streets are so big in Salt Lake City?" James asked.

"Why?" Daveed asked.

"They were built wide enough so that you could drive a chariot down them and have enough room to turn it completely around," James said. "A chariot! So, all this space is just so people could have enough room to change their minds if they were going the wrong way."

Hitomi disappeared into the back alley with the dude. I felt a tinge of panic in my stomach. The bile started churning.

"Are *we* going the wrong way?" I asked.

James drank from his soda. As the firelight flickered on his face, he looked like a kid.

"I don't know," he said.

The patio was so quiet. The few people who had come to the show had already left, and Hitomi had wandered off around the corner.

I pulled out my phone to text Robert, saw the last text from Robert's mother, and put the phone back in my pocket.

54. A Dinner Party in Idaho

A DAY OFF.

Deep in the woods somewhere in the giant caldera of Idaho, we drove to a dinner party. It wasn't just a night without a show but a night away from our normal selves. Smoke the dread away. Turn off the switch.

"Cassandra and Torrin are their names," James said as he adjusted his tie in the van. "These are respectable people. Let's try to tame our wilderness a bit."

"Cassandra like the van?" Daveed asked.

"Yes," said James. "Like the van. I hadn't thought of that. I went to school with them and—they've done well for themselves."

"What, are we going to embarrass you?" Hitomi asked.

"This rain is intense," Daveed said as he squinted through the windshield. "It was dry like half an hour ago and now we've hit this, like, wet pocket."

"Wet pocket!" I said.

Daveed looked at me.

"I challenge you," I said, "to work that phrase into conversation during this dinner party."

"Guys, no," James said.

"Okay, challenge accepted," Daveed said. "But you have to use the phrase . . . 'Knitting committee.'"

"Knitting committee?" I asked.

"I don't know, it's just what came to mind."

"Guys," James said. "These are university professors. Torrin is a published author. Ian, you should talk to him about writing a book."

"Okay, then I need a scarf," I said. "Does anyone have a scarf?"

"I might have something," Hitomi said as she dug through her bag. "Here."

She passed forward a piece of clothing. I tried to see it in the dark. It was the pair of leopard-print tights she had worn at the party back in Brooklyn. I looked back at her.

"It's the best I've got," she said.

I tossed them around my neck.

We ran through the rain from the van into the house, squealing as we scampered over puddles. Once inside we felt hushed by the very grown-up decor. Soft music was playing, and there was a floor-to-ceiling bookshelf in the foyer. I thought about the one book I owned, how I wished I were reading something else.

Daveed, taking off his coat, said to our hosts, "It's raining pretty hard out there. My coat has a wet pocket now."

I looked over at him like he had cheated. He gave me a shrug.

We took our shoes off and slid in our socks across the hardwood floors. James tried to engage in proper conversation with them. Cassandra offered me some wine and I accepted. I didn't know what the point of holding off was anymore.

We all gathered at the dining room table. I took my napkin and put it on my lap. It was like we were three on three, kids versus adults.

"What is eating?" I asked as I speared an asparagus. "Isn't it kind of weird? You take some food and put it in a hole in your body and mush it up and then it becomes more of you."

"Ian is a writer," James said. "So—"

"Ian, what are you writing?" Torrin asked.

"I am just getting started," I said. "I'm trying to write about love."

"Oh, *love,*" Torrin said, like it was a unique concept. "Yes. What about love?"

"Well," I said, "just a certain kind of love. Not the kind people usually write about. Just a love that is soft and quiet. That isn't dramatic. Or. Is dramatic, but is dramatic inside while calm outside. Like a fire in a bank vault."

"A fire in a bank vault," Cassandra said.

"Yes," I said. "I hadn't thought of it that way before, but yes. It's also about how love is the opposite of grief, but they're really the same. Just wondering if you can grieve for someone if they're not really gone."

"Grieve for someone next to you?" Cassandra asked.

"Not next to you," I said. "Like, grieve for someone without for sure knowing if they're gone forever. Also." I looked at Hitomi from the side of my vision. "Can you adore someone without possessing them? Like, can you really just appreciate someone for the beauty they bring to the world, but not have to, like, I don't know. *Be* with them. In most stories love is presented as this victory march, and in my experience it's much more awkward than that."

"Are people going to want to read that, though?" Torrin asked.

"Well," I said. "I just. I don't know. It's what I have right now. Maybe it'll change." I poked at my asparagus again. "What kind of books do you write?"

"I've written eight books—" Torrin said.

"Nine—" Cassandra said.

"Yes," Torrin said. "I suppose nine. But eight books in a series of detective stories. They've each been a modest success, and I teach in a creative writing program at the university."

"Ian is a great writer," Hitomi said.

Everyone stopped and looked at Hitomi.

"I looked at a page of his notebook while he was asleep in the van," she said, and then turned to me. "I looked at a page of your notebook while you were asleep in the van. It was wonderful. You should share it with people."

"Yeah!" Daveed said.

"Let's hear something," Cassandra said.

"My notebook's in the van," I said.

"Oh, too bad," Cassandra said. "After dinner though?"

"Perhaps," I said.

Hitomi looked at me from across the table. I guess I should have felt violated, but really, I felt special, like she had seen me for the first time.

"How's the tour going?" Torrin asked James.

"It's—we're getting by," James said. "There have been some good shows."

"This will be our last tour," Hitomi said.

"What?" Cassandra asked.

"No," James said. "That's not true. Hitomi, that's not true. Last night was rough, so that's all we remember."

"I don't want to do this anymore," Hitomi said. "It's too sad."

"It's just a tough time," James said, "after a bad show."

"It's not that," Hitomi said. "I just don't want to give away my preciousness anymore to people sitting in a bar who don't care."

"Look, 'Tome," James said. "You realize we're making obsolete music, right?"

"*Great*," Hitomi said.

"Okay, no," James said. "It's not obsolete. But. You know. Fuck it. My favorite things are obsolete. *Moby-Dick* is obsolete. Walking is obsolete. Being irrelevant takes the pressure off. You can just enjoy it then, right? Don't you still enjoy the actual singing part, aside from all the other stuff?"

"Of course," she said as she pushed her asparagus.

"Everyone's just into up-tempo music these days because they're all afraid of dying," James said.

The old house seemed to shudder at that.

"I'm not afraid of dying," Hitomi said. "I'm afraid of being old and muttering about my aching back. It's the muttering I want to avoid."

Everyone was silent. There was just the meager scraping of Daveed's knife on his plate. He looked up at everyone and seemed to want to say something positive.

"This whole thing," I said, holding my glass of wine and sitting back, like I had seen James do so many times. "Being in a band on the road. It reminds me of one thing."

"What's that?" Hitomi asked.

"It feels like—" I said as I took another sip, straightened my leopard-print scarf, and looked directly at Daveed. "And don't take this the wrong way, but this whole business of music and touring and all that, it feels like we're just a part of this big, I don't know—*knitting committee*. You know?"

Daveed smiled big, like I had knocked down all the bowling pins.

"Cheers to that!" Daveed said, raising his glass.

"What—" James asked.

"Is that," Torrin asked, "a pair of tights around your neck?"

55.
Pendleton

AT THE WESTERN EDGE OF THE HIGH DESERT was the town of Pendleton, Oregon. Portraits of bucking broncos and their riders graced the brick buildings. I tried to park the van in front of a café as James explained music to us.

"Do you know what the number one song of all time is?" he asked, looking at his phone. "The fucking 'Twist' by Chubby Checker."

I put the van in reverse and looked behind me.

"So, that's what we're talking about here," he said. "A dance craze. We should come up with a dance craze."

My view was blocked by instruments. I didn't know what I was expecting. There was never anything to see if you looked behind you.

"I mean, what else are we out here doing?" he asked.

"Expressing grief at the loneliness of being human?" Hitomi asked.

"Okay! Let's turn that into a dance craze, though. *Come on, let's do the Expression of Grief!"* James sang, moving his arms around.

"Like we did last summerrrr. Let's do the Expression of Grieeeffff!"

I looked over at Hitomi to gauge her reaction.

"See? Nothing to it," James said.

I eased the van back, just like James did in Yonkers when Bill was telling us how Cassandra wasn't as big as she seemed. What had he said? "Surprisingly compact?"

CRUNCH.

I had gone too far. We all heard that gross sound of twisting metal. I pulled forward a few feet and put it in park. James jumped out first.

"Cassandra," he moaned. I had backed into a telephone pole. The pole was fine, just as chewed up as any other telephone pole. *Cassandra,* however, now had a big dent in the bumper and back door, spoiling the smoothness of those lines hammered out years before in a Chevrolet factory.

James pulled at the rear door and it wouldn't open. He shook it with a furious rage, and I thought he was going to turn into Thor right there and hammer us all into the ground.

He finally popped the door open and fell back from the momentum. He looked inside.

"Christ," he said.

My hands were covering my face. I didn't know what horror could be in there.

James turned to me and said, "Well, this is what you deserve."

The Wurlitzer. The poor, noble piano replacement. The regiment of soldiers waiting to be played. James's instrument that he had lent me because I didn't have my own. It was dented in the same way the van was dented. I closed my eyes.

"Come on, let's check it out," James said.

We dragged it onto the sidewalk and opened it up to see the damage.

"This," James said, "is not good."

"I'm—" I said. "I'm so sorry."

James stood in front of me and looked me in the eyes. He put his hands on my shoulders. I was ready to receive a speech from him. Something about the abundance of America. How we can't get complacent about it and start backing vans into telephone poles and destroying our Wurlitzers. All the great, warm, vintage instruments were made decades ago. We can't go around breaking them, ruining them, discarding them like old toothbrushes.

James didn't say this. I looked at his punchable face. It was only then that I saw he had the same chin as Robert's. Somehow, in the context of James's face, it was all wrong, like he had just pulled it out of a Mr. Potato Head box. Now that chin looked so delicious to punch. I always feared there would be a time when it would come to that, when we'd get in a fight. Not just him crashing into me on the dance floor, but an actual fistfight. Even though I had never punched someone in my life, we would have to fight each other on the sidewalk of a rodeo town, right in front of the Working Girls Hotel.

It would be strange for me to strike first, though, seeing as I had just dented his van and his Wurlitzer in one swift action. Could I just go with that feeling, go into a frenzy, strike first and second and third? Preemptive strikes? And then run off into the streets of Pendleton?

Still James stood there with his hand on my shoulder.

"*Now* is when we need a dance craze," Daveed said.

Hitomi laughed. James kept staring at me.

"*Let's twist that metal,*" Hitomi sang under her breath. "*Like we did last summerrr...*"

I fell into James' eyes, like he was subsuming me. I don't know if he had really looked at me since the moment we first met at the diner. Up until then I felt like another object of his, just another thing he needed to pack into the van. But if he loved his objects this much, maybe he could find something redeemable in me. But could I find it in him?

"You're a good kid," he said, probably quoting a Western he had seen once. "Let's watch where we're going from now on, okay?"

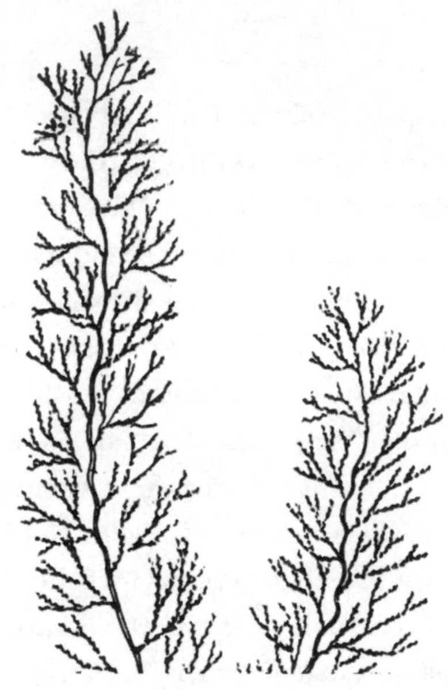

56.
Seattle

THAT NIGHT WE HAD A CELLIST JOIN US from the other band, and something about the classical seriousness on her face gave us all the liberation we needed. We were no longer just a bunch of fuckups. We were fuckups with a purpose. We tried to surprise and upend her expectation of where the song was going, and the four of us felt closer together than we had in at least a week.

I've loved so many things
kisses under a blanket
the shadows of elm leaves
I've wished they would keep flowing out
like water spun through a turbine
I've wished they would love me too
but then I realized it didn't matter
my love was my own creation
we were together
because I said so

I didn't know who was with whom. If you try to find the through line in a collection of poems, you'll go crazy. I knew that.

There was a piano onstage somehow. Somehow a Ludwig upright knew to show up to the gig and be a little out of tune, just out of tune enough to give grist to everything, to drive the cellist mad.

Robert had wandered off and left his phone behind. I suppose in the modern age that is a declaration of suicide. What life is there if you don't have your phone with you? But then, maybe he had evolved to a higher state of being. Or maybe he just lost the phone.

Objects we lose track of, they still exist somewhere in the big world. They still keep living. *Life goes on,* as a famous Cougar from Indiana once sang. Life goes on even after your belongings get broken and are taken away from you. Long after the thrill of pounding on those keys is gone.

But I had a piano to play in Seattle, and the sharpness and clarity of it pulled us all together. That, along with antagonizing that poor cellist.

"See?" James said to Hitomi after. "A better show is always around the corner. We just have to live through every painful hour of the day to get there."

Afterward James led us to a place called Denise's. The cellist came with us. James wouldn't tell us what it was going to be, exactly, and with a name like that, it could have been a diner just as easily as it could have been—

"Is this a strip club?" Hitomi asked as we walked up.

"It's an adult drinking establishment," James said.

"God, why didn't you just say so?"

I looked at the neon sign with the *e,* the *n,* and the *s* burnt out and wondered how I could've ever thought James might be taking us to a diner.

"Ladies and gentlemen, give it up for Amberrrrr!" said the DJ into a distorted microphone.

We walked in to see Amber step out on stage, lovely Amber, swinging around the pole, getting warmed up. In a flash, she climbed up the pole and linked her right leg around it. She hung there upside down, smiling, as she removed her top. Danzig was on the speakers singing *if you wanna find hell with me.*

Hitomi and James sat up front, while Daveed, the cellist, and I sat in the back. Amber hung on the pole and Hitomi turned back to look at us with a satisfied smile. James looked back too and raised his glass of vodka grapefruit. Amber was so still and peaceful, safe at the very center of the spinning world. All around her was the madness of rushing forces, coalescing into hordes to enact revenge on whoever had wronged them. Meanwhile Amber, now having removed her bottoms, was as naked as you could be, and so comfortable in that nakedness she seemed more clothed than the rest of us.

I thought, *as much as she takes away, she still remains Amber.*

The cellist poked at her drink with the tiny straw. She shoved an ice cube beneath the gin, which caused another cube to spring up.

"We don't do this—" I said to her.

"What?" she said, pushing her hair behind her ear.

"We don't do this every night," I said. "We don't usually do this."

She nodded and looked up at the ceiling, like, *I'm here now.*

Daveed clinked his glass to hers and said loudly, "Just another Tuesday night for Tashtego!"

Amber slid down the pole, the Danzig song now finished, and she walked offstage while collecting dollar bills from the floor. Hitomi hollered and handed her a bill.

Only when Amber had stopped performing did I feel comfortable in looking at her. I thought how strange a thing the human body is when it is all revealed, when it is all shaved and pruned and presented on a stage with spotlights. How the more we try to get to the forbidden thing, the more it looks plain and clinical.

And then Hitomi stood up. Her legs were so elegant in her stone-washed jeans. I closed my eyes and tried to calm myself.

57.
3 a.m. People

I WANT 3 A.M. PEOPLE. I want unlit, vulnerable people. I want uncrowded people, smoldering people. I want to be with those people in their natural state at 3 a.m.

I want people smoking cigarettes when they never do. I want people saying things they'll deny the next day.

I want standing-in-the-parking-lot people, outside-some-all-night-diner people. I want people gone, people unleashed.

It's at 3 a.m. when you see the whole shape of the people you've only ever seen during the day. It shows you their shading and their depth.

(God help you if you meet a person for the first time at 3 a.m., if all you know of a person is 3 a.m. Then you only know the shadows, you only know their trouble.)

But for however long I'll have known a person, I don't feel I really know them until I know them at 3 a.m. Even just to see them once at 3 a.m., sitting on the hood of a car that isn't theirs, the reflection of the neon lights bending on the bumper. Even just to see them lose their domesticity, entertain the squalor. It all happens at 3 a.m.

Daveed in the 3 a.m. was unwrapped, all of us cringing at what might break.

"Watch this, man," he said as he jumped up onto a newspaper box, didn't quite make it, and then flopped over it like today's mackerel.

He was not embarrassed. He put his arms out wide and turned it into a trick. We sculpted a statue of him in our minds.

Rosy-cheeked James marched on, unloading some soliloquy into the air. How often we seem to reach our end, feel there will be no good times left, and then we keep staggering on past heartbreak, and there's something joyous. How did we ever find it? And thank God we didn't stop long ago, say, back in Utah. Thank God we didn't give up.

Hitomi was dancing a quiet dance deep in her body. A one-third-energy version of a dance, like she was rehearsing it in her head for a later recital. This was the dance she had to keep to herself. And when would she unveil it, and would we be invited?

This was our band in the 3 a.m., our band in the not-morning-but-not-night. Maybe for the last time would all of us be happy at the same time, which seemed crazy to say, which seemed impossible, but I did indeed think that exact thing at the peak of an exhale of laughter, the streetlights bursting just so, right as the clock hit 3 a.m. I thought, *Maybe this is it.*

It was an odd thought I didn't say out loud, because we were only halfway through our trip, and hadn't we just figured it all out?

Then Daveed jumped up onto another thing, as graceless as a lump of laundry, and with even less guile, and I forgot all about everything.

Hitomi tried to follow along, but just as she started to skip down the sidewalk, she fell down right on her face.

"Are you okay?" James asked.

"I'm okay," she said, and her hands were covering her mouth, and we were all wondering what the new Hitomi was going to look like.

"Let's see," James said.

She revealed it and it glimmered in the streetlights: a chipped tooth. Just a tiny bit of the corner of one of her teeth was gone.

She felt it with her tongue and asked, "How bad?"

"Not bad," James said.

She looked at me.

"Not bad," I said.

"God damn it," she said and walked off.

Portland

WE DRIPPED DOWN TO THE FOREST CITY OF PORTLAND. In the sky was a great black rainbow, as the sun, blocked by clouds, pushed its strongest strands of light through the raindrops. It was Robert, from somewhere beyond, shrugging his coldest shoulder at me, pushing me out of the party.

Gordo was on the radio talking about whales.

"If I'm supposed to care so much about saving whales, I'd like to know when a whale has ever built a hospital."

Was he . . . was he reading *Moby-Dick* too? Or were the whales a symbol of environmentalism?

We went to the great, towering bookstore of Powell's to feel dry, to feel the soak of our skin tempered by all that paper and cardboard.

I walked through the poetry aisle at an andante pace with my arms down at forty-five-degree angles. *Here is the specter of Death himself come to call another to his chambers.* Except I would be the opposite of Death. I would give life to all the books on the shelf that hadn't been read out loud in ages.

A bookstore not as a mortuary, then, but a greenhouse. A bookstore as a place you go on dates to read out loud to each other the poems you love and the poems you've never tried before. See how it goes. Classes meet at a bookstore so the teacher can wave his hand at random and knock a masterpiece off the shelf, just to emphasize the point that *magic is literally falling on top of our heads.*

Exiting the poetry aisle, I saw Hitomi in periodicals, under the lights.

I walked up to her and said, "What are you doing here?"

She smiled and said, "What am I doing *where?*"

I laughed. We were deep in the labyrinth. And yet there we were, standing right next to the earlier versions of ourselves, dancing in that living room.

"Are we supernatural?" she asked.

"Maybe," I said.

But wait. I had never entered the labyrinth. Was it too late?

"The first thing I thought when I met you," I said, "was *finally.*"

"What took you so long?" she asked.

"I got lost."

"How's *Moby-Dick?*" she asked.

"It's okay," I said. "We're searching for that whale."

"I hope you find him."

"I think we will."

She laughed and looked down.

"Do you not enjoy such stories?" I asked.

"I just think," she said, "everyone's always telling stories of these big quests. And I feel like they always involve swords or harpoons. Someone always has to die."

I glanced at the back of a book to see an author photo that I could swear was of Robert. He hadn't ever written a book though. Had he?

"I just wish we could, you know," Hitomi said. "Quest *inward.*"

"Yeah, I understand."

"Or downward," she said, and she twisted down to the floor.

"Do you think you'll ever write a book?" I asked.

"What? No," she said, straightening up. "What do you mean? What would I write?"

"A book of poetry," I said.

"No. I would never."

"Why?"

"I don't know. James thinks I should stick to writing songs."

"I disagree."

"Okay," she said, looking around. "I'll make one copy of a book and you can have it."

"Okay."

"I mean, it'll cost a thousand dollars."

"Deal."

We crossed over to the east side, past big, dark condos full of beautiful people leaning over railings and taking photos. The buildings seemed like the planted footprints of an invading robot horde, a mutiny that was not fought off, but instead welcomed. On one balcony I saw a cactus in a pot. Daveed saw it too and said, "What's that guy doing here?"

We stopped at the Doug Fir, our venue for the night, and went into the restaurant upstairs. The walls were long logs lit from beneath with yellow light. It was all interspersed with mirrors and glass. I touched one of the logs.

"This is like Lincoln's Disco Shack," Daveed said.

"All these trees," Hitomi said.

We loaded our gear into the basement, where the show would be. Outside it was still dripping.

James had somehow found a keyboard for me, on loan from someone he knew in Portland. We would be able to borrow it for the rest of the trip.

I pulled it out of its case. Eighty-eight keys of digital sound from Yamaha, engineered to be more in tune than anything could ever be.

Daveed helped me put the keyboard on its stand and I tested it out. It sounded like a piano. I hit louder and louder notes, and they sounded like louder and louder notes of a piano. I turned to the "Electric Piano" setting, and it sounded like something Mariah Carey would vomit up on New Year's Day. I went over to "Grand Piano," and it sounded grand and thin at the same time, like a picture of a piano.

I looked over at Daveed as he tuned his toms by hitting them with his stick and turning a drum key on the rim. The drumheads were plastic, but they were still *there*, vibrating in the room.

"Is it okay?" James asked.

"I mean . . ." I said as I looked down at it.

"Look, it has four piano sounds," he said. "And eighty-eight keys!"

That night, on that stage amongst all that lumber, I played "Piano 1" and felt a thousand miles away from the band. I thought about the thrift store with Robert, when he asked me if I knew why a piano has eighty-eight keys. I really didn't know. It's not even an even number of octaves. There's one more A, B-flat, and B than any other key. That always felt odd to me.

sometimes
when you look at me
like you're looking at a sweet-ass motherfucker
I wonder if you know
that I stand in the bathroom mirror
cursing my own face
for its mistakes
or that I'm terrified
that one day my uterus
will just keep sliding down

and fall out of my body
and you'll move on
to someone else

I'm not sure I had ever heard a woman speak about that specific fear. I always thought a uterus was pretty secure in there.

I sank into a booth after the show, my whole life spent in a series of booths, booth after booth after booth. Behind me I heard a familiar voice.

"It's just good to talk with another woman. All I have is dudes around me every hour of the day."

"Are you guys still hooking up though?"

"Yeah. What else are we going to do?"

"So you're not broken up?"

"I don't know. It's just gravity. It's easier just to have sex than to argue."

59. Wednesday

Easier. To have sex. Than argue.

We stayed that night in a big house where the trees were old and brave and spread their branches over the streets.

"Just don't use the shower in the downstairs bathroom," our host said. "There's an injured crow in there with one eye. His name is Wednesday."

Daveed walked into the bathroom and shouted, "Oh snap! She's right! There's a crow in here!"

Our host gave a patient look to us, like, *well yeah.*

She ran a sort of hospital for wounded animals in her house. All around were the bones of animals who hadn't made it. A squirrel skull on the mantel. The pelvis of a magpie. I suppose the person who has saved the most animals is also going to be left with a lot of skeletons.

We slept upstairs on the third floor. There were two beds and plenty of floorspace for us to spread out. Amongst the boxes stored up there I found a bunch of old *National Geographics*. I leafed through them and wrote down the titles of the articles in my notebook.

"Someday we'll all be skeletons," James said as he flopped down on a bed. "I mean, we already are. But we're covered up by a bunch of meat."

"I think it would be beautiful," Hitomi said, "to have my skeleton displayed in a case in someone's house after I'm dead."

"Really?" James asked. "You were horrified at the Mütter. You couldn't get out of there fast enough."

"I know, but that was, like, too much. I mean, if I were the only human skeleton in a house. You don't want too many."

I arranged the National Geographic titles and numbered them, trying to find an order.

"I think it's beautiful," she said, "when we're all stripped down to our bones. It's pure structure. But structure can be beautiful too."

"Any news about Robert?" James asked me.

"I—no," I said.

"I'm sorry," he said.

"We should do something for him," Daveed said.

"What do you mean?" I asked.

"Just a ceremony," he said. "Some way of speaking to him."

"No," I said. "That's okay."

"No, I agree," Hitomi said. "You should make an offering."

"I don't have anything to offer," I said.

"It can just be words," she said. "It's something you put in the air and give away. I do it every night."

"I don't know," I said.

"What do you have written there?" she said. "Read that."

"It's just the titles of articles," I said.

"Stand up," she said.

I stood up.

"Just read it and really believe in it," she said. "The words don't matter."

I laughed about words not mattering. Didn't we both agree that *only* words mattered? James was the one who didn't care about words, who tossed them out like he was chumming for sharks.

I looked up at the ceiling. I looked out at everyone, looking at me with such expectant faces. I felt sorry for them, for caring so much about this tiny moment.

the wonder city that moves by night
captured the first-ever albino gorilla
and, riding the outlaw trail,
they reached the funeral of Winston Churchill
they gave him the best full measure
of gold, the eternal treasure
and said goodbye to the stone age

Everyone was quiet after. There should be something to say after a poem instead of *mmmm*. The rain dripped down on the roof above us. Two stories below, we heard the crow let out one sad, plaintive caw.

I looked at Hitomi. It was like she had vouched for my writing back in Idaho, and then I had come forward with *this,* and everyone tried to think what to say.

"It's more of a collage," I said.

"It's beautiful," Hitomi said. "But I want to hear what *you* think about the world."

"It was just a collage," I said.

We all slept that night in the same room, slumped on different mattresses like an army who had been marching for reasons they couldn't remember. A single blade of moonlight cut across my eyes. Daveed was next to me, on his side, an eyeshade covering his eyes. James was snoring lightly. Hitomi shoved him in her sleep every few minutes.

I couldn't sleep, didn't want to sleep, didn't ever want to sleep again. Maybe I just wanted to be alone. I craved it so much I would stay up late just to have it.

The moonlight seared into me. Its sole design was to keep me awake. James's snores were the only reminder that anyone else was alive on the planet. I listened for the crow but heard nothing.

I looked at my phone to check the date. It had been five weeks since the night of the party, since my car was towed and Dennis was carried off to the hospital.

All around us were suffering animals about to die and hardly able to make a sound. I thought of the moment when Dennis's son made the decision to take him away. All those steps, those painful steps, of getting him packed up, taking him downstairs. That must have taken forever. All the while, with every step, Dennis would have known he was leaving for good. Leaving that sad piano for good. Leaving that kitchen drawer forever unfixed.

The whole city around me was quiet. James had stopped snoring. I thought maybe if Wednesday, the sad crow, would make a sound, I could fall asleep. It's only when the world is at its quietest that I worry everything has stopped, that it's all over.

I thought about the trout in the cooler in the back of my dad's car that one time, flopping to get off the ice. I didn't want to hear them flopping because that meant they were suffering. But I didn't want to hear them stop, because that would mean they were dead.

The only bearable fraction of a second was when the trout were midflop, floating in the air. Everything else was suffering or death.

At the time I was calmed by Gordo's words. Why are we wringing our hands about what animals need when we're so much smarter than them? Yet now I was in a house in Portland where every creature mattered, and they didn't have to pass an IQ test to be loved. They just had to exist.

Also, animals don't pay medical bills. Sometimes you do work not just in spite of it being for no pay, but almost *because* it is for no pay.

Like with poetry.

The moonlight finally slid off my face and onto Daveed's head. I could now start to drift off.

The next morning we had to leave early, and I didn't want to wake up. I didn't want to walk down to face that crow. We crept out quietly so as not to wake anyone, least of all that sweet Wednesday, who was either asleep or dead, or halfway in between. Every floorboard creaked as we all stepped out, and creaked some more as we turned to look back at a bandmate to give them a stern look about all the creaking they were doing. It was no use, the house being a collection of old boards, just a ship that had been on too many voyages and was now at rest.

As we passed the downstairs bathroom, I looked at the door, half expecting to see a note explaining Wednesday's removal to the hospital where crows die. Instead there was nothing, and we all crept past and got in the van in the dewy fall morning.

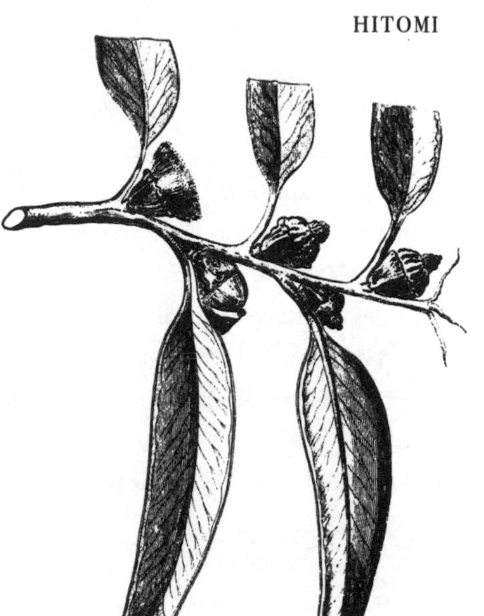

60. San Francisco

We set up on the narrow stage of the Hotel Utah in San Francisco, which had an overhanging balcony as close as you could ever expect a balcony to be. That room must have been a good place for burlesque or boxing back after the failure of the temperance movement. There was a wooden mermaid above the stage, a creature released from a tree trunk to remind future spectators in this ultra-gentrified city of a time not long before—maybe a hundred and fifty years, but what's that?—when you could ram your boat into the shore and just open up business as a bar, no license needed.

"Let me show you how to adjust that," the sound man said to Hitomi as he grabbed the mic stand in front of her.

Hitomi was wearing that baby blue baby doll dress she bought in Detroit. It was like the evil twin of Christina's pink dress. Or. Not evil. I don't know why I mentioned evil.

There was an upright piano on the corner of the stage. At the beginning of the show, James finished tuning his guitar and nodded at me to start. I placed my hands on the piano and played a chord, but the microphone for my instrument wasn't turned on. I shaded my eyes from the spotlight and looked back at the sound booth.

It was empty.

This was the kind of venue that employed only one person for the joint position of sound man and bartender, and at crucial moments like this, when someone really needed a negroni served to them in a pint glass, the musical act of the evening might have to wait a few minutes to have their piano mics actually operable.

"God damn it," I said. I walked offstage looking for the overemployed man while the rest of the band started the set. He was behind the bar.

"Hey," I said. "We're starting."

"Okay," he said.

"Can you turn the piano mics on? Please?"

"Just a minute."

I walked back to the music room and stood near the sound booth watching the band while I waited. There was a decent crowd in that small room, probably the best crowd of tour. I never know what leads a group of people to show up for something, what snippet of a song they heard somewhere, what mystery they've built up in their heads.

Hitomi walked up to the mic.

"Hmm-mmm," she said, clearing her throat.

I looked next to me to check in with whoever was sitting there, to see if they agreed that this was the most beautiful way anyone had ever cleared their throat. A man looked back at me with suspicion that I was trying to steal his french fries.

I rarely got to see Hitomi's face as she performed. I saw it back in the practice space in Brooklyn, when we were huddled in a semicircle. When you practice with a band, you face inward, and ever after that, you face outward, toward the crowd. Suddenly everything is less intimate. This thing you shared with each other is now spread out to an audience, who sometimes adores what you do and sometimes is indifferent to it.

She had that look of pain and torture as she sang. It was almost embarrassing. Her eyebrows raised like she was thinking, "I don't understand this any more than you do." I looked around to see how other people reacted to it. I wanted to cover it up, prevent people from seeing it.

But it wasn't embarrassing. It was true and anguished.

Daveed looked at me in the audience and smiled, as though he were noticing an old friend who happened to come to the show.

James had a look on his face like he was monitoring a tiger. Hitomi flipped through her book and found the right page. She looked at it and contorted her brow to take on the emotions of it.

how to love more:
      pull out your death,
        your embarrassment,
your hands covering everything shameful,
   you, in that purple dress
      sitting at the lemonade stand
         take all of that out
and slap that whale on a cold metal table
      gut it   eat its heart
        bathe in its blood
   that embarrassment, that shame
                it is actually death
         and you are alive
 so
      no contest, my friend
                no contest

I was stuck watching her next to the sound booth. I was spectator and admirer. The sound man / barman stepped behind me and turned on the piano mics.

"You wanna give that a try?" he said.

"Yeah, just a minute," I said. I didn't want to stop watching.

While Daveed drummed, the symbols on his hands sped through space and time. They animated themselves, and I saw their meaning. I didn't need him to explain them to me anymore. They were fire underwater. Something brief and challenging that still had some time to exist.

It wasn't just Hitomi's beauty, her physical beauty, that transfixed me. I didn't want to devour her. My love for her was different. I didn't want to place her under glass.

I wanted to know her, and to be known by her. For such a solitary person as myself, that felt like a grand realization. I had walked through the jungles of a corrupted world, everyone acting like an imitation of someone they had seen once in a magazine, and I had stepped away from the clatter of perfume samples and fizzy drinks, into a clearing in the silver moonlight to see this creature I had thought was extinct, or rather never even dreamed could possibly exist. And there she was, just living and breathing as though it were not a miracle: Hitomi, *Hit-OH-me,* assembled brick by brick to be her own towering figure.

It is the casual unfolding of the greatest miracles that makes us want to sit down and breathe them in. The seagull on the breeze, navigating with hair-trigger pulls of his muscles to swoop this way and that, cliffside for a brief second and then thrusting into the water to harass some poor sardine. If there was any preening to Hitomi, or calling attention to herself, if she ever held a frame around her own beauty, affixed a placard that explained the medium and date of completion for viewers, I wouldn't have stood for it.

It's the ones who are standing off to the side, next to the elevators, not presented as anything at all, even though they are in fact worth millions. Those are the artifacts I love.

"Ian from Indiana," Hitomi said from the stage. The music stopped. Everyone in the room turned to look at me.

"Would you please grace us with *one note* on this piano?" she asked.

Everyone in the room held their breath in anticipation. I stepped slowly through the crowd and up on stage.

"Ian from Indiana, everybody," Hitomi said, and everyone gave a polite applause, for who even was this Ian, some lucky contest winner from the audience?

Everyone went quiet as I sat at the piano. I thought of the row of pianos stretching back in time that I had played in my life, a hall of mirrors of pianos upon pianos, eighty-eight keys multiplied by, let's say, two hundred and thirty-four pianos. How many keys was that? I'd have to multiply it later.

I looked back at Hitomi. She nodded. I felt my eyes water up, thinking of that particular piano back in the thrift store in Valparaiso. What was it Robert had been saying about the lower keys? They're not meant to be played? I still didn't understand.

I looked out in the crowd and saw someone grab the forearm of the person next to them. Was it that easy? Could we achieve the forearm grab just in an extended silence?

I put my foot on the sustain pedal, found the middle C, and pressed ever so lightly. Good old emotionally stable piano, she purred back a middle C in the San Francisco evening. The bartender / sound man had pushed the "on" button after all. I played just that one note, in literal adherence to Hitomi's request. One tiny note. It started to die out. Everyone kept holding their breath, probably about to turn blue. Two laps in a non-regulation pool.

Then Daveed—bravely and accurately, but not without a bit of humor to it—called out, "Three, four!" and came in with James. Hitomi howled a pained vocal line and we were off.

61.
Monterey Aquarium

EVERY KIND OF BLUE.

The bowl of blueberries at the house in Idaho. The watery parts of *National Geographic* maps. The dark denim of Hitomi's jacket. Every cyan button, every azure bead and swirling marble that held the entire world inside of it. The navy blue of the sparkly, plush sheets in Cleveland. The blue that doesn't fade even after you wash it. The blue that swallows you whole.

"Look," Hitomi said to me. "It just. It really sucks that I told that story and you guys didn't say anything."

She was standing in front of a tank of moon jellyfish. It was distracting, those alien creatures billowing and glowing in the water behind her. A young woman stepped up with a camera and took a picture of the jellyfish.

She was referring to that morning, when she had told us about how she'd had a terrible night after the San Francisco show. She had stayed with a friend of a friend, somewhere separate from the band, and he ended up being a creep and saying weird shit to her, and she slept on the couch all night holding her keys in her hand, terrified he was going to try to get on top of her.

She hadn't said it all like that to us right away. She was understandably embarrassed and tried to make it seem like not a big deal and started crying in the middle of a coffee shop in the Mission.

Now we were in the swirl of blue at the aquarium.

"What were we supposed to say?" I asked.

"I can't tell you what to say. You just have to say something. Anything."

"I'm sorry," I said.

"I needed you to say something," she said.

"I know."

"If I were on tour with a group of women, they would've taken me to a spa today. Instead of this."

My face got red. I looked around. We were in, let's be honest, Fish Jail. It seemed like a fun activity on a day off, but now that she mentioned it, why were we there? We turned a corner to a big room with a two-story-tall tank. Daveed was standing there looking at a big, awkward fish who looked like a Staten Island garbage man. The fish had an odd arrangement of fins that didn't look at all to be an efficient way to get around the ocean. But that's what he had, so he did his best to get around the tank.

Only, there was nowhere to go. I wished there was a way to tell that fish, that sad fish, that he was never going to find the opening.

You are a wild animal who has been domesticated, I thought. *You are not crazy.*

"I'm sorry," I said. "That must have sucked."

"Thank you," Hitomi said as she bent over to stretch out her back. The carousel of creatures swirled in the tank.

I looked over at Hitomi as she looked up. All the shades of blue cast a mottled light on her face. Teal tissue paper, the frozen hearts of glaciers, toilet bowls that are trying too hard to prove that they're clean. I couldn't tell if she was tired or crying or what.

62.
The Material World

ON OUR WAY DOWN THROUGH CALIFORNIA, I thought of a conversation I had with Robert earlier that summer. We were in a bar, he with a beer, me with an iced tea. They looked almost the same color as they sat in their pint glasses on the table in front of us.

They. Them. Us.

"This is my problem with the material world," Robert said as I took a sip.

This statement had, I thought, not followed anything particularly material.

"What?" I asked.

"The material world. It's just so . . . insistent."

"What other option is there?"

"Look," he said. "If you're going to be another part of this *insistence . . .*"

"No! I'm not being difficult. I just. I don't understand."

"Okay," he said. "It's like if you drew a circle. Here, let me draw a circle."

He grabbed a napkin and took a pen out of his coat pocket. He drew a circle on it, which cut into the napkin. He tried to hold it together with his other hand. The ink of the pen gave out and he had to go over the circle a couple of times.

"Okay, there," he said, slapping down the pen and the torn-up napkin. "There it is. That's the world. Any questions?"

We both laughed.

"No, alright, look," he continued. "This circle represents everything. Everything in existence. The totality of matter, consciousness, everything. Name a thing."

"Iced tea," I said stirring the ice in my glass.

"*That's* in the circle! Name another thing."

"Jay Leno."

"He's in the circle. Believe it or not! Okay. So, let's say there are two parts to the circle. There is all this"—he gestured wildly at the bar around us, picked up his glass of beer and put it down, touched my nose—"you, me, iced tea, and Jay fucking—ha. Leno. And then there's everything else. Let's call everything else Dream Land, okay?"

"Okay," I said.

There was a *Jurassic Park* pinball machine at the other end of the room. A plastic tyrannosaurus was under the glass, frozen in mid-howl.

"Now, let's just for starters say that those are the two basic parts of life, and they both are equal. The Material World and Dream Land." He drew a line through the center of the circle. "Now, don't say anything yet, let's just imagine this is true. Think about all the things that are not in the Material World. Every dream you've ever had, for starters. That's like a third of your life. But also every daydream. Every idea you've had that didn't get built or realized. Every desire, every memory once the action is gone. Everything, you know . . . liminal and weird: falling in love, laughter . . ."

"All the dead people," I said.

"Yes! All the dead people!" he said.

The one other man at the bar looked up from his phone for half a second to check on us.

"There's a lot of them," Robert whispered. "All *that* goes into this half we call Dream Land. Now, it's starting to seem like maybe half isn't big enough to hold all that. But, let's stick with half. Now. Everybody in our lives, every parent and teacher and boss, everyone talks to us about things in this half." He pointed to the Material World. "It's safe there. And it's scary. But at least we can touch it, we can knock on it, we can prove it to be real. That's comforting, even when it's a total hellscape. So, we get a lot of support to buy into this life in the Material World, and not much for Dream Land. But we're saying for now that Dream Land is half of everything. So, what do you think that does to people, when half of reality is only hinted at, scoffed at, or demeaned?"

"It'll make you get real frustrated," I said.

"Yes," he said. "But also. Your body doesn't know. Your body doesn't listen to mechanical time, or laws, or cultural taboos. So your body seeks out that balance no matter what. So it wants to be in Dream Land half the time. Now. There are conveniently still eight hours of our day when it is acceptable to sleep. And even that is being shaved down. But still, even with sleeping and dreaming, I suspect our bodies try to find more of that sweet, sweet Dream Life somewhere. And maybe that creates problems in a world so occupied with the material."

Robert put the pen down and sat back in his chair, his argument presented. He took a sip of his beer, which glowed in the sunlight.

"I mean. I'm just throwing that out there," he said.

63. Los Angeles

I STARTED LISTENING TO *MOBY-DICK* ON AUDIOBOOK, which really sped the story along. I could keep moving through all the chapters about nautical details without having to worry too much about whether I was catching everything. There was a whale at the end of the book. The whole point of being on such a long and boring voyage was that you could lose focus, you could lose days, you could get lost in yourself, lost in your sickness, lost in your menial work. Eventually you'd encounter the whale, and all you had to do in the meantime was prepare yourself for that.

Just get to the whale. Just get to the whale.

I fell asleep as we coasted down the spine of California. I woke up to us moving through a nameless town. Daveed looked out the window and said to me, as though he could feel that I had just woken up, "Do you know what 'alma' means?"

I blinked my eyes and saw a street sign out the window in the blasted-out sunlight that said ALMA.

"Is it a kind of tree?" I asked.

"No," he said. "It means 'soul.'"

On the radio, James was finally listening to music, but it was only because Gordo was playing a parody song based on "Royals" in which that word was replaced with a city America was currently bombing, I suppose as a way of mocking people who were against the bombing. I could only laugh a maniacal laugh of exasperation.

"You guys okay with this?" I asked as I turned to Daveed, who was somehow already asleep, and back at Hitomi, who had her earbuds in.

James looked back at me and turned the volume up.

There was an upright piano onstage at the Hotel Café. It was just a Yamaha, which made me skeptical. That's the same company that makes fake pianos, and I always wonder how close those two parts of the factory are to each other. But if Wurlitzer can make electric pianos as well as jukeboxes, maybe it's okay.

Hitomi read from her book in the spotlight.

you could not pay me to run on the bluff tonight
it's not mountain lions or coyotes I fear
but that I would be eaten alive
by your friends
or by your coworker, the distant one
or
to be honest
to be sweet and honest
I am afraid
of you

After the show we lost track of James. His guitar sat on stage, leaning on his amp, like he had been Raptured. I carefully packed his guitar up for him. His phone was sitting there, too. I thought of telling Hitomi, but instead I just slipped it in my pocket.

"Let's just go to that bar he wanted to go to," Hitomi said. "D'Antoni's? I'm hoping that's not a strip club. I'll text him to meet us there."

On our way out I quietly asked the doorman to send James to us if he should return.

A walk down urine-soaked sidewalks, a smoke of a joint with Daveed, and then we stepped in to see red leather booths, tables with white linen tablecloths, and red napkins that matched the booths. The napkins were folded into tents, which sat on opposite sides of the tables as though they were on opposite sides of a battle, with the slender salt and pepper shakers acting as emissaries, running across the battlefield at cease-fire to broker some kind of peace.

We sat at one of the booths, three of us without James.

"I assume we'll find him again?" I asked.

"Sure," Hitomi said. "Los Angeles is a small town. We're bound to run into him."

"I always think I'm looking at someone famous," Daveed said, "and then they turn out to not be. Like that guy over there."

We all looked at the bar where there was a guy who looked right on the border of being famous.

"I think fame," Hitomi said, "would have to be, by definition, something that you were sure about."

"Okay, then *I'm* famous," Daveed said.

"Look at these," Hitomi said as she looked at a couple of black-and-white photos on the wall next to us. "It says this one's from 1912. Holy shit. It's so hard to believe these people really existed. Look at these two people. The way she's folding her arms and leaning back on her friend? I always think of people from the past as just working in factories and marching. Like, fulfilling their historical duty. But they loved each other. I mean, look at that. How many times do you think they were photographed in their lives? A dozen maybe? I've been photographed more times today."

A band was playing Eagles covers on the small stage. At one point in their set, a woman got up and started tap dancing, not particularly on the stage or with any blessing from the band. She danced her way around the room in a show of goodwill.

"I'm seventy-three, and I started dancing when I was seventy," she said as she drifted past our table, anticipating our question. "I tried to stay away from show business, but I just couldn't."

She shrugged her shoulders and tapped over to the next table, smiling.

"I wonder what I'll be doing when I'm seventy-three," Hitomi said.

"I need to call my girl," Daveed said as he looked at his phone. "What do I say to her? She says she's been sitting in the garden looking at the dead sunflowers and crying."

"Oh, poor girl," Hitomi said. "Tell her you'll be cooking her breakfast in less than two weeks."

"Two weeks? God, this country is too big."

"I propose a water slide across Kansas," Hitomi said.

"Alright, I'm gonna step outside, you guys will be here for a bit?"

"How could we tear ourselves away?" Hitomi said, waving at Eagletopia, or whatever they were called.

"Which would you rather be stuck watching," I asked Hitomi, "an Eagles cover band, or the Eagles?"

"Oh, definitely this," Hitomi said.

I smiled and took a sip of my drink. Behind me the band was singing about a particular corner in the town of Winslow, Arizona.

"You know . . ." she said. "You know when you go see a musical or a play and there's a bad guy in it? And through the whole thing he's scowling and evil? And then they finish the show and they have a curtain call and all the actors come out and wave and smile, and it's kind of a relief to see the bad guy smile? Because now he's just the actor and he's getting applause?"

"Hm. Yes," I said. "Okay. What about it?"

"That's what it's like when you smile."

"Oh."

"It's so rare that I start to think it's not possible. But then I'm glad I stuck around for the curtain call."

"Oh," I said. "Wait, so I'm . . . the bad guy?"

"Don't take it too literally," she said. "I'll be back in a minute."

She walked to the bathroom, and after she rounded the corner, James's phone buzzed in my pocket with a text from her:

Where the fuck are you?

I looked at it, not sure what to do. Such a private thing, someone else's phone, their thumbprints on the glass.

I thought about typing a response to Hitomi, but what would I say?

I love you.

No.

I hate you. Fuck you. Go be with Ian for all I care. I give you my blessing.

My thumbs levitated over the keyboard, wondering at the vast power they had. Would it be that easy? Was there a sentence I could write that would make a difference?

I'll be back soon, I texted.

Another text from her came quickly.

But where are you? I'm stuck talking with Ian.

Stuck? Jesus. I had made a mistake in texting her. Stuck? Was I supposed to stand up for myself as James? How would that sound? What did she mean by *stuck?*

I felt gutted. A whale on a dock, cut open and left for the flies to gnaw on.

I started to type out a response:

What do you mean stuck—

But before I could send it, another text from Hitomi:

Fine. I'm just gonna make out with him.

Okay. Now that. I didn't know what to say. I texted back just these words to her:

Good luck!

I put the phone in my pocket as she walked back to the table. The Eagles cover band started what seemed to be the last song of their set, *the* signature Eagles song, the song that is essentially a Yelp review of a hotel in California. I looked over at the guitarists, judging whether I thought they could handle the epic closing guitar solos.

"So what's with this book you're writing?" she said as she sat down. "Is that a real thing?"

"Didn't you say you read it when I wasn't looking?"

"Just like a sentence."

"Well, it's a real thing."

"Is it about our band? Are you just going to write about James being an asshole?"

"No, no. I'm writing about Robert. I was *just* writing about something I remember him telling me, how half the world is made up of dreams and death and imagination, but we diminish its importance compared to the Material World."

"I like that," she said. "I think I'd like Robert."

"I think you guys would be friends."

"Hey, I want to say something. Since we're alone."

Wait. Part of the joy and curse of being a writer is feeling like you can pause and expand certain moments of your life. In retrospect, rarely does anything pivot on one moment. There are car crashes and slipped scalpels, sure, but you can't receive a favorable gust of wind and suddenly have someone be in love with you.

I mean, you can't.

Can you?

Still, Hitomi was in the middle of that thought, the band was still in the first verse of "Hotel California," and I was there still, too, living in that moment, living in the blubber of the whale, all around me a sea of blubber, the majority of the thing that I hunted being composed of whale fat, so much fat, all around me fat.

What would we do with all that fat? Light our lamps? Why were we hunting that thing, again?

"I just," Hitomi said, looking at me. "I appreciate you. And I respect you."

"Wait," I said. "I'm sorry. I just. I really need to pee. Can you hold on to that thought?"

I suppose I wanted the moment to extend in actuality, too, in the Material World, but I also wanted to clear something up. I raced to the bathroom and pulled out James's phone and texted:

Why did you say you're stuck with him? Is he really that boring?

She texted back:

I was just trying to get a rise out of you. Where. Are. You?

I tried to think of something ambiguous but not completely infuriating. Was that the calculation going on in James's head at all times? Ambiguity that almost-but-doesn't-quite piss everyone off?

I texted:

I'm with some people from the show. I'll be there soon.

And then I added:

Look, Hitomi. I'm sorry. I love you.

I raced back to the booth to sit with her.

"You have James's phone, don't you?" Hitomi asked.

Damn.

"You do!" she said.

"How did you know?" I asked.

"James would never say sorry," she said.

I considered this for a second and then sat back and laughed. She laughed, too.

"How are you going to get his phone back to him without him noticing?"

"Well, we'll have to find him first, won't we?"

The band was reaching the end of the singing part of "Hotel California" and about to get to the whole point of the song: the guitar solos.

The guitar solos. The guitar solos that tamed a continent, that raised a nation.

"Were you going to say something," I asked as I pulled out James's phone, "before I went to the bathroom?"

The first guitarist was adequate. Then he handed the solo off to the second guitarist, and that guy biffed a note right in the opening.

"I just wanted to say," Hitomi said, "I see you. You're processing this grief while you probably hear us argue through the walls. I just. I see that."

I did hear them argue through the walls. I did hear that, and I would wait to fall asleep until I heard their tone calm down and Hitomi's laughter spill out. Was I a fool for being emotionally invested in that? Could I check out any time I wanted, but never leave?

She sat back in the booth and grabbed her glass of wine and looked at me, like someone would look at a chunk of fallen satellite on the lawn. Nothing to do about it, particularly, other than look. *And maybe we can find a serial number . . .*

"Thank you," I said. "I see you, too."

Well, obviously. One thing for sure was that I saw her. God, I was Dennis, wasn't I? Talking about a meaningless broken drawer instead of saying, *Don't just see me, damn it, love me.*

The Hotel California was on fire. Not in a good way. It was collapsing on itself. All hotel guests were given a blanket and a voucher for one free future stay at any affiliate hotel.

"That time in Indianapolis—" I said, just barely above the volume of the guitar solos, which were clumsily but defiantly going on just over my shoulder, surely signaling the coming end of something.

"When you shocked me—" I said, trying to come to a conclusion, as the cover band tried to find a way to end a song that famously fades out and has no ending, because for all we know Joe Walsh and what's-his-name are still somewhere trading licks.

"I'm just glad I came on tour," I said.

The song finally found its end with an epic clatter of cymbals and toms and strumming, followed by double hits to signal to the audience that not only was the band finished with the song and the set, but the night was over, music was over, conversation was over, please pay your server and get out.

So. There.

We found that the only thing worse than the sound of a mediocre Eagles cover band was the sound of nothing at all.

"I guess that's it," she said.

We paid for our drinks and stood up. Daveed walked back in, looking sad.

"What happened?" Hitomi asked.

"Nothing," he said.

And then, right then, at 2:07, as the bar staff was almost literally shoving us out the door, James finally showed up, not looking the least concerned. He glanced at the stage, then over at the bar, and said only, "Are they still serving drinks?"

"No, we need to get out of here," Hitomi said as she walked toward the door.

James had found us a place to stay in Hollywood that was apparently an upgrade from the place we were going to stay but were unable to go to because it was now so late. He told me the cross streets and I put it in my phone. This did not seem to have been the purpose of his sojourn away from the band, but rather something that came together by accident. Still, he claimed it as a badge of honor.

After getting into the van, Hitomi and James negotiated the subtle differences between being a go-getter for the band and being a thoughtless wanderer.

"The *fuck* were you all night?" Hitomi asked.

"I was finding us a place to stay," James said as he patted his pockets. "Wait, where's my phone?"

"I put it in your guitar case," I said.

"What a responsible band mate," Hitomi said. "Wait. You were *not* looking for a place to stay that whole time."

"In a way I was," he said. "You have to follow threads to see where they go. You never know when you give someone a smoke or go with them to check out their ride just what it will lead to. That's my job."

"You went to check out someone's ride?"

"I was following threads," James said.

I drove the van down Hollywood Boulevard, and I finally had control of the sound system to listen to Joni in her natural habitat.

"Guys," Daveed said, "I'm afraid I'm losing my girl."

"What do you mean?" James said.

"Phone calls aren't enough."

"Did you tell her you'll be cooking her breakfast in two weeks?" Hitomi asked.

"I just wish I could see her in person."

"Well, we are about to turn left and head back across the continent in her direction," James said.

I saw a street I recognized and swerved right.

"No, Ian, New York is to the *left.*"

"Just a little detour first," I said.

"Well, I tried," James said to Daveed.

"What's the address?" I asked James. "You only told me the cross streets."

"I'm not sure," James said. "He texted it to me. Where's my phone again?"

In my pocket, but—

"Oh shit!" Hitomi said, loving the moment. "Where did you last see it, James?"

"Um, it's in your guitar case?" I said, with that question mark at the end as though I weren't sure.

"Oh, that's right!" Hitomi said. "Ian kindly placed it in your guitar case for you."

"Thank you, dear Ian," said James.

"What a nice keyboardist we have," Hitomi said.

"You really can't find a better one these days. Shame he has such a sour expression all the time."

"Aw, I like his face."

"Ian, can you please pull over so I can get that phone?"

"Right," I said.

"Like, now?" James said.

"Just looking for a safe place to stop," I said.

"It's not like it's going anywhere!" Hitomi said.

"Yeah, but *we* are," James said.

I stopped in the driveway of a Wendy's and James got out.

"It's just that time is so different out on the road," Daveed continued.

I tried to figure out how to get James's phone back to him without him knowing that I had been holding on to it. I was too scared to get out of my seat. I looked back at Hitomi and she just smiled.

"Like. I know that only three weeks have passed," Daveed said as James looked through his guitar case. "Which is not that long. But so much happens in those three weeks that they feel like three months."

"Astronauts had the same problem," Hitomi said. "And you know what they did?"

James came back.

"Hey, it's not in the guitar case," he said. "You said you put it in there?"

"Should be," I said.

"I'll call it," Hitomi said.

I quickly pulled off my seatbelt and jumped out.

"I'll look for it!"

I ran around to the back before James could get there. I opened the back door and pulled his phone out of my pocket right as it started vibrating with Hitomi's call. It slipped out of my hand and splashed on the pavement as James came around.

"Okay," he said as he looked at it and then back up at me, seeming to figure out what happened. "I guess there it is."

He picked it up and it glinted in the streetlights, somehow not shattered.

"Hello, Hitomi," he said into the phone. "What were you saying about that great keyboardist of ours?"

We pulled our belongings inside the apartment, and it wasn't equipped to handle all four of us. A roommate was out of town and his bedroom was offered to the couple in the band, which by the force of momentum was still James and Hitomi. Daveed—sad, drunk Daveed—lay down on the couch in front of a window that revealed the shining tower of Capitol Records. I looked at that building, wondering what possibly still went on in there. Like, were they just constantly packing up boxes?

"I'll sleep in the van," I said.

64.
Los Angeles Morning

I woke up to a quiet dawn in Hollywood.

I thought about Hitomi. I thought maybe, in the silence of the van, maybe it would be okay to relieve some of the tension built up from weeks on the road with this person.

The blinds were down. It could be a short journey, and no one would have to know.

Not to try to make it sound more noble than it was. I had been suppressing and indulging a feeling for weeks. I didn't know which was worse. Either way, it had consequences.

I touched my hip and considered the logistics of it. Not just the action itself, but the reality of having to look someone in the eye after you had fantasized about them. But also, maybe it was a way to be a better person, to try out a notion and see that maybe that wasn't how I felt about her.

I figured it was okay to do once. I would've tried it in the shower, where it would have seemed more understandable, or at least cleaner, but those things never occurred to me in the shower. Besides, there I was in the van, all alone, thinking of her. I unbuttoned the top of my pants.

Suddenly I heard a crunch and the van rattled. An earthquake?

I looked out the window to see a red car driving off. It had rounded one of the narrow corners and rear-ended me.

I stepped out barefooted into the cool morning and looked at the back of the van. He had hit the same spot where I had backed into the telephone pole in Pendleton. I suppose I had just received the answer to my curiosity about Hitomi.

A man jogged past and I looked at him like I was looking at a dragon. He had earbuds in and didn't look at me directly, but I could sense him at least consider my reality for a second.

I grabbed my journal and walked down the hill to the lobby of the apartment building where the band was staying. I realized I didn't have a way in. I stepped back and looked up at the windows, as though I could execute some sort of free climb. Did I need suction cups? A crossbow?

Instead a businessman stepped out of the door, and I slipped in despite his nervous look.

The lobby was decorated with chandeliers and nice furniture. In the corner was a grand piano. I remembered James saying the night before as we walked through, "Don't be fooled. This is all prop furniture. Nothing is real in LA."

I wondered if that were true. Prop furniture is still furniture though, right?

Prop pianos are still pianos?

I sat down and thought about playing it, but it was still before eight in the morning and I didn't want to wake anyone.

I set my hands on the keys without pressing them down, feeling the mountainous blacks rising out of the valley of white. The lid was propped open, and I looked at the gleaming wires and the dutiful hammers. I thought of Joni herself sitting down at such a piano, smoking a cigarette, looking at her notebook.

I closed the cover and put my journal on top and wrote a letter.

65.
Why Is It Like This?

Hitomi,

Why is it like this, hanging out with you?

Why is it like a lamp being plugged in?

Why is it like petting a cat all over, and not wanting to stop?

Why is it like a projector, with an endless reel of film, the beginning attached to the end, looping forever, and as soon as the bad guy gets tied up and the good guy kisses the girl, we go right back to the girl in the village and the bad guy plotting his scheme?

Why is it like the waves of the ocean, never giving up?

Why is it like the dirty dishes in a 24-hour restaurant?

Why is it like the mail?

Chemistry tells us molecules form because elements will have a certain number of electrons, and they're more stable if they share one with another element that has what they lack.

Maybe it's like that.

Maybe it's like a part in a play, and you've been auditioning actors for weeks, and no one gets it, and then someone walks in, and before they say a word, you just know it's going to work.

Maybe it's like music, when two notes are not in harmony and they create this wobble in the air that just doesn't feel right, and then they adjust a bit and they just fit, and you can feel it in your chest and in your head, the resonance of the sound, because two waves have matched up.

Maybe it's like no one wants to talk about anything interesting, and they only want to talk about money, or the things that money can buy, and they really are talking about how scared they are, what's it like when we die, why did I believe all the lies my mother told me, but instead of saying that, which would be really interesting, they bury themselves deeper in the lie, and they talk about the lie, because that's what seems right and proper and inoffensive, and uncovering it even a little, dusting it off for even a second is just too terrifying, because maybe underneath there is a big chasm you'll fall down, and you'll lose all your friends and your comfort, and you'll fall behind on your favorite TV show, and you won't know how to get back, and maybe it's too scary to take even one step down a hallway you're not sure about.

Maybe it's like having already been dead, because you lost something you thought gave you life, and you've come so close to losing your own life besides, that there's nothing worth holding back, there's nothing to protect, there's nothing to be afraid of, except for the fear of being bored and being boring and being with boring people and falling asleep and not ever seeing all the colors in *Christina's World,* the silver strands in her hair.

Maybe it's like falling asleep, in that middle period where it really feels like you're falling backward out of your body, and how is it that everyone does that every night and then they wake up and go to work and act so straight like the world can all be figured out and pinned down and there's nothing spooky about closing your eyes and losing your mind every night.

Maybe it's like making love, your boundaries melting, feeling pleasure but not knowing what's yours or who started it, feeling like every move is toward your own pleasure and someone else's, feeling like a bee plunging into a flower, not because it's his job but because he sees beauty and just plunges.

Maybe it's like a game, like What Am I Thinking, throwing out possible points and determining where the other person is, finding that middle ground that neither of you discussed.

Maybe it's like stretching your shoulders in the sun.

Maybe it's like the earth, whose spinning congealed the dirt into one whole, whose path is through darkness yet somehow not scary, who orbits the thing that burns with life-giving light, but whose path is always away from it, solitary.

Maybe it's like God, like all the coincidences and unexplained magic that you felt in your bones, all the ways you needed something and someone gave it to you right before you gave up, and them giving that to you happened right when they needed to do that, and that happens a billion times over every minute and who could plan all that out or even have the compassion to try but God.

Maybe it's like feet in the surf.

Maybe it's like a heart drawn on the back of your hand.

Maybe it's a game.

66.
Joshua Tree

I CAREFULLY REMOVED THAT LETTER FROM MY JOURNAL and folded it three ways, the way you do with letters. I didn't have an envelope, so I put it in the chest pocket of my blazer. It was nice to have it close to my heart. I would read it to her that night.

We drove east from Los Angeles into the high desert.

I did the driving. I chose the music. Merle Haggard.

I forgot to look at the ocean, I thought, right at the moment it was too late.

I watched as tumbleweeds spilled across the landscape at a diagonal to our van. They tore through like kamikaze pilots, bound to hit their target because they weren't aiming a weapon, they were aiming themselves. I'd see these balls rolling through and try to adjust our path so we didn't hit them, then realize this was stupid and plow on ahead, and the weeds would smash into the grill of our van and disintegrate, and it felt like I had extinguished a life.

We were quiet the whole drive until we got near Joshua Tree National Park and passed a sign that read FRIED LIVER WASH.

"What a weird thing to put on a sign," Hitomi said. "Are they joking when they call this a wash?"

"I think," James said, "maybe you have to imagine the one day of the year when the rains come."

We camped that evening in the park near large boulders and cholla cacti. Daveed started assembling firewood in the pit. They passed a bottle of wine around. They were so used to me refusing drink that I had to pluck it out of their hands to get some.

"What's your fire-building technique?" James asked.

Nothing can happen without a technique, I thought as I unconsciously reached up to clutch the letter and my heart in one handful.

"Care for it like a baby bird who fell out of a nest," Daveed said.

"Do what?" James asked.

"That's my technique," Daveed said. "For building a fire. Care for it until it can walk on its own."

"That's. Well, sure," James said.

It felt like we were marooned on another planet. The still air was clear. The clear air was still. A constant stream of lights traced a line in the sky overhead, all those airplanes on a flight path to Los Angeles.

"Fire needs to be nurtured," Daveed said. "Think of how you'd feel if someone brought you to a party. You'd need encouragement."

"But do you build a structure for it or—" James asked.

"Sure, man. A little cabin. Like for wounded soldiers."

I don't think he was purposely being difficult, but I loved how much Daveed confounded James.

Daveed bent down and lit the paper underneath. After a while of staring at it, he looked away, slowly sucked in air, and then breathed on the fire. It glowed with gratitude. A warm red light highlighted all the crevices of his face. He looked like one of those stone demons above the New York City streets, watchful, patient.

"I guess that's an effective method," James said.

Hitomi stared into the fire and seemed to realize something.

"How did we get here?" she asked.

"To California?" James asked. "Remember when those people a few days ago asked if we had any fruit? That was the front door of California."

"No. Not California." Hitomi looked into the dark. "How did we get to this point where we travel the country and play music?"

"Interesting question," James said. "We both loved music. And we loved each other. And we played an open mic together in Queens once. End of story."

I pulled the letter out of my pocket and thought of reading it there in front of everyone. What did it matter if I did? It wasn't a gooey love letter. It didn't say anything explicit. It was just a series of questions. If it embarrassed James, he would've only been embarrassed because what he had with Hitomi was no longer anything magical, or it never had been.

"But does it need to be at such a breakneck pace?" Hitomi asked. "It's so nice when we get a night like this away from the city."

"If you like," James said, "we could just do a whole tour of camping and only play one show."

"I know you're joking, but I think I'd actually like that."

I looked over at Hitomi, with the light flickering across her face. She seemed neither happy nor sad. I thought of what Daveed had once said about his tattoos as protections, and I thought of hers not as aesthetic decorations but as warnings to the world to leave her alone.

Every miracle causes suffering. Every miracle comes from suffering. Shoot. I couldn't remember it now.

The victims of the disease are the same as the disease itself.

No. That wasn't it.

"This is already too long as it is," Daveed said. "You guys don't get it because you travel together."

"Oh like this makes it easier?" Hitomi said.

I took a long drink from the bottle of wine. I thought about those movies you watch when you're a kid, where someone is trying to save a life and they ignore all the warnings and crash through gates to get there. Like, literally smash through them in a stolen truck. Those people are framed as heroes. But you could make a movie from another point of view about how they're just assholes crashing through gates. What about the responsible people who have to rebuild the gates?

"Okay, look," James said. "Just imagine if we had real shows booked by someone like Mary Cornish. The pressure wouldn't be on me to set up everything. None of us are complaining about the travel when we have good shows."

I looked over at Daveed as I held the letter in my pocket. Who considers the feelings of the owners of gates? What kind of reverse sociopath garbage was that? I felt like a repressed little domesticated bird around these people. I hadn't put it together until then. These were three people who did what they wanted, took what they wanted, lived the life they wanted. I just went along with what other people asked of me. Go on tour, when music is the thing that hurt you most? Sure! Ride along for five weeks in a bumpy van next to someone with gorgeous legs? Sure, okay! What kind of repercussions could that possibly have?

I felt the purple crust accumulate on my lips as I drank more wine. I wanted the freedom to be an asshole. *The medication for the disease causes the same effects as the disease it's trying to cure.* Was that it? I had it written down somewhere. *Every miracle is, at its heart, actually suffering.* What a concept to put in a bible.

Hitomi had her head on James' shoulder now. Daveed was still in half-light. I had a blanket around my shoulders and I held that bottle of wine in my hand. I had removed it from the circle. They didn't need it anymore. I needed it.

"We're gonna get there," James said to Hitomi.

She closed her eyes and curled up to him.

Where were we going to get to? Back home? To exactly where we started? All the instruments splayed out on a sidewalk in Brooklyn?

"We're gonna get there," he said again as he patted her head.

My head started to hurt. Like a hangover coming before any of the good parts of being drunk. The wine was gone. I held the bottle up above my head. I wanted a big crash, a shattering of the moment. Everyone would look at me and I would pull out my letter and read it and everyone would see that I was someone who acted, not someone who was acted upon. "You are a doer," they would say. "Bravo."

I smirked a little and dropped the bottle. It hit the ground with one thud and it stuck there. No one noticed. Not one needle of one cactus fluttered. The Joshua trees held their arms up.

I looked back at Daveed. "Good job on the fire," I said.

"Thanks," he said as he poked it. "Soon it'll be all grown up and ready to start its own family."

James and Hitomi slept in the van that night. I heard the coyotes howl down the hill. Their cries sounded like a circle of witches conjuring a spirit and stirred the faraway neighborhood dogs to bark. The dogs sounded like they wanted to join the party, but they were stuck. The coyotes were expressive and wild. They played fretless instruments that ran loose through the tonal range. The domestic dogs made short, dumb sounds. The coyotes were talking. The dogs were trying to join the conversation but were across a great divide.

After the fire died down, I saw Daveed playing in the dirt. He had taken several rocks to make a conglomeration: two overlapping circles.

"That was *you* making these?" I asked.

He looked up at me, with a joint in his hand, and exhaled.

"Yeah, of course."

"Of course," I said.

"How about a game?" Daveed asked.

I heard from the van Hitomi's laugh, melodic and free. I wanted to transcribe it on a music staff. All the grace notes. All the slides.

"Sure, sure," I said. "Yeah, a game."

"What's wrong?"

"Nothing," I said. I took the joint from him and took a puff. "It's. Nothing. Okay. How about a Math Path?"

"What is that?" he asked. "Does it involve math?"

"Yes. Math is kind of baked into the game."

"Alright. It sounds hard."

"No. I can keep it simple. All you have to do is just follow along and do the equation."

"Equation?"

"It's not hard. Here, just. Try. Just follow along. Okay, so start with the number of keys on a piano."

"I know this! Eighty-eight."

"Yes, but. Keep it in your head for now."

"Okay, sorry."

"Okay. The number of keys on a piano. Minus the number of cards in a tarot deck. Divided by the number of fingers on your right hand. Minus the number of hearts you have in your chest."

"Wow, that got personal."

"I don't know for sure how many hearts you have."

"Yeah, you don't."

"Okay, but what's the answer?"

"One, right?"

"Yes. Nice work!"

"I got it?" he asked.

"Yeah! Okay, I'll give you another one. Okay. The number of legs on a spider. Take half of that. Take half again."

"Wait, you can't take half of zero."

"What?"

"You started with eight. And then you said half. Half of eight is zero."

"Half of eight is zero?"

"Yeah. You take two circles and remove one?"

I stared at him. I couldn't tell if he was joking or not.

Half of eight is zero.

From the van I heard a yelp. Hitomi's voice. Not a laugh. Not a nightmare. Not singing. The sound of her suppressing an orgasm. Maybe now I understood what it meant to be afraid of a uterus falling out of your body.

The distant coyotes howled, and I wondered what even separated us from them. The marijuana had been stronger than I thought. The coyotes had been howling all along, and might have been getting closer and closer, might have even surrounded us. They could teach us how to sing out of key. Finally we could unlearn all those rigid pitches we had tied ourselves to on the piano, like boards on our backs to keep us straight. Why had we forsaken wilderness?

From the van came another yip. She wasn't even trying to hide it after all. I scrunched my face into a painful grimace, like I was passing the moon through my urethra. Daveed looked at me and smiled, determined to turn it all into something positive.

"It's okay," he said. "You can try again."

What did it even matter? The coyotes had moved on and forgotten us, had become a story we would tell others who would think we were crazy.

I took the letter out of my pocket and tore it in half with a clean rip. I set it in the fire and watched it ignite. I saw the word *harmony* before it all burned up.

67. Tucson

THE NEXT DAY A SICKNESS GREW IN ME. It felt like my guts had split open and released all that bile I thought had dried up. Instead it had crawled into my heart, and my heart, the poor sieve, was leaking it back into my body. It felt like the fat in my cells had spoiled.

Tucson offered a dry wind that coasted through the whitewashed buildings. The buildings are the skeletons. The people are the blood. A town can learn a sickness, can repeat a pattern, can get stuck in an eddy, just like a person can.

Us travelers, then, passing through these bodies at such a high rate. What are we? Neutrinos? B-12 shots? Pathogens?

There are places in the country that feel closer to a distant past. New York City is not one of those places. The furthest time period you can imagine is maybe the 1960s. But in the desert your mind can stretch back centuries. Things are not so far away. You can look over at a butte and, as Daveed said, squint a bit and imagine a rushing crowd of animals coming over the hill.

In the desert cities you can see the bodies laid out more plainly. Or at least you can see the skeletons. All soft tissue is burnt away and chewed off. Most of what sticks out are the bones.

Melissa called to say Robert's mother was going ahead with the wake. I could fly in for it if I skipped the last show of the tour.

At the show in Tucson, the band started with a dirge. I hadn't admitted to myself I was sick. I lay on the stage, next to my keyboard, because I didn't want to be vertical. I didn't even realize we were starting. Every show we played on tour was different, but they all started with the same phenomenon. The three of us played music and waited for Hitomi to finish her drink and come up onstage to launch into her poem. By the time she got onstage and opened a page to start reading, everyone in the room had shut up. No one would shush anyone or give an eye, it was just a collective decision by the room each time.

That wonderful moment of calm was so thrilling. She'd stand there and read what she had written, and it would be new to us, too.

I built you out of garlic and tobacco
ruby and scarlet
I built you so I could know myself
but
you slipped out of my hands
and shattered on the riverbed
I thought I was on top of you
but you were on top of me
I thought I was the queen of the underground
but I was the tumbleweed
traveling
only
after
my own death
I remembered my promise
I sent you dead flowers for your wedding

but you forgot
    to put
        roses
            o n
                m y
                    grave

I saw her wobble that night in Tucson the same way she wobbled in Indianapolis.

"Okay," she said. "Okay, hold on."

She stagger-stepped. Behind her I saw James swinging his guitar, rocking with impatience. She smiled a bit and the light caught her chipped tooth.

"Pick a song, 'Tome," he said.

"Shut up!" she said. "Of course! What else would I do?"

"You might just stagger off into the desert."

"Really?" she asked, and she said it right into the microphone, clearer than she had said anything in the whole set. You could feel every person in the audience tighten up like they thought someone was about to hit them with a belt.

"You think I'm going to stagger off and ditch the band? Have I ever done that?" she asked.

"Not yet."

I wish he hadn't said those words, but it was even worse how he said them, like he was goading her.

"Fuck. YOU!" she said. She put her hand to her temple and she closed her eyes.

"You guys just play something," she said, and walked off the stage.

Without any hesitation James called out, "Three, four!" But instead of it being a magical coming together like in San Francisco, we all just flailed at our instruments, not knowing which song and which key.

"Okay," he said. "Let's try that again. Daveed, you count it off?"

"Which song?" Daveed asked.

"Doesn't matter," James said.

But now it was just some boring instrumental song by a bunch of dudes. And it hurt. It hurt throughout my body. How shitty the music we made was. How ugly and stupid it felt. I didn't want to be up there. I wouldn't have wanted to be in the audience. I wouldn't have wanted to be anywhere in the same city as that thing we were doing.

I know a rotten sickness in me was twisting my objectivity. I know that. But also, sometimes it takes a vile thing to release you from a responsibility and really tell the truth.

In my heart that night on stage, I felt how stupid we were, and I honestly thought, as a reaction to that, as a way to run the other direction, *Maybe Gordo is right.*

68.
Queen of the Night

WE STAYED THAT NIGHT ALL TOGETHER in one room and couldn't avoid being a part of the argument. I lay down on the floor with my hand on my forehead. Daveed sat on the couch like a child of a divorce. He eyed a Jenga tower on the table in front of him, but seemed afraid to start playing, maybe because of the ruckus it would cause when the tower would fall.

All I heard from the argument was Hitomi saying, "Why can't I just sing in a garden?"

And James saying, "'Cause then who would get to listen?"

And Hitomi saying, "I would sing to the garlic bulbs. I don't know. Why does anyone have to hear me? I don't care if anyone hears me."

Then Hitomi stepped out for air. I imagined she would have been far away five minutes later when I stepped out too, but she was still there, sitting on the ground.

"I want to get some cigarettes," she said. "Will you walk with me?"

"Okay."

The streetlights gave the world an odd glow. The air was so dry I felt like we were stepping across a newly populated Mars, trying it for once without helmets on, to see if we could survive or—

"Do you think I'm overreacting?" she asked.

"No," I said. "No, I don't think so."

"I walked offstage in the middle of a gig. You think that's normal?"

"Nothing's normal. We're beyond normal. We're in the middle of the desert. Is that normal?"

"No. It's a fucking apocalypse."

I laughed.

"What's so funny?" she asked.

"It's just funny that you don't like the desert."

"Why?"

"Just. When I met you. I thought. This is weird, but. I thought about this flower out here called the Queen of the Night. Do you know it?"

"No. Is it an asshole like me?"

"No," I said, laughing. "It's not. It's not an asshole flower. If that's even possible."

"Oh, it's possible."

"It's just this really rare flower. It only blooms one night of the year. And that night—I've never seen it. But that night is really special. People get the word it's going to bloom earlier in the day, and everyone gathers around to watch it bloom. And it only blooms at night. And then in the morning it's gone."

"And I'm like that?"

"Well, no."

"Only good for one night of the year?"

"No, no. I mean. That night I met you. Before I knew your name. That moment just felt so special. And, I guess, in my head I called you the Queen of the Night."

"Oh."

"It's a good thing. To be that. You see."

"Hmm."

We stepped over crumbled cement into the empty parking lot of a convenience store.

"I'm not that, you know," she said. "The Queen of the Night. I'm not just something that blooms and then is gone. I've known people like that, and it's not any way to be. I want to be a sunflower, spending my day tracking the movement of the sun across the sky. Can you call me a sunflower instead?"

"I'll make a note of that," I said.

"If I warrant a mention in your book."

"You might come up in the margins."

We walked past a pickup truck idling with no one in it.

"How are you feeling, Sick-o?" she asked.

"I'm feeling like . . . I really don't feel good. I feel like my blood is filled with lead."

"Let's get you something at the store to knock that sickness out of you."

69.
El Paso

THE SICKNESS MUTATED INSIDE ME. It wanted things. It wanted to take over my body and be its own person. I wanted to fight it, but the more the sickness became a part of me, the more I would have to fight my own self, the more I would have to declare war on my own body and turn over every cell looking for the enemy.

"Someone told me once," James said, "that there are three magical states in this country, and New Mexico is one of them."

"What are the other two?" Hitomi asked.

"I'm trying to remember," James said. "Michigan, I'm pretty sure. And, I think . . . Mississippi? Does that sound right?"

I heard this discussion muted and strangled while in my bed of sickness in the back seat. I sat up to see a series of road signs spaced a few hundred feet apart.

IN A DUST STORM
PULL OFF ROADWAY
TURN VEHICLE OFF
FEET OFF BRAKES
STAY BUCKLED

I slid through modes of consciousness in the back seat, a dead body they were hauling to the morgue.

But.

I'm.

Not.

Dead.

Everything surrounding me was reduced to flickering shades of light while I battled off the pressure in my head.

That drill they use to bore into the whale's skull. I could use one of those.

And then I heard Gordo's voice, now as comforting as hearing my own father's.

"Anyone who tells you the world is ending is trying to sell you something. Worse than that, they're trying to take something away from you. They're trying to take away your freedoms. The world is going to be here for a long time. Liberalism is just an unfortunate splat on the windshield of progress."

We stopped at someone's house and everyone got out. I stumbled inside, feeling gallons of whale oil sloshing in my head.

"The kids are at their father's house, so you can have their rooms."

"Let's give one to Ian."

Someone helped me into a bed. The sheets were printed with pink cartoon characters. The mattress was narrow, like it was cut to be the exact width and length of my body. The pillow was flat, and I couldn't imagine having the energy to lift my head and fluff it. The bed faced east, like all the best graves do, so the dead can face the rising sun on Judgment Day.

"Do you need a bedtime story?" James asked.

The pastor's grave should face west so he can address his flock.

I heard the soft negotiation of books. Then a creak of a chair.

"Okay," James said. "Let's learn about hearts. 'The smallest heart in the world belongs to a hummingbird. It pulses so fast it sounds like a modem trying to connect.' And then there's a picture of a smiling hummingbird. So cute."

The turning of a page. Thick pages.

"'The largest heart in the world belongs to the blue whale. It is about the size and weight of an upright piano.' Hey, *you* play piano. I wish you could see this picture. Do you want to look? Okay, well there's a whale with a piano in his heart. What a thing! He could accompany his own whale songs with it."

I tried to look up at the picture. I pried open one tired eye because opening both would have been too much. I couldn't focus on the picture, but instead I saw James's face, and for a second it looked like Robert's.

Then another voice from outside the room:

"James, do you want some dinner?"

"Okay, just a second," James said. "Alright, I'm going to leave you with that image. Dream about a whale with a piano heart. Now *that's* a whale worth chasing around the world."

Then he patted my head softly, as though he were doing it sarcastically, but the result was he still did it.

"Good night," he said as he gently closed the door.

70.
A Fog

I WOKE UP IN A FOG IN THE MIDDLE OF THE NIGHT. I needed to pee, though I dearly wished I didn't have to move my body at all. I wrestled myself out of that little bed with the thin sheets. I pushed open the bedroom door, wondering if the rest of the band was out at a bar or what. I heard the muffled sounds of what might have been a television.

I tried to find my way in this house I didn't know. Tile floors and smudged reflections in pictures. I tried to look at the faces of the children, tried to know them a bit, since I was an invader in their bedroom, this big, buggy, diseased beast who was moaning and twisting up their sheets. Why was I allowed to do that, why was I allowed to be anywhere? They should've buried me in a metal drum in the desert.

A muffled song was playing somewhere. I couldn't tell if it was a man or woman singing. It sounded like it was coming from the underworld. The words were familiar.

Southern trees bear strange fruit

I couldn't tell which door was the bathroom. Sometimes it's hard to know. Would it be stupid to have a sign in a house? To point you to the restroom? Yes, that would be stupid. Some sick animal would just ogle the woman silhouette anyway.

There was one door ajar. I pushed it open and looked inside.

I saw two figures moving on a bed. Someone lying down and someone over them. The one looked like they were mending the other, a rhythmic mending with their mouth. Chewing a poultice that would pull out the stinger. They moved so beautifully in the moonlight, in the blue of the darkest corner of night.

This was not a bathroom. It was a tableau. It was a painting more beautiful and tragic than anything at the MoMA. Certainly more real than that prim picnic-going lady in pink. The sheets and the darkness obscured any recognition of faces, and for a second I told myself this was the couple of the house, married people with kids who had thin beds in which I was sleeping.

And then the door gave a shudder as it hit the rubber backstop and went *f-d-d-d-d-d-d*. The hunched figure on top looked at me. And I saw that familiar face. Hitomi in the moonlight. Silver-and-blue moonlight.

Strange fruit hanging from the poplar trees

I looked for too long. I thought it was a painting. A painting of Hitomi. And then my stomach dropped and I felt stupid for everything I was. I felt stupid for being in this band, going on tour around the country, being in the desert of wherever the fuck we were. What was I doing?

I tried to say, "Sorry," but I couldn't form any words. I backed out of the room and closed the door, hoping I could just make the whole thing go away. I went down the hall and found the actual bathroom. I closed and locked the door behind me and lay my face down on the cool tiles. They were dirty, but those tiles were so cool on my face.

71.
Return to Dream Land

I FELT ROSEMARY-SCENTED HANDS PULL ME DOWN into the shadow, which became sunlight.

This time Robert saw me. He faccd me. He was wearing a blue checkered shirt. We were together and talking. He was funny and kind and teasing.

"You're a musician again?"

Again, again, again.

"I—heh . . . I don't . . . hehheh."

We talked about why he went missing and how it was all just a misunderstanding.

We were in a kitchen. His kitchen. But not his kitchen. Yellow linoleum-flowered floor. Like coffee filters were cut into snowflakes and pressed in amber. I held a cup of coffee close to my face to feel the warmth of it. Sunlight gushed through the windows, yellow and thick.

"Why?" I asked him as I smiled. "Why? Why? Why?"

"Don't be so dramatic," he said. "I just needed to step away for a while."

A while.

A while, a while.

A whale.

A whale? Did he say he needed to step away for a *whale?*

Suddenly the sunlight was thicker because it was pushing through water. Strands of kelp waved in between us. Still, it was warm and amniotic. It felt so good to swim in the same waters as him. Did we need to go up for air? He didn't seem worried about it, so I wasn't either.

Suddenly we were in the lobby of a big building, but still underwater. It was a hospital, but it was built like a train station, with big, arching ceilings that inspired you with their grandeur. Taller than any space needed to be, so that they could inspire us to dream.

But it wasn't just that. The doors and ceilings needed to be so high because this wasn't a hospital for me. It was a hospital for whales. I realized this as one humpback swam right behind me and swirled up in a beautiful, posed comma above me, then alighted down at the reception desk. I wasn't even mad that she had cut the line, because her arc and her grace were such a gift.

The nurse whale swam up to greet her, and they touched noses or snouts or whatever you call them, and then they swam off together through a grand hall, deep into the darkness, their tails rhyming as they churned through the water. I sat there in the lobby, drifting backward and looking up, looking up to the ceilings to see the light streaming in from above, thick and pale light from above, sprinkled with dust and little creatures. Maybe I would just stay in the waiting room. Maybe my sickness wasn't as critical as I had thought. Maybe I was being dramatic.

Robert was still there. I wanted to stay forever. It was warm and everything was okay. Can it just always be okay?

But then. The water turned cold.

I shivered.

No.

No, I just want this. To be here. In the warmth.

The sun was blocked by a passing boat.

Or was it a whale?

No. I want to stay. I don't need my body.

Just. Please.

Just more time.

Just. No. Please.

Robert drifted up. His face looked so peaceful. Why wasn't he scared?

Please. No. Just. Just let me have more time.

I know it's just a dream.

It doesn't matter.

I know it's the only way.

Just. Please.

"You're a good salesperson, I have no doubt about that."

I started to resurface to the waking world.

"I don't know if you've read the whole email."

I was back in the little kid's bed in El Paso.

"I don't even intentionally send people out in that market, because it's such a hard job."

I had twisted up the sheet into a rope that wrapped around me, a pink cartoon noose.

"I'll gauge some understanding from them about it."

I just wanted to be back in the water with Robert. But someone was in the kitchen talking on the phone, some adult, someone I had never met, and it was over.

"No problem, no problem, stay in the game."

72.
Making Repairs

"DAVEED! HOW'S IT GOING UP THERE?"

"Okay."

"Is it okay?"

"Yes, James."

"Okay. If you need me to come up—"

"No."

"Can you see where the thing screws in?"

"Yeah, it's just hard to get my fingers in there, man."

"Do you need pliers? Daveed?"

"I don't think pliers will help."

"What will help?"

"Just. Give me a second."

"Okay. I just don't want to do any more damage to Cassandra, like ol' Ian did back in Oregon. Remember that, Ian? She can't take many more holes in her."

"Let's not. Gah. Give Ian. Fuck. A hard time. Rrrr. When he's sick. And. I don't even have a hammer, man. How would I put a hole in her?"

"Okay, you're right. Sorry. I should've been the one up there. I would've if it weren't for my shoulder. Sore from last night."

"It's okay, man. Almost got it."

"Okay. Thank you, Daveed. Let me know if I can help. We're making repairs at sea, Ian, like a real live *Pequod*. Fixing on the fly. You do see that, right? I wish we could just open up a sail and coast through the desert. It would save us a lot on gas. Of course, there's no wind. There's not even like one—what is it? Knot. Not even one knot of wind. Not a knot. No wind at all. Is that even possible? Isn't there, like, an iguana farting somewhere nearby? How is there no wind? Maybe the earth stopped turning at noon. That would explain how the sun is just sitting there baking poor Daveed to death and there's absolutely, pathologically not any wind. Is that possible? How hot is it up there, Daveed?"

"Not as bad as tarring the roofs of houses when I was young."

"No, sir, not as bad as that. Though why did they have to make that storage thing out of black plastic, you know? That sure makes it hotter."

"It's not too bad."

"I wonder if they ever tested an atomic bomb around here. This seems like a good place to just . . . *SHHHFFEWWW!* Just set off the biggest explosion in the history of the world. Just to try it out. Yeah, why not out here, where there's nothing? Earth is our dominion anyway, for us humans to do as we please, because we're so goddamn smart."

"James. You got that socket wrench?"

"Yes, sir."

"Pass it up."

"It's going to be okay, though, right, Ian? You probably haven't made any more progress in the book. I imagine the whole ship is just waiting for you to get better so they can resume their hunt of the whale. Everyone in the crew is paused in midstep. The sun is hanging in the sky. The winds are still. Ol' Ahab is in mid ball scratch. Just waiting for you to get better so they can all get back to their singular purpose in life. Are you almost there, Ian? You feeling better? Seemed like you were able to walk around last night a bit."

"Can you give me the next-size-bigger socket?"

"What size would that be, Daveed?"

"I don't know. Bigger than five-eighths."

"What's bigger than five-eighths?"

"Just. James. Come on."

"Alright, here, try one of these. Anyway, don't say a word, Ian. Get some rest. Did you think about that piano in the whale's chest? Just imagine those men on the *Pequod,* cutting into that whale and finding a *piano* in there. And then old Queequeg pounds on it. I wonder who in that crew could play a tune. I bet ol' Tashtego could play. Maybe that's why I named this band after him. What say you, Daveed?"

"Got it!"

"Alright, he's got it! We can get back on the road and not have our belongings fly off. Ian, you're supposed to jump back to life! That was your cue. God damn it, does anything ever happen on time? Is there even *time* anymore? Alright, get down here, Daveed, let's get to Austin and see if ol' Mary Cornish finds us slightly tolerable."

73.
Van Horn

IN A GAS STATION IN VAN HORN, TEXAS, I found my soul again. I found my body. The bathroom mirror was dirty and cracked, but it gave me self-confidence. If that mirror was doing enough to reflect, despite its damage, then maybe I was, too.

I stepped out of the bathroom and saw Hitomi in the aisle of the convenience store. The fluorescent light gave everyone in the store a monstrous green hue to their face.

But there she was, the Queen of the Night, blooming for the one time of the year. Blooming in secret, blooming in a stupid convenience store. She was wearing those leopard-print tights. I couldn't believe I was encountering a celebrity in the middle of Texas. I almost pointed at them and said, "Those. Tights." Not with any intonation, just like a zombie would say. Her leggings were dirty, and one leg rode up her calf. But there they were, the magical leopard pants from that person I had danced with.

She wasn't looking at me. She was just standing in the aisle grabbing a bag of marshmallows and squeezing them. She squeezed them hard, to the point where they wouldn't just spring back to life.

"What are you doing?" I asked.

"I just like to leave an impression," she said.

"Literally?" I said.

"Yeah," she said. "Literally."

I still didn't have much energy to push against this.

"They don't have tampons in there, do they?" she asked.

I stared at her, trying to parse where *there* was, what tampons were. Who *I* was.

"You didn't notice," she said. "It's okay. I'm sure they don't. It's not like it's a body fluid we regularly expel"—here she gave a little curtsey—"like piss or shit, where we'd want to offer supplies to our fellow humans."

"I hadn't thought of that," I said.

"Nobody does," she said.

She searched the shelves and grabbed a box of tampons and tucked it under her hand with a smooth motion. She started to put it under her sleeve. She looked back at me. Was she getting ready to steal them? I wasn't judging or anything, I just loved watching her. Was I part of the problem?

"Can you ask him for the bathroom key?" she asked.

I held out the bathroom key in my hand, which had a funnel attached to it so no one would walk off with it.

"Oh, right," she said.

"You know what I like about whales?" she continued. "You can never see the whole whale at once. You know? They're always concealed somewhat. There's something so thrilling about that. You know all the best pornography is from the time when an ankle was considered obscene, right?"

She grabbed the bag of marshmallows again and squished a few more. She did a little spring step and walked up to the counter.

"Just this, please," she said.

74.
Fort Stockton

We got a motel in Fort Stockton, which, as prophesied by James, turned out to be the only motel of tour.

Hitomi and I were mistaken for a couple by the old woman at the front desk. She had thick-paned glasses and she barely glanced at us, but it felt like a validation of some sort, and Hitomi didn't directly resist the characterization.

The band wanted to go to a bar, even though this was the one night of the week we didn't have to go to a bar. I told them I would meet them there after I took a shower. I wanted to wash all the dust and pollen off me. Sometimes the body feels like a big billboard on which every creature on Earth likes to post its messages.

After the shower I stood naked in the steam of the bathroom. A television in the next room was arguing with itself.

There was a centerfold pinned to the back of the bathroom door. It was that type of motel. It was a photo of a young woman at the beach wearing a pink bikini with her back to us. She was so tan she looked like a browned sausage.

On the horizon was a beach house. She didn't seem to want to go there. She looked so lonely. She was smiling in the sun, but it was a desperate smile and a desperate sun. Her eyes said, "Is this good enough?" I could picture the photographer standing where I stood, cajoling her to look sexy.

Do we ever know what's good enough?

I took the centerfold off the wall, folded it once, and put it in the garbage. Then I thought of *Christina's World,* and I wondered how I had slipped out of such beauty into the ugly world again.

I walked down a dusty street to join the rest of the band at the bar. Outside, Daveed stood with a cigarette in his hand. A neon sign advertising Coors glowed bright.

"You made it," Daveed said.

"I did. How is it in there?"

"Well, it's no. . . What was that place in Los Angeles?"

"D'Antoni's?"

"Yeah. It's not that."

"Well," I said. "I guess I gotta go in."

I thought of a water tower on a rooftop. It can't hold water until it starts to hold water. I grabbed the handle of the door to the bar.

"You like her?" Daveed asked.

"What?" I said.

"Hitomi. You're into her?"

"Um."

"It's okay. She's great. I'm just asking."

I let go of the door. The water was spilling out the slats. How could this ever work?

"I. I don't know," I said. I patted my pockets, like there would be something in there that answered the question. "Yeah. I do. I guess I do."

He looked at me and smiled. I looked at his cigarette.

"I thought you didn't smoke?" I said.

"This isn't a cigarette," he said.

"Yes, it is."

He looked at it for a second.

"So it is," he said.

"I feel like I haven't seen you in a year," I said.

"Yeah. You looked pretty dreary there for a while. We seriously considered just leaving you to the coyotes."

"Do you think they would have me?"

"One way or another," he said.

He closed his eyes. The water tower was full. The wood was swelling.

"What's wrong?" I asked.

"It's just. It's been too long. That fourth week. It's too much."

"Why? What's happening?"

"I don't know."

"How's that horn coming along?"

"Ah, I can't get anywhere with it. Do you see anything poking out of my forehead yet?"

"No, not yet."

"What are you going to do about Hitomi?"

"Do? What? There's nothing to do."

"You should tell her you like her. What do you have to lose?"

"Just. Like. Everything."

"Naw. You don't have anything at all, so what's the risk?"

"Thanks," I said. I looked at the door and then out at the town.

"Want to play Pushing Hands?" I asked.

"Nah. I'm too wobbly."

"Math Path?"

He took a drag of his cigarette.

"Alright, man. Hit me."

"Okay," I said. "I'll keep it simple. Okay. Four times two. Times three. Divided by four. Is?"

"Heartbreak," Daveed said, shaking his head.

"No. It's six. Okay. Six divided by two."

"Heartbreak."

"Minus one."

"It's all heartbreak."

"I guess," I said. "You're not wrong."

Inside was something I was not expecting: two rows of people facing each other. Hitomi saw me walk in and motioned me to stand in one of the lines.

"Alright, everyone, join hands," said a man into a microphone onstage. "Step to the center. Then head back home."

We were in a contra dance. Like a square dance, except you keep switching neighbors and moving down the row and then back up again. Hitomi was wearing a tie because there weren't enough men there, so she had to dance as one of them. One of us.

James danced too, and Daveed joined in. We moved like latticework across the dirty floor of that bar in Ft. Stockton. The people mostly wore hoodies or T-shirts. It was like we were reenacting the memory of something that had happened a hundred years before, back when couples would've come with matching outfits, their names embroidered into them.

But in that weaving of dance, as I moved throughout the room, I went from feeling sorry for the clumsy people, the people who weren't trying, to realizing it didn't matter if I got the dance quicker than they did. We all had to swing with each other in this intricate knot, and we lived and died by the weakest among us. Hitomi laughed as she do-si-doed, that big, broad laugh I'd heard many times, dotted across the country, in Philadelphia and Seattle and Joshua Tree. We were free in our movements because we were participating in something communal, something so ancient that nothing dangerous could ever happen. Besides, she wore a tie and was a man, and therefore I never even got to promenade with her.

75. Austin

AUSTIN WAS THE COOL OASIS IN THE VASTNESS OF TEXAS. Subtle green hills greeted us like a pod of dolphins to escort us to a safe port. We coasted through the desert to the greenery of the capital, which was a jar of stardust sitting on a table. Just sitting there. We could shake it up and see what happens or just roll around in all that dust.

From Arizona through New Mexico to Central Texas, I was so sick I was barely a person, so much so I couldn't remember our allegiances and squabbles anymore.

Let's not forget the whole point of the tour, the real oasis for us: Mary Cornish. I wondered what she would look like, if she would have curly or straight hair, if she would have a clipboard and tick off all our good qualities, or if she would just hold a glass of whiskey to her lips the whole time we played, and as soon as we got offstage and asked her what she thought, she'd say, "Exquisite," and we'd say, "You mean the whiskey or our performance?" and she'd wave her hand like she was summoning a great new kingdom out of thin air and say, *"All of it."*

I watched Hitomi in the bar in Austin writing in her notebook. I was impressed she had stuck to her commitment to write a new poem every night. It's hard to keep any promises on the road—of diet, exercise, writing postcards to friends, taking vitamins, bathing. Everything falls overboard in the endless expanse of the journey. The only goal is to get to the next town and play the show. In that dreaminess, all that waiting, sometimes you forget to wake up.

I stood at the bar as James walked up next to me and ordered a drink.

"Monopolowa and soda," he said as he looked around the room. "How am I supposed to know if Mary's here? I just realized I don't know what she looks like. She'll probably look very obviously like a booking agent, right?"

He looked at me, holding my journal.

"Writing anything good in there?" he asked.

"Sometimes some of it seems good and some of it seems horrible," I said. "And then the next day, it's like the good and bad parts reverse."

"Read me something horrible," he said. "Read me the worst you've got."

"Okay," I said.

I flipped through a page and found a description of Hitomi's voice. Would he know who I was writing about? Did it matter? Didn't we all love her voice?

"I love the way you sing," I said, pushing through the vulnerability in my voice. "I can hear the melody in every sentence you say. Every time you sing, there is a flock of birds opening up their wings, getting ready to fly. Not flying yet, but able to, and intending to."

A few seconds passed in the clatter of the bar.

"Well," James said as he took a sip. "I really have to give it to you. You're right. That's no good at all."

We heard a microphone being tested onstage. Hitomi was up there already with Daveed.

"Are we starting?" James asked as he looked at his phone.

Indeed, she started her poem while Daveed was still adjusting his hi-hat.

If I'm the queen of the night
who's gonna lay the dawn at my feet?

"'Queen of the night?'" James said under his breath as he set down his drink. "Since when?"

James got to the stage looking like he wanted to fix something. But there was nothing to fix. Was Mary Cornish going to show up? I walked onstage, too. Hitomi read another poem as we joined in.

God used to be in everything
and everyone
so much so
that it wasn't even worth mentioning
and then God was a group of quarreling figures on a mountain
and then God was an angry father in the sky
and then God
was a heartbroken man on a cross
and then God
was a reminder to do good
and then God was the guilt of being bad
and then God was just something you screamed
as you blew yourself up
and then God was almost nothing at all
you asked me, "why do I need a god?"
and I saw a little boy asking
why he needs to eat his dinner

maybe you should think about
how the gods might need you
maybe they are out there
envying our bodies
wishing they had birthdays
wishing they could dance or drink milkshakes
maybe they tap on our jar sometimes
to remind us they're out there
and they're not mad at us
and they're not taunting us
they're saying, "Hey, motherfucker.
Dance!
Don't forget to dance!"

We played a very disconnected, distracted set. We all watched the door for every person who came and went. James removed his guitar as the last chord was still ringing and walked offstage.

"Well," Hitomi said to me at the bar after. "I wonder if she came."

James was gone.

"Maybe he's out talking to her?" I offered.

"Maybe," she said.

The warm night air pressed through the door of the bar.

"I just hate the waiting," she said. "And wondering."

"We could go swimming," I joked.

She smiled and breathed in.

"I don't know," she said. "That would be nice. I don't like leaving the venue without knowing where we're staying."

She looked over at Daveed talking and laughing with someone in the corner.

I pulled out my journal. I had written something new that morning. I cleared my throat and tried to gather all the courage I could.

"You asked me a few thousand miles ago what I like about your dancing," I said, referring to a conversation in Salt Lake City when I had tried to explain why I felt so drawn to dancing with her.

"Yes," she said, facing back to me.

"I wrote it out."

"Read it to me," she said.

I shuffled to the right page.

"The first time I met you," I read, "you were wearing leopard-print pants and bunny slippers. And my first thought was that the leopard was going to eat the bunnies. But then I watched you dancing across that living room floor, gliding through shapes even genius mathematicians hadn't thought of. And, in watching you, I thought maybe the bunnies had a chance.

"And then I danced with you. It was only ninety seconds, but you invited me into the architecture of your dance in such a generous way. I felt like I belonged. I felt beautiful too.

"And then I was inside the swirl of leopard and bunny. And that's when I realized: I was the one in danger. I was the hunted.

"Here is what I like about your dancing, and I'm not even joking: You have a sense of humor about it, and it's in your shoulders. The angles you make with your shoulders. The sudden shift from one plane to the next. The descending lines.

"But it's more than that. Dance is about intention. It's not about form. If you go through the steps of a salsa like you're filling in footprints on the ground, you are not dancing. You are also not dancing if you think, 'Left, right, left, right.' You're not dancing if you ask someone after, 'Was that dancing?'

"Joni Mitchell said all you have to do to dance is close your eyes, feel the music, and express that feeling with your body. It sounds simple, but 95 percent of people don't do that. Most people dance like they learned it, as Elvis Costello sang, from a series of still pictures.

They are imitating forms instead of feeling intention.

"But you. You have no trouble with intention. When I see you dance, I see you telling a story about the music with your body. You are telling about the late-night drives, and your father who couldn't play guitar, and all that's beautiful about music. And you tell it with your body, which is a beautiful medium of expression. It's much more beautiful than any musical instrument or pen. It's more beautiful because your body's sole purpose isn't expression. It is locomotion and respiration and automaticity and all the things that keep you alive. That your body can also express such beautiful things makes that expression ten times as beautiful. I love the range of your movement, how you dip down to the ground, how you raise your arms, how you smile. You brighten the dance floor. You encourage others to dance.

"You make people near you feel beautiful. *You make people near you feel beautiful.* That's good dancing."

We stood there silent for a few seconds. Her smile was as subtle as the tilt of an italicized comma. The smallest things hold their center.

"You're a weirdo," Hitomi said. "Let's go swimming."

I stood there looking at her for a second, thinking it was a joke, but she didn't change her expression. I went over to Daveed.

"We're going for a walk," I said. "You're the man of the house now."

He looked at me and smiled and nodded.

"Be careful," he said.

"Really?" I asked.

"Nah," he said. "Be uncareful."

Hitomi and I walked down the street together in silence. We passed the bar where I had played a South by Southwest showcase a few years before. That show had seemed so important at the time, and it had mattered so much who was in the audience and how in tune we were and that we not screw anything up. And that only led us to play out of tune and screw everything up. Now it was just another bar in Austin.

We walked down to the river and found a darkened access point with a dock. The water reflected back the light of some of the brightest stars. I thought about how far that light had traveled through the universe to splash upon that section of the river.

We got to the end of the dock. I got nervous, wondering what would come next.

Hitomi started to take off her clothes. I turned to the side so I wasn't facing her. I started to take off my shirt. The moonlight was silver and it brought out the silver dots in her hair. They were like meteorites flung across the universe long ago. They only came alive when their brothers and sisters were out to watch them, and their long journey was a lesson to us all.

She took her shirt off, and she had a beautiful violet bra on with little scallops in it. I pictured her going into a store and buying it. She would look through the racks of clothes and roll her eyes at the preciousness of it all.

She reached back to unclasp it, and when she did, it lost its tension and loosened on her. She put her hands in front to hold onto it for a second, and then she dropped it to the ground.

I turned a little further as I took off my pants. I was now worried about the management of my excitement, something so natural and yet so embarrassing.

She took off her skirt, and she stood there in her light-pink underwear and faced the water. A bit of her underwear rode up. She had a beautiful tattoo down her thigh of an orange flower.

"What's that?" I asked, hoping it was okay I was observing her body.

She touched the tattoo with the back of her hand.

"It's a tiger lily," she said. "I love the idea of a tiger mixed with a flower. So strong and delicate."

I stood there behind her in my boxer shorts, looking at the back of her leg, at the curve of her back. She hesitated a second and pulled down her underwear. They had a spot of blood on them.

"Sorry," she said.

She stepped out, naked as anyone ever, and dove headfirst into the river.

I took my boxer shorts off, held myself, and jumped in feet first.

The water was so cold and sudden, and I went down farther than I thought I was going to. I thought about what would happen if I kept going down to the muddy bottom. What if I hit my ankle on a rusty piece of metal, on the head of a fish, on some forgotten treasure or horror?

I pushed up to the surface, my breath compressed by the cold, and I got to the top and breathed in. I brushed the hair off my face and realized I wasn't going to be able to tread water for more than a couple of seconds.

I grabbed the dock and hung on as I looked over at Hitomi. She was swimming across the river, her head bobbing in the starlight. I was shivering and cold. I realized we didn't have towels. I looked at our crumpled clothes on the dock, next to each other in their dishevelment.

I climbed onto the dock and sat there naked and curled up. The beads of water prepared themselves for a very slow evaporation. Hitomi swam back over to me and climbed up onto the dock.

She stood naked and proud and looked out over the river like she owned it, like she owned all of Texas. I looked at the tiger lily on her leg as water dripped down it. I counted the spots on that flower, fierce and orange in the soft starlight.

"What's your tattoo say?" she asked.

"'Philharmonic,'" I said. "It means *devoted to music.*"

Hitomi cleared her throat. A soft *hmm-mmm* , with that pause in the middle. You could take all the stars out of the sky and put them in that tiny space.

76.
In the Middle of the Night

I AWOKE TO JAMES CRYING. I had been in the middle of a dream of Hitomi and me as ten-year-olds in a community swimming pool, her smiling at me and singing, "When the water rushes past us in the springtime," and then pulling me under, where she continued the line, "Glub glub glub glub glub glub glub glub gluuuuuub."

I sat up in a panic. I was in a dark room. My first thought was that James had discovered me and Hitomi wrapped in a naked embrace. The sheets were twisted around my legs like seaweed. Was I naked? I wasn't naked.

I tried to piece together where we were, to orient myself in space. Was it the desert? The room I was in had big windows. I patted the floor next to me. Hitomi wasn't there.

James was across the room, crying. I looked over in the dark and tried to regain my focus. Okay. We were in a big room with big windows. We were in Austin. Hitomi and I hadn't slept together. Hitomi was sitting next to James on a leather couch.

"She didn't fucking come," James said.

I had never heard his voice so broken before. He was definitely drunk, but he had lost all confidence and his voice sputtered out with snot and blubber.

"It's okay," she said. "It was a shitty set anyway."

"It was shitty because she didn't come."

"I don't know about that."

We were in a sunken living room. There was a big painting over the couch, but in the darkness I couldn't tell what it was. The frame seemed nice.

"This whole fucking tour was to take us here to play at her feet," James said. "And she couldn't get off her lazy ass and come down to the club. I just. God, I hate booking these tours."

"It's okay," she said, stroking his back.

"I've lost so much money on this."

"Me too," she said.

"All the shows I thought were sure things didn't work out. And all the shows I thought were long shots didn't work out. It's just so hard to make it all work."

James wept in the still night air of Austin. Now I was wide awake. Now I remembered where we were. We were in James's friend Nessa's house. Nessa had left a key for us in a flowerpot under a basketball. The next morning, Nessa, a divorced woman with a six-year-old son, would tell us about a parent-teacher conference she went to recently where the teacher, Mr. Green, was hitting on her, saying something about how he could see where her son got his good looks, and Nessa's response to him was, "Well, I disagree that my ex-husband is homely," which was blunt and presumptuous and made us all laugh over migas and coffee in her ranch home with the sunken living room and the big painting.

But in the long, endless night, with me so thoroughly awake, James was weeping a rhythmic, plaintive sob. I felt lucky to be in the presence of it because it was so ugly and true.

I looked at my phone, and of course it was 3 a.m.

77.
Orange

THERE IS A HARDNESS TO TEXAS you lose perspective on as you drive through the state, because Texas is so enormous you forget there is anything else outside it. Especially when you drive through during the morning, especially when some of your party is hungover, especially when most of them are hungover and you are the only one in any condition to drive.

But right around the border of Louisiana—past the town of Orange, Texas—the environment softens. The plants all around you relax, relieved of their militancy. Everything turns to willows and oaks draped with shawls of Spanish moss. You feel all the brutality of Texas slip away.

"That's better, isn't it?" James said as he looked around, coming out of a dream. "Thank God we made it out of Texas."

The trees around us seemed to celebrate along with us, stringing their garlands in a canopy of fertility.

"But at the same time," James said, adjusting his pillow. "I kind of miss it."

78.
New Orleans

HALLOWEEN IN NEW ORLEANS.

The moon was a leftover decoration from a high school dance. We had only an hour to pull together some costumes, as we had forgotten what time of year it was. Fortunately, New Orleans is a city ready to assist your last-second costume needs.

James decided to be Gordo, of course. He wore a blazer on top of a sweater. He put a throw pillow underneath to give himself a paunch. He put on cheap glasses with thin gold frames, and he slicked his hair back.

Daveed had two incomplete costumes he combined into one—the ears and tail of a lion and the suit of a clown. He painted red circles on his cheeks to contrast the whiskers.

Hitomi dressed as Frida Kahlo from that family photo where Frida dressed as a man. The intense brow; a three-piece suit; a big, red, silky tie; a scarf billowing out of the pocket; and a paintbrush tied around her wrist for those who couldn't piece it together.

I was a skeleton pirate. I found a one-size-fits-all skeleton costume and a cheap pirate hat. The costume was designed like a wetsuit, where you step through a hole in the back. I put my legs in the bottom half and tried to pull the top half up over my chest, but it was too tight, so I had to cut it in half, which left me looking like some creature who had grown inside of someone and slowly eaten his way out.

We were joined by Hitomi's friend from high school, who was dressed as D'Artagnan from *The Three Musketeers*. Introduced by that name, never given another name; wearing a big, floppy hat and a beautiful black cape with red lining underneath, a black mask, and a plastic sword at their side.

The sun was setting at Audubon Park. The leaves of every plant were so big, and their roots pushed up through the concrete of the sidewalk like it was nothing at all.

D'Artagnan had some little squares of paper and shared one with Hitomi. Daveed and I took one and split it. James stuck with alcohol.

"How long does it take to start working?" I asked.

"It's always different," D'Artagnan said, adjusting the mask.

Bugs ambled past. In most places the bugs scurry to get out of the way, but in New Orleans they are so large they wait for you to scurry. Big, heavy beetles you could put a saddle on and ride around, except the bugs wouldn't allow it.

After a few minutes the colors around me were somehow both muted and vibrant.

"Do you guys feel it?" I asked, kicking at the ground.

"Not yet," D'Artagnan said. "It takes time."

"Where I come from in Florida, we have mangrove trees," Hitomi said. The vowels in mangrove seemed to stretch out longer than usual. "Mangrove trees can survive in saltwater, which most trees can't," she said. "They expel the salt out of their bark. You ever see those burls? That's where she heals herself."

I saw the word SHE in big letters as Hitomi said it, like a ticker tape.

We got back to the van, and I offered to drive down St. Charles to our gig, which seemed impossible, but I didn't want to let on I felt that way.

Besides—if you do something impossible, you have power over it.

Besides—drive the speed limit, stay between the lines.

Besides—everything is impossible when you think about it.

I sat in the driver's seat and the seat grabbed on to me. The steering wheel bent and twisted in my hands. The road curled around us to keep me on it.

"Thank you, road."

I was driving for the first time ever. I was the first person to build an engine and attach it to a wagon and rumble down a dirt road, his family watching while they clutched linens and wildflowers in their hands, watching the world move into the modern age.

The song on the radio was the only song that had ever existed.

That's the difference between us

The Flaming Lips, who, thank God, knew. Their song seemed to wink at me and hold me as surely as the driver's seat held me. It was on the college radio station, and it had started playing before we were born, and it would go on until the planets crashed into the sun. Every drumbeat could host an entire species.

Turn on the turn signal. Hand over hand on the steering wheel to turn left. Every bump on the steering wheel was alive. Stay between the white lines, even as they slithered.

Frida and D'Artagnan shared the back seat. Gordo and the Lion-Clown sat in the middle seats and turned them around so they could all drink and play cards. I, the humble skeleton-pirate, piloted us through the city.

"Are we lost?" Frida asked me.

"I'm following this road," I said.

"Yeah, but all the roads curve with the river here, so you can't just go straight," she said.

"I know, but," I said. "Do I need to turn off?"

"No," D'Artagnan interrupted, "just keep going until I tell you to turn."

What flips the switch to lead someone to like someone else? And can a person flip it on or off themselves? If a little piece of paper with chemicals on it can change your whole perception of the world, is it really that much to think there's a way to do it?

"So—what is up?" Frida asked D'Artagnan.

"I'm not getting along with Austin right now and it's really upsetting."

"We had a great time in Austin," I said, looking in the rearview mirror as I adjusted it.

"We're talking about a person, Ian," Frida said.

"Oh."

"We just," D'Artagnan continued. "We have these great nights where I'm like, 'You are the miracle wonderbeast of my dreams,' and then some days they're just sitting there on the couch and I'm pushing a vacuum cleaner into their feet and I just wish they were dead."

"I know that feeling," Frida said.

The whole van shuddered. Did we have a vacuum cleaner? I looked in the rearview, half expecting to see one tucked in a side closet next to a picture of Uncle Randall.

"Okay, what are we playing?" Daveed asked.

"Hearts," D'Artagnan said.

"Cool. Is it like Clubs?"

"It's nothing like Clubs," Frida said.

"It's pretty much like Clubs," D'Artagnan said. "Every card game is basically unshuffling the deck really slowly."

Cars on the street were weaving into each other like cards in a deck, shuffling and reshuffling and unshuffling themselves. Every movement felt so urgent and desperate before, and now it all made sense.

"So what are you going to do?" Frida asked.

"We're taking the week off," D'Artagnan said. "Which unfortunately coincides with Halloween, which unfortunately means I'm going to make out with like six people. Turn here!"

"Fuck," I said, missing the turn. "Sorry. I needed more notice."

"Okay, just stay on this then," D'Artagnan said. "So have you guys had a good tour or what?"

"Yeah, it's been alright," Frida said.

Alright. Had it been alright? I couldn't gauge what it had been, or what our goals were, or what we were even looking for.

"I was on tour in the spring and we had some tight shows in Texas," D'Artagnan said.

"I forget what happened to us in Texas," Frida said. "And it was just, like, yesterday."

"Austin?" I said, thinking I was going to get it right this time.

"What?" Frida said.

"Austin. The city. We played in Austin last night."

"Right. I know. That's not really Texas."

"Yeah," D'Artagnan said. "I'm talking Amarillo. Fucking Dallas. We had some crazy shows where everybody was just going off."

"We don't ever have people dancing." Frida said.

"What kind of places are you playing?"

"What kind of places are we playing, James? I mean. Gordo."

"We are playing in the worst of the worst," Gordo said. "The blight of the inner city. Places that should be torn down."

"Why are you playing those places, then?" D'Artagnan asked.

"He's just kidding," Frida said. "He's that guy. Gordo."

"I don't know who that is," D'Artagnan said.

"Buh," Gordo said. "You need to tune in, my friend."

"Is this guy for real?" D'Artagnan asked.

"He is definitely *not* for real," Frida said. "Say you're just kidding."

"I am *not* kidding," Gordo said. "There is nothing funny about it."

An uncomfortable pause.

"He's doing a bit," Frida said. "He just wants to antagonize someone. Don't fall for it."

"Anyway, you have any good shows?" D'Artagnan asked.

"San Francisco was alright," Frida said.

"Did you play Oakland?"

"No. We skipped Oakland. Why did we skip Oakland?"

"San Francisco is just a bunch of investment bankers, man," D'Artagnan said. "What are you guys doing? Did you play Chicago?"

"We played in a church."

"You played in a—what! Why the fuck are you fucking with a church?"

"They had a pipe organ. Ian bled all over it."

I looked in the rearview mirror again, but I didn't know what to add. Should I have held up my hand? Was it still bleeding?

"I don't know what the fuck you guys are up to," D'Artagnan said. "Turn here!"

"Fuck!" I said, as I looked helplessly at the street fading away.

"Alright, just keep going," D'Artagnan said. "Anyway, I've just been losing my mind thinking about Austin and—okay, now, turn right at the next block, okay, man?"

"Yes, okay."

"I just want to—yes, here."

"Got it," I said.

"I just want to not think about Austin tonight."

That's the difference between us

I saw a flash of red-and-blue lights in the rearview mirror. I figured it was an ambulance racing across town, so I started to pull over. The lights stayed behind us and got closer. I pulled to a stop and they bled into the van, casting us all as blue-and-red versions of ourselves.

"Um," I said. "I think we've been pulled over."

"Shit!" someone said.

"It's okay," I said. "I'll just. It's okay."

"Here, let me get the registration," James said. He dove through the center to reach into the glove box and rifle through the papers.

I tried to calm myself in preparation for the cop. I put my hands on the wheel in an unthreatening way.

The cop came to the window. His skin was the color of a sequoia, like that nice man back at the impound lot in New York.

"License and registration, please," he said.

"Just a seconnnnd," James said as the papers spilled out on the floor.

"Just a second," I said. "How are you, by the way?"

"Just fine," the cop said.

"James?" I turned and said.

"Okay, here we go!" James said. He handed me the papers.

Then from the back:

"We're not doing anything wrong here!" D'Artagnan said.

I handed the papers to the cop.

"We're, uh," I said. "We're on our way to a gig."

"Okay," the cop said.

He took the papers and walked away.

Everyone burst out laughing.

"Okay, guys," I said, turning around. "Come on, can we just hold it together?"

I looked back at everyone and felt helpless. I wasn't sure I could hold it together myself. I looked over at James sitting in the front seat, dressed as Gordo. The pillow in his shirt was bunched up in such an awkward, unnatural way. I started laughing at the earnest expression on his face, and then he started laughing, too.

"Okay, he's coming back," I said. "Please."

I tried to pull the smile off of my face, to smooth it down.

"From New York, huh?" the cop said.

"Yes," I said as I closed my eyes.

"Look," he said. "The reason I pulled you over is you crossed two lanes without signaling. I'm gonna leave you with a warning. Be sure you signal next time."

"Okay," I said. "It's just—"

"THANK YOU!" everyone shouted at once.

And then, quietly, I said, "Thank you."

I wanted everyone to die. I wanted to die.

"I'm sorry," I said to the cop. He walked away.

That's the difference between us

God, was that song still going?

even if
we fuck this all up
and the war birds circle around a charred landscape
there will still be one of us comforting the other
that's the end of this story:
love

The audience danced for the first time all tour, as though personally ordered to by D'Artagnan. Mario danced with Jasmine while she sipped on hibiscus tea and rum. A politician with fake money falling out of his pockets and a bright red poppy on his lapel spun Marge Simpson around as she laughed and grasped her pearl necklace.

The effects of the medication are the same as the symptoms of the disease. That's what Dennis said to me once. God, what sense did that make?

The medicine only gets us back to where we started.

Our set merged seamlessly into a dance party. I searched for Hitomi. Why were we always on dance floors? Was that the only way to talk about anything? My entire time with her was spent pushing through people on a dance floor to find her, like some anxiety dream.

I thought maybe there was still something I could say to her that would mean something. Los Angeles plus Austin (the city) equaled—what, exactly?

Instead she found me. She pointed at James and yelled at me.

"Do you know this guy is having a book signing the day we leave Florida?" she said.

"What?" I asked.

"Yes," he said in his Gordo voice as he danced. "And it will show everyone, finally, how they ought to live their lives."

The people around us understood who he was and started laughing.

"Oh my God," Hitomi-as-Frida-as-a-man said as she stopped dancing in what was supposed to be mock anger but looked very real. "You politicized the fucking environment. Do you know how fucked up it is to turn the natural world into a political issue?"

"Look," he said as he kept dancing. "I played by the rules. I did what I had to do to get ahead. I shouldn't be punished just because of my superior intellect."

"You don't know shit, though," Frida said. "You just ate a bunch of garbage and opiates and fucked some whores. And now you're just a sad old man."

Wow. Somehow that didn't bring the dance party to a complete halt. It barely even registered to the room.

The music played on. To olly olly oxen free. To the cows coming home, or in this case, a person in a cow outfit, rubbing their udders in a horrifying manner. In New Orleans, you could always slip out of facing something, duck down, loop around the back, and then walk right into the face of Death himself.

At one point at the end of the night we all sat around a table in the corner. Daveed's clown makeup was smeared all over his face. Frida sat down on Gordo's lap.

"I want to tell you something," James said to Hitomi.

She gave him a sarcastic smile.

"No really," he said as he took off those thin glasses. "I'm serious. I want to say—"

The music still vibrated around us. It took great force to say anything at an acceptable volume.

"I just want to say I'm sorry," he said. "I know how scared you were. Back over there."

He gestured toward San Francisco. I pictured a dove flying out of his hand to touch the Golden Gate.

"I'm sorry for everything," he said. "I don't know what happened. I only wanted to adore you. I'm sorry I fell out of that adoration."

Hitomi looked at him and smiled. The music ended, and there was a respite where he could lower his volume.

"I just. I'm sorry," he said, his voice scratchy from all the shouting.

She dropped her head down to soak in his words.

"I love your voice," he said. "I can hear the melodies, your melodies, in everything you say throughout the day. Every time you sing, there is a flock of seagulls opening up their wings and getting ready to fly. Not flying yet, just getting ready to. About to."

Motherfucker stole my words. I wanted to tackle him into a swamp and never let him up again.

"Why is it so difficult?" Hitomi asked.

"I don't know."

"It's felt like we've had nothing to say to each other but arguments."

"I know," he said. "I'm sorry."

She held her head down and he kissed her lightly on her ear.

I went to the bathroom and took my skeleton gloves off to wash my hands. That soapy water felt so strange, like I was massaging a snail. In the formerly serene vessel of my body I felt everything rising to a boil. I felt it burning in the black hole where my stomach should have been if I weren't just a skeleton.

I tried to pull a paper towel from the dispenser over the sink, but it was at the end of the roll and I was given only one tiny corner of paper. I threw that piece in the trash and wiped my hands on my rib cage. I thought of how in cartoons a rib cage always sounds like a marimba, but my chest didn't feel musical or bright.

I looked at the stupid paper towel dispenser, stationed in a bathroom in a bar in New Orleans for its whole life with orders to dispense towels to people with wet hands. How sad that it couldn't even do that.

"You fucking worthless fuck-up," I said.

I slapped it once and it barely budged. I glared at it. No one else was in the bathroom. In the bar, the music still throbbed for those who were in the mood for throbbing.

I took a big breath and slapped it again. I saw a flash of red on my hand from where it cut me open, and the red looked so beautiful highlighted against the black and white of my body. I wiped some of the blood on my ribs and I kept slapping the towel dispenser. With each hit it rattled and then regained its composure to accept another slap.

"Do your job. Do your one job."

In the mirror I saw Batman and Robin walk in behind me, chuckling to each other about having defeated a bourgeois criminal by deciphering riddles. When they saw me and what I was doing to that poor metal box, they looked horrified, like they had never seen a real beating before, like they had never watched a bloody skeleton beat the shit out of a useless towel dispenser. Whatever they had come into the bathroom for, they were now too scared to do it, and they stood there with eyes wide behind their cheap plastic masks.

I turned around and held up my bloody hand.

“Get out of here!” I shouted. “Hsssssss!”

I actually hissed, which I’m not sure I had ever done before. It felt necessary. I was now the bad guy, but it felt so good.

They ran out and I went back to wailing on that stupid machine.

79.
A Massage

SOMEHOW I ENDED UP IN THE BACK OF THE VAN with a woman. She emerged from the ether. Not someone James had tried to set me up with. I brought her back to the van like it was my luxury apartment. The chemicals I had taken hours before in the park were wearing off. The world's colors were going back to their normal stations.

Her name was Lara, which I kept repeating to myself so I wouldn't forget it. So many names passed through my fingers; in the late-night exhaustion I promised myself I would remember hers.

"Can I give you a massage?" she asked. "Just in a friendly way."

"You don't have to—" I said.

"I'd like to," she said.

"Now?" I asked.

"Sure," she said.

"Well, now that you mention it," I said, as I flopped down on the back bench of the van, "there's something going on in my lower back that could use some attention."

"Good thing I can see each and every one of your bones clearly," she said, as she started to prod in my back. "What happened to your hand?"

"An encounter in the bathroom," I said.

She stopped.

"A towel dispenser," I said.

"Okay," she said, and resumed. "I'll just assume the towel dispenser started it."

"You know, I think it did."

"I hope it's not weird to do this. I'm not someone who, like, goes home with bands every night. I just thought you looked really interesting and wanted to get to know you better."

"I. Thank you," I said.

"What music would you like to listen to?" she asked as she held her phone.

"Colleen," I said.

"Is that someone's name?" she asked.

"Yes. Just Colleen. She's French."

She put the music on and soft arpeggios pelted at the side of the window. I didn't expect her hands to be so firm. Any time anyone has ever asked me, "Is this too hard?" I would always say, "No, you can go harder." But she pressed into the clay of my body, and I felt every ache of every mile driven on that tour. All 6,103 of them, as catalogued by James.

But I didn't tell her to stop.

I thought about what it meant to die. Maybe it's just the great releasing of all the emotions you've held bound up in your muscles and fat. All those creatures who felt sunshine on their bodies, who ran through fields with the joy of a pounding heart, they all ended up as oil in our machines.

Millions of creatures die every day and we don't mope around ruing their deaths. Killing is what nature does to keep the world meaningful. Death is a curator. He shapes the living world. You might question his taste, or think he removes all the best people, but who knows what siren call he hears.

And, in the course of time, he takes everyone. So, in fact, he is just a curator who eventually drops all his standards.

I wanted to talk to Robert more than I ever had. I had thought before about all the ways I would yell at him, punch him in the arm, tell him he was being a son of a bitch. But really I just wanted to say I'm sorry. And thank you. Those two things, back and forth, over and over again. I felt a storm of tears grow inside me. I wanted to say the same phrases to everyone, like they were a magic spell I just learned that could unlock every frustration.

I'm sorry

Thank you

I wanted to run through the streets of the Bywater like I was selling vegetables. But instead of radishes, I would have forgiveness. Instead of corn, I would have gratitude. I would've done that at that moment of inspiration, I would have run through the streets and shouted like an escaped five-year-old, but of course I was in the van with a kind woman on top of me. Instead the storm cloud of tears overtook me.

The music ended and we were there in silence as she kept rubbing my back.

"Anything else you want to listen to?" Lara asked.

"Joni Mitchell?" I said.

"Okay. Any particular song?"

"Oh, you know. 'Last Time I Saw Richard' maybe."

"Okay."

She typed it into her phone and set it down and went back to massaging my back. The music sounded strange. I thought for a second she had misheard me, like she thought I said Johnny Mitchell. It sounded like a more modern recording with strings. A woman's deep and husky voice came on.

I realized that, as much as I loved Joni Mitchell, I hadn't advanced past the album *Blue*. This song was on that album, but this was obviously a more recent live version. I had a vague understanding that her voice had dropped as she aged, because how could someone's voice stay so high for so long? But this voice was deep and rough and about seventeen octaves lower than what I was used to.

This was wrong. I did not want to listen to this.

I sat up suddenly.

"What's wrong?" she asked.

"I can't—" I said.

"What?"

"I don't know."

"I'm sorry," I said. "I just. She's so old. I don't—"

"We can change the music," she said.

"No, it's okay. This has been good. I really appreciate it. I just. Fuck," I said.

What was it? Was I going to walk out on someone during Joni again? Why was it never right?

"I'm sorry," I said. "Thank you. I'm sorry."

But there was nowhere to go. I would have to kick this nice woman out of the van.

I took a deep breath.

"Maybe we could just have silence," I said. "And just lie down here in the dark."

"Of course. That sounds lovely, actually," she said as she took off her coat.

"It's just been a long day," I said.

"I know," she said, and curled next to me on the bench.

"And. Thank you."

"You're welcome."

"I'm sorry. Thank you. I'm sorry."

80.
New Orleans Morning

IN THE BRUTAL LIGHT OF DAY after the nighttime parties in New Orleans, no one knows anyone. No one remembers pledging devotion, saying they were best friends, saying that night would never end. Sunglasses and foundation can hide some of the splotches, but they can't make us go back in time, make us take back the things we said. We are left in our hollowed-out husks of bodies, and we find it's true we keep moving forward. There are no cycles. There is us in our bodies walking down the sidewalks of Decatur, garbage everywhere until someone comes to clean it up. We have ten nails driven through our skulls.

"Don't. Talk. To me," James said as he crawled into the back of the van. "Ever. Again."

So, like any great hangover, you have to just get through it and then pretend like nothing was ever promised. Wash off what can be washed off. Put nutrients into your body, even though your body will say, *Why now all of a sudden?*

And then slip out of the city. No texts, no rendezvous. Just get out and don't come back. There is nothing there for you.

81.
Mobile

WHALE SPOTTED.

The chase was on, and I suppose I could feel the purpose now of all that waiting, because the actual hunt was always going to be so short.

I drove the van most of the day again, as it seemed to be my job now to haul hungover bodies along the Gulf of Mexico. We traced the arc of that shoreline when the freeway allowed us to, and the hunters lost their minds at finally seeing the creature they had dreamed about, prepared for, and mythologized. Maybe they had lost their minds long before. Maybe they had lost their minds the first time they stepped on the boat.

James was in the front seat, asleep, with his disheveled Gordo costume on. He had turned on the radio to listen to the real Gordo and left it chattering as he fell asleep. We lost the station for a glorious minute, and then that voice stumbled in again from another station. It was like James was tuning in to the home office, like he was looking to connect with the original iteration for further refinements on how to be that thing.

"All of this stuff about global warming," said the voice on the radio. "They're just trying to—to wrap their hands around the economy, and their goal is to have us all living out of grass huts."

I thought of the sad one-finned fish at the Monterey Fish Jail, how he chased no one and no one chased him. How we all want safety and protection, want to provide it for others, and understandably so. *There there, you're safe now here in these walls; no one is pursuing you.*

"Man is the true owner of the earth, the true steward, the highest expression of God himself. And do you know how I know that?"

But. What was the game we all loved when we were three?

Chase me.

All of us laughed at the thrill of being wanted.

Chase me.

"Because never once has a whale built a hospital. Not once. We have idiots over at Sea World giving Shamu a chalkboard to see if it can add up two plus two. Geniuses. But when has a whale ever contributed anything to society? Seriously. When?"

82.
Tallahassee

THE ACTUAL KILLING OF THE BEAST IS DANGEROUS. And it turns out it doesn't matter at all how much you know about every inch of its body, the muscles of the fluke, the curious cavity in its head. It still has a tail like a steam shovel. It can still pull you under the water and dismantle you. But somewhere past Tallahassee, as the radio finally submitted to a storm of static and I turned it off, as rain Pollacked our windshield, there he was. The whale. Instead of an excited crew, I had a van of sleeping bandmates.

In my earbuds, though, the crew was shouting. They found the whale and they found themselves. Five hundred and fifty pages of whale particulars, twenty-four hours of audiobook narration, and then it was over. A struggle of white water and splintered oars. Who even won, after all that? Why does there have to be a winner? There are no winners.

After the last line of the book, I took my earbuds out.

"I'm done," I said to James.

"Done?"

"The book."

"How was it? Did we get the whale?"

"I'm not sure. We had a lot of casualties."

"Yeah, maybe next time," he said.

He stared out the window.

"I remember reading it when I was eighteen," he said, stretching his arms. "And I couldn't figure out why it was called *Moby-Dick*. You know. Why wasn't it called *Ahab*? That's what the whole book is about."

A semi truck whooshed by us, parting the seas and causing them to crash down on us.

"The narrator has an interesting way of describing things," James continued, "but he doesn't do interesting things. And the whale is only there at the end. So, really, the whole book is about Ahab. That's what I thought when I was eighteen. And then I read the book again a few years ago, right when we were putting the band together. And. I got it. I understood why it's called *Moby-Dick*. The whale is what he's obsessed with. Everything else falls away when you're obsessed. It's like your object of obsession sits there on a pedestal for everyone to see, and you're just the one holding the spotlight. You know?"

The rain stopped and the sun broke through the castles of pink clouds. I looked in the rearview mirror to see Hitomi asleep.

"It's like," he continued. "There's a reason they didn't call the *Tonight Show,* like . . . *Johnny Carson's Spotlight Operator Show.* You know? Am I making sense?"

And then he fell back asleep, and I was alone again in Florida with nothing to listen to except Gordo.

"This pit of grief and guilt and shame, it's just an invention. It's a cauldron of tears that liberals can always turn to when they want to feel horrible about the world. But the sun is shining, America is still the best country in the history of the world, and we still have the Constitution, at least for another day."

God, what if we didn't have to feel any guilt or shame about anything? Almost tempting, if it weren't for all the carnage around us.

"He was a Native American, you know," James said, still with his eyes closed.

"Gordo?" I asked.

"No," James said. "Not Gordo. Tashtego. The harpoonist from *Moby-Dick*. He was Native American."

"Oh. I didn't catch that."

"That was no small thing back then," he said, "to treat a Native American with such dignity. Even in fiction. That's why I named the band that, you know. Back before Hitomi joined, I had some naive idea that a band could do something for social justice. And then I realized that you can't change anything with art. There will always be some horrible machine that tramples over your little daisy patch. But it's still important to do, to go around the country and sing for those who will still listen. I mean, we think of government as being in charge, as being so important, but there's never been a congressional hearing to discuss ways to stop a species from going extinct, or to come up with a solution to homelessness, or to do anything to help people be more free. It's just. I don't know. What we do is so unimportant to the world, but we still have to give our whole lives to doing that very unimportant thing."

He fell back asleep, and snored almost immediately. Very softly, in the fading sunlight of Florida, I said under my breath, "I agree."

83.
St. Petersburg

We drove through orange groves in the beautiful sun of Florida. I reached my hand out the window to catch some of it. It felt like a different sun than we had felt in New York, or Chicago, or in the Southwest desert. That sun bleached the bones of dead animals. This sun was kind and forgiving.

Except it was still Florida, that place that chooses you more than you choose it. No one particularly tries to go to Florida, any more than a spider tries to circle down the drain. It just happens, and then you're there.

Hitomi stuck her hand out the window and said, "I used to run through groves like this as a kid with my cousins and pick oranges. Sometimes an old man would chase us off by shooting saltpeter at us. Now they just let these oranges fall on the ground and rot."

We checked in to a campsite south of St. Petersburg. It was almost full, but we slipped into the last open spot. We went down to the beach, where we saw an old wooden shack that rented canoes. Hitomi and I got one and carried it over our heads.

"You guys going to just escape, then?" James asked as he lay on the beach with his hand on his forehead.

"You can rent your own canoe, too," she said.

"I'll remember this," he said, holding up a limp fist.

We launched the canoe on a muddy bank of an estuary, and the metal bottom slid over reeds and stones into the water. We stepped in, Hitomi in front.

It did feel like we had escaped, like we were alone on a secret adventure.

"Have you noticed that flip-flops don't flip or flop?" she asked. "If anything, they flap. Seems like they really blew it on that name."

I wanted to ask Hitomi a question. I thought this would be the last time I would get a chance because I was flying out the next morning to go to Robert's wake. I knew exactly what I wanted to ask, though I couldn't figure out how to ask it.

"They should call them flap-flaps," she said.

Maybe it was best to just wait. We paddled through the estuary.

"There is this flower growing around here," Hitomi whispered, like she would surprise it if she talked too loudly. "It's called the *belladonna.*"

Drip. Drip. Drip. What was dripping?

"It looks pretty," she said. "But don't touch it. It's very poisonous."

Her shoulders twisted as she paddled the canoe. She wore a tank top, and I could see her tattoo of a fish circling around her neck. Then, in the water, some small creature jumped and was back in before I could see what it was.

"You'll see," she said. "There'll be one around here somewhere. Every year someone puts some on a birthday cake because the flowers look so pretty, and a whole roomful of kids dies."

The swamp was cool as we passed by mangroves and live oaks.

"It's typical, though," she continued. "All these nonpoisonous plants have these plain names, and this one dangerous one—oh, there it is!" She pointed to a sprawling plant at the elbow of the river bend. It wasn't blooming, but I pictured the lavender bulbs with their lips pursed, pointed down. It was so quiet as our canoe drifted.

"Anyway, *belladonna* means 'beautiful woman,'" she said. "Because, you know, watch out for those beautiful women."

We paddled around the curves of the estuary. Fallen logs jutted out, little birds scurried around. In contrast to the desert, everything was to the bursting point with water and life. Everything was thrashing and pulsing and trying to drag something else down into the bog with it.

"Have a good night last night?" Hitomi asked.

New Orleans felt like a previous lifetime.

"I . . . did," I said, not sure how much to divulge.

"That's good," she said. "Anything bite you?"

"I don't think so."

"How's your hand?"

I looked at the bandage on my hand.

"I think I don't need this anymore," I said as I took it off and saw the wound underneath.

We kept paddling through the swamps, and I thought how the farther we went, the longer the trip back would be. I pictured the curve of the estuary from above, and it was exactly like the F-hole on a cello. Starting in a circular pool, curving around a sharp bend into a long straightaway with a barb in it, then curling back around into another pool that seemed to have us turned around in the opposite direction. All those curves made it hard to know where we were going.

"I just crave silence sometimes," she said. "I know I'm ruining it by talking about it. But it's important to know. Some people can't stand silence. Like James, it seems like. With you, it's okay to be silent."

I let a beat go by, thinking this was almost a trick.

"Thank you," I said.

A paddle in the water.

Drip. Drip. Drip.

"I don't know how other people do it," she continued. I wasn't sure what *it* was now. "Or if anyone does actually do it. If it's even possible. To match up with someone in every way—physically, emotionally, intellectually, musically, logistically. I just. It seems like it would be such a miracle, and everyone talks about it like it's a thing that's supposed to happen by the time you're thirty. But meeting someone who fulfills all those things, I don't know. That sounds like shooting a bullet and hitting another bullet in the air. Like, it's technically possible, but. Not something to get upset about if it doesn't happen. And yet. God. People get so upset about it. Including me."

This was not in response to a question, at least not one that I asked. It seemed to bubble up from a conversation she was having in her head, or one she was having with the swamp itself.

"But," she said. "It's all around us. This, like, encouragement, to try to hit the bullet out of the air. Every song and movie is about it, right? Even the ones I sing. It's like a cult we're all stuck in. A suicide cult."

The hissing of the swamp soothed me, whatever was behind it, like there was a collective desire on the part of the swamp to quiet down. Like there was a show about to start. I wondered if there was a way I could record that sound and have it sound like anything.

I thought maybe I would try. I put down my oar and pulled out my phone and opened the voice memos. I scrolled backwards through all the recordings of our shows. "New Orleans," "San Francisco," "Denver," "Indianapolis." At the end of the list, right after "Philadelphia," was a file called, "Sequoia." I didn't know what it was, so I pressed play.

All the turtles and snakes and bugs stopped their hissing and listened. The sounds of the swamp were replaced with a rumbling on the recording, and then a deep voice spoke.

you are not crazy
you are a wild animal who has been domesticated
you know what happens to animals when they are put in zoos
they pace
they worry
they fall asleep to themselves
those who encourage you to stay put are afraid too
they fall asleep to themselves
they worry
they pace
you know what happens to animals when they are put in zoos
you are a wild animal who has been domesticated
you are not crazy

Hitomi set down her oar, but she didn't look back at me. I saw her back relax.

"The night I met you," she said.

"Yes," I said. "Wait, how did you know?"

"Because I was there."

"Were you?"

"You forgot? I was wearing bunny slippers."

"I know. I remember meeting you. How did you know when this was from?

"At that party," she said. She kept her back to me, but I could feel her smiling. "I wrote that poem in your notebook when you went to the bathroom."

"What? What do you mean?"

"Yeah," she said. "I guess maybe that's a rude thing to do. I forgot I did that. But I just had a whim and I did it. Is that a rude thing to do? Is it like masturbating in someone's bed?"

"No, I—wait, *you* wrote that?" I asked.

"Who else would have written it?" Hitomi asked.

"I thought maybe I did."

"I mean . . . no offense. Don't you think you would have remembered writing it?"

"I—" I said. "That's what encouraged me to finally start writing. I didn't see you grab my notebook."

"It was something I was working on in my head that day and I thought I'd surprise you by writing it in your book. It didn't seem like there was anything else in there. Who did you get to read it for you?"

"He was this guy at the impound lot," I said. "My car got towed that night, and my notebook was in there."

"Oh," she said. "Right. That's funny."

"I begged him to get the journal out of the car and read me the poem in it," I said. "There was something I had written in there too, but I guess he flipped to your poem. Honestly, all this time I thought maybe he had just made it up on the spot."

"Sorry to ruin it for you."

"No. No, it's so much better this way. Damn. I'm glad we figured this out."

Still I wanted to ask her a question. How would it start?

"Do you think there's any way . . ." I started. And there it was. Now I had to keep going with it.

"Do you think there's any. Room . . ." Room? Where was this going?

She stopped paddling and held the oar for a second, even though we were in a hurry.

"I love you," I said. I tried to remember what I wrote in that letter back in Los Angeles, but nothing came to me. Did I even write that letter?

She turned around to look at me.

"I just love you," I said. "The way you clear your throat. The way you hold your arm when you read onstage. I love the way you squish marshmallows. Why do you do that? I love the way your brain works, and how you process the world and hold yourself together. I felt terrible that morning in San Francisco. I wanted to punch that guy who was a creep to you, but I know that wouldn't solve anything. I wanted to just hold you and protect you. I wanted to—"

She had tears in her eyes.

"I wanted to hug you," I said, "and kiss you and tell you everything was going to be alright. I was afraid. I didn't know what else to do. I was afraid so many times and I wish I could be a braver person. I just. From the moment I met you—I just loved you right away."

She closed her eyes very slowly and opened them again and had a tiny smile in one corner of her mouth.

"I think you're wonderful," she said.

"Are you back with James?" I asked.

"I think we're going to give it a try," she said softly. "I think I owe him another chance."

We turned a corner and saw an egret stretching in the sunlight. She was stalking some tiny prey in the grass. She stood still. So still that she looked like a carving of an egret made from an ivory tusk that hung in a museum. She lowered herself, shimmied, and stabbed at some poor creature in the grass.

I thought of Hitomi reading that six-word poem back in Salt Lake City.

"There you are," I said. "There you are."

84.
How Long?

WE PLAYED IN A BAR IN A STRIP MALL IN THE SUBURBS. I laughed when we drove up to it, as the plastic sign above could have easily said NAIL SALON or CHINESE FOOD but instead said the name of the bar.

"Hey, Tome," James said as he looked at his phone. "I just got an email from Mary Cornish. She says, 'So sorry to miss your show. I came down with a horrible flu and didn't leave bed for three days. I'd be happy to come see you next time you're in Austin. Kindly, Mary.' The next time we're in Austin! The next time!"

That is where the tour ended for me: in a strip mall in Florida, playing a digital keyboard. Maybe all the things that we try to wriggle out of, thinking we deserve better, maybe we slip out of those and end up falling into a pot of boiling water.

At sound check I held my face close to the digital keyboard as I pressed the keys, trying to find some mechanical connection to it.

Daveed stared at me. "What are you doing?"

"Did you ever see *Stand By Me*?" I asked.

"Yeah."

"I'm listening for a train."

"What do you hear?"

"Nothing yet."

I looked at the keys and wondered what I was even saying.

"Tell me something you learned today," I said.

"Do you know how many days it takes Mercury to orbit the sun?"

"No. I don't. How many?"

"Eighty-eight. And . . . isn't that how many keys are on a piano?"

"Yes, actually. It is."

"Yeah," he said. "I thought so. I thought you'd like that. It reminded me that, you know, time isn't linear. Everything is just a cycle. It's not like Mercury cares about how long something takes. Anyway, I've been trying to tell my girl this. That time isn't linear. That I'm already home, that I've always been home, that I'll always be home."

"How is that going?" I asked.

"It's not working so far."

That evening train. That evening train. Any question about how to move forward with music had to face the question of that evening train and wonder at how long it had been gone.

I looked at James and thought of him just a few days before reading me that children's book in El Paso.

The largest heart belongs to the blue whale, about the size and weight of a piano.

And I tried to think of what pianos and hearts have in common.

Maybe I could make a list:

> Both are thought of as melodic.
> Both are masters of harmony.
> But both are actually percussive.
> Both have hidden strings.

And maybe both have strings that were never meant to be played. Both have a capacity that borders on redundant. They vibrate when another nearby string vibrates.

That was it.

The answer to Robert's riddle. Why a piano has eighty-eight keys. The low keys are just there for support. To vibrate in sympathy.

"Hey," I said to James. "I just figured out why a piano has the low keys."

"Yeah," James said. "Sympathetic resonance. Everyone knows that."

What a dick. He stepped away, and I sat with those keys. All of those lovely, sympathetic keys. Well, the ones in front of me were just plastic, but it was good to finally know what they were emulating.

"Ladies and gentleman of Florida," Hitomi said as she got up to the microphone. "This is normally the part where I read a poem over this music that my band plays. But I want to do something different tonight, and it's a bit of a surprise."

She turned and looked at me.

"This is our keyboardist, Ian," she said.

People politely applauded.

"He's a writer too."

I looked at her and froze. Is this how the stories of Medusa started? Someone scared stiff of a beautiful woman?

"I want to invite him tonight, in my home state of Florida—"

Oh God.

"If he's willing."

Oh God, oh God.

"To read something of his own. Right now. Would you do that for us, Ian? My mom drove an hour and a half to be here, and I'd like her to hear you read."

What. Why.

I stopped playing. I grabbed my journal. I stood up. The light shone in my face. I felt dizzy from all the sun I had soaked in that day. I read the first page I turned to. James and Daveed played something sweet and spare. Hitomi stood to the side and watched me.

I'm writing it down so the world can know:
I once loved someone beyond all sense
beyond all reason
I loved their broken parts
I loved their darkness
I'm writing it down
because it makes me feel like
I have control over something
just to write the words
I was here
in the world
and I loved someone

And, there in the front row—in the state of Florida, of all places—someone grabbed the forearm of the person next to them. I looked over at Hitomi to see a smile of recognition. I went back to my simple keyboard, black-and-white keys arrayed before me, and they looked so straight and rigid. For a second I was confused what they even meant at all.

85.
A Ceremony

"Is this about connection or closure?" I asked.

"You tell me," Daveed said.

We were walking down a dark, winding path at one-thirty in the morning. This was still Florida, so I felt like any tree might be the grabbing kind of tree. Daveed had a headlamp on that would shine in my eyes every time he turned back to look at me.

"Closure," I said.

"Okay."

"No, wait," I said. "I meant to say connection. Connection."

"Okay, good. That's what I need too."

We were looking for a stream behind the property of the house.

"Have you ever been present when someone died?" he asked as he walked on.

"No."

"It's really something. I've been there for two. My grandma and a chicken."

I thought how right then would be a hilarious time for an alligator to appear. We hadn't even told Hitomi and James where we were going. If an alligator popped out and ate us both, we'd just be gone and they'd have to figure it out through contextual clues, and they'd try to track down our parents and tell them, "Alligators, we think."

"It wasn't at the same time," Daveed continued. "The chicken and my grandmother didn't die at the same time. We had chickens in our yard when I was a kid, and one time—I was maybe nine—this one got sick, and I tried to nurse her back to health. I brought her inside and fed her and stroked her feathers. And just when it seemed like she was getting better, she croaked. And she really made a croaking sound right when she died. That's what I'll always remember. It was just the most unearthly sound, like it was being broadcast through her. Just this 'GWWAACKKK!' And then she was dead."

We got to a clearing next to a stream. I was holding a bottle of olive oil and a blue-and-white checkered dish towel from the house. Blue for Joni. White for the Beatles. Me and Robert.

"And then a few years later, I was the only one in the room with my grandma as she passed."

Daveed knelt and set down a dish and a couple of oranges.

"And the funny thing is—well, it's not funny. But. You know what I mean. When my grandma died, she made the same sound as the chicken. Maybe it was lower in pitch, but not much. It was just this final exhalation where she let go."

He nodded at me to pour the olive oil over the oranges in the dish, which we placed on the dish towel.

"Those are the only two deaths I've seen, and I've always wondered if everyone lets out that same sound when they die, or if some people never get the chance."

I thought about that sound, the sound of death. Maybe I had heard it somewhere but I didn't think it was real. When people hear gunshots in real life, they never think they're gunshots, because they're used to the big sound they make in movies.

We stood up and Daveed spoke, almost as though he had written it out before.

Dear Great Spirits,
the unknowable ungoogleable spirits
you push the tulips out of the ground
you made Froot loops and Fruity Pebbles
you made penises and vaginas
(thank you for that)
Spirits, please hold back the alligators while we pray
we don't know whose land this is
or who died here a thousand times
we're sorry we don't know
but we call on the people of this land tonight
we're in a tough spot
we've forgotten how to touch the ground
we have nothing to offer you
you'd probably love crystals from the canyon
we have Flaming Hot Cheetos
you probably want frankincense
we have baby wipes
you want holy water
we have Dasani
take these oranges
I know y'all got plenty of oranges down here,
but I promise you these are extra sweet
we need your help
we don't know how to find the people we love the most
and we keep running into the same assholes over and over again
you nip at our heels like the coyote
and we're trying to slow down
we ask for your help tonight
we ask you to protect Robert
to give him a blanket and a glass of water
he's a good man

my friend Ian says he's the smartest motherfucker he's ever met,
and Ian is the smartest motherfucker I've ever met,
so that must be one smart motherfucker
I'm sure Robert doesn't need help figuring things out
maybe he just needs to be reminded
that he doesn't have to figure it all out
so please give him a nip at the heels
trip him up and wrestle him in the dirt
we're so grateful for the mystery
that we don't understand any of it
we're here to listen
we won't give up

When he was done we stood there in silence for a minute. The stream sounded like it had gained twice its volume of water. Now it sounded like a band of warriors rushing past us.

And that was it.

"Good idea," Daveed said as we started back. "To do a ceremony."

"Thank you," I said.

"I'm gonna miss you when you're gone."

I thought about it for a second.

"You mean, when I leave the tour?" I asked. "Or when I'm dead?"

Daveed laughed, which made the light on his head shake, which made all the trees around us look like they were laughing too.

86.
St. Petersburg Morning

"COULD I HAVE A MINUTE?" I asked Hitomi. "Like. Just one minute."

"Sure," she said.

They were dropping me off at the airport to fly to Indiana. I nodded over to the side where we could talk.

"Do you think—" I said. "Do you think." I looked down the terminal where someone else was saying goodbye. "Do you think that we'll know each other after this? Back in New York?"

"Of course. Why not?"

"I know, of course," I said, looking down. "I just. You never know. And. I would. I would like that. To know you."

"Yeah. Of course."

"I just. Sometimes you don't know if you'll know someone. Sometimes you just don't know."

Inside someone's car a dog was barking. I thought of the coyotes back in the desert, howling a song in detuned harmony while the domesticated dogs gave their brutish rebuttal.

"I always feel like . . ." she said. "Something gets torn away from me whenever something beautiful happens. Like I'm a bus full of people, and I get emptier and emptier as everyone leaves at their favorite place, until everyone has gotten off the bus, and there I am, just an empty bus, and then I have nowhere else to go."

We stood there looking at each other for two seconds and then laughed.

"So there's that," she said.

Ten feet away, James interrupted.

"Do each of us get an individual goodbye? Or . . ."

"No," I said, "I'll do the rest of you as a pair."

"Okay," he said, looking at Daveed. "I guess we're next."

"Fettuccine Cortado," I said to Daveed.

"Oh!" he said. "I forgot about that!"

"Our race is run . . ."

"Damn. I'm trying to remember your name," he said.

"We'll always have the Grand Prix in Kankakee."

"Don't tell me—" he said.

"And, it's a miracle we both survived that crash in Pendleton."

"Linguine Breve!"

"Always at your side," I said as I bowed.

He hugged me.

"Come back to the diner, yeah?"

"I don't live near there anymore," I said. "But. Yeah. Definitely."

"Kid," James said, looking at me. "You did good. But. We're gonna have to let you go. Budget cuts. We're putting you on a plane to Indiana. Don't take it personally."

"How could I?" I said and hugged him.

I grabbed my bag, and for some reason gave a salute to everyone and then went into the terminal. Only after making it to security did I realize I forgot to hug Hitomi.

87.
Valpariso Again

Melissa picked me up at O'Hare and drove me straight to the wake.

"They have punch there," she said.

"Oh good. Punch."

The wake wasn't what I wanted at all. It wasn't what Robert would have wanted, if he were actually dead. It was what his mother wanted. She wanted a time to be still and sad, to have boxes of tea and coffee and pastries. I guess I wanted that stillness and sadness too, but I wanted it to have certainty, and I didn't want anyone else around, and I certainly didn't want any God damn pastries. I didn't want a finish line to his life, an artificial one like in the marathons where two people are holding up tape.

I wanted to see Robert alive in that gorgeous fading sunlight of Indiana. I guess I wished it was a surprise wake, that his mother knew all along he was okay and she was just saving him to build up the suspense.

Instead it was a waking dream. Heavy sunlight pouring through half-opened windows. Feet shuffling on hardwood floors. Heads tucked to chests. There were no words I could say to his mom, really, or that she could say to me. I sat with relatives deep in couches, plates of food on our laps, frozen in our pain.

"You've got a six cylinder on that Toyota?" someone's dad asked another.

"V-8," he said.

"You have a tow hitch on that?"

"No, no, I drive it around town for errands."

Everyone wore black, except for one girl in a lavender linen dress. Old enough to dress herself, young enough to not care about such things. She was a crane in a field of crows. Brilliant in plumage, ridiculing us.

Robert's mom put his camera on the mantel. Why would he leave his camera? Why would she put it on the mantel, like it was proof of something? I felt like she wanted him dead, that she would rather have him be dead than be between two worlds. A camera case as a cenotaph, the casket that holds no body, only memories of light.

"How was the tour?" someone asked.

"It was fin," I said.

I had my notebook open, and I was drawing figure eights over and over again, with the circle on top first and then the fat one on the bottom.

"Did you say *fine* or *fun*?"

"I don't know. I think I tried to combine them."

"Did you guys have any big shows?"

"No. They were all small. Smaller shows are better."

"What kind of music do you play?"

On the couch a young boy was playing checkers with an old man. I didn't recognize either of them.

In my head I stood up. I stood up in my head. It was time for a eulogy, in my head. No one would ever ask me to do such a thing in reality. But I wanted to. I would never have tried to make it happen, in the still air of that house. But I wanted to. So I imagined I stood up, on top of the coffee table.

"I have a few words," I would say. The checkers players would stop and look up at me. "Um." I would say um. Even in my fantasy, I would stumble.

"Robert was a rainbow."

Is that how it would start?

I suppose it is.

"Robert was a beam of light separated into colors. He was the gentle slope of light tumbling off the clouds. He was the clouds. He was the change in pressure that allowed the clouds to form. He was the laws of physics. He was the universe. He was the moment before the universe began, which was never a moment because the universe created everything. The universe created our appreciation of the universe. *The universe created our appreciation of the universe.*"

I was still sitting on the couch thinking all this when Melissa came up and put a hand on my shoulder. I started to cry. I had wanted Robert to be real again, to be with me in the physical world, and maybe I had built him into something he wasn't. He had chosen to walk away. And there were people who were actually present, people offering a soft hand, or curious questions. And I hadn't been able to be present for them. I cried, like it was a recap of all the tears, cried and uncried, of the past month.

A cauldron of tears.

My phone buzzed.

It was a text from Hitomi. I stood up to look at it. It was so strange to see her name on my phone, instead of looking at the back of her head as she wrote.

We canceled our last show. We're going to the Gordo reading. Walking up to the bookstore now.

Oh no. Why would they do this?

"He was just so full of spirit," I overheard Robert's mom say to someone.

Another text from Hitomi:

This wasn't my idea, btw, but the show tonight was going to suck anyway.

I tried to text back, but Robert's mom interrupted me. She put her hand on my arm.

"I want you to have something," she said.

Oh no. She was going to give me something I didn't want, something I didn't deserve because he wasn't really dead. She was going to give me something I would never sell or throw away, that I would be stuck with for the rest of my life.

My phone was in my pocket, pulsing with texts.

"It was on his kitchen table when we came into his house," she said.

She handed me a porcelain bell. A little one that you could cover up completely in your palm. Something he had bought at the thrift store that day, probably just to make the woman behind the counter happy.

"Thank you," I said.

She hugged me. A tight hug in which I couldn't participate because she did all the hugging. It lasted longer than I wanted.

After she let me go, I turned away and pulled out my phone to see three texts from Hitomi:

He's dressed like Gordo. I mean, James is. I'm not sure who is who.

He's in line to get a book signed. I'm going to photograph it.

I can't believe we're doing this.

And then Robert's mother, still focused on me, said, "I thought you'd want to have it."

"Thank you," I said as I jingled the bell in my hand. It made the tiniest muffled ring.

Again from Hitomi:

He's talking to him!

And:

They look like they're bonding?!

I rang the bell faster to see how loud it could get.

“I don’t know,” his mom said. “I don’t know why I thought you should have that. Maybe it’s strange.”

“It’s okay,” I said over my shoulder.

And from Hitomi:

Phone is dying but going to send a pic.

And then a photo.

In it James was leaning over, with his slicked-back hair, the sweater underneath the blazer. The photo was blurry, and Gordo’s face was in shadow. Gordo was dressed less like himself than James was. I couldn’t tell what the look was on Gordo’s face, what he was thinking. *Is this a long-lost son? Is this a superfan, someone about to shoot me?* A man behind James was smirking, like he saw through the game.

I sent Hitomi three exclamation points and kept waiting for more.

But that was it.

88.
Last

CENTRAL PARK THE NEXT SPRING was full of anticipation, like when someone is so excited to tell you good news and they are just waiting for you to shut up and look at them, just look at their face for one second and realize they have something important to say.

A pregnant pause. Like an egg. Like the character zero, so inessential it's not even a number and it gets put right at the start of everything.

Also. Half of eight is zero.

I played music with Daveed every Wednesday night, just me and him as a duo, alone in a rehearsal space. We got high and built towers of ridiculous rhythms and tore them all down. His arms blurred in a fit of blendered math as he played, his tattoos dancing from one arm to the next. I felt safe with him, like I could never play a wrong note, like there wasn't a wrong note in the world.

Whenever I thought of texting Hitomi, I thought of the Rocky Mountains. How they looked like frozen waves. How you could never be sure if they would unfreeze at the perfect worst moment. I danced alone in the backrooms of clubs, and I felt outside of anything anyone would call beautiful, but in a way it was like being in true wilderness for the first time.

I never used to dance before I met her.

The cherry trees of Prospect Park had something important to say, and they weren't going to wait much longer. Even as crumbled piles of dirty snow lingered on the ground, the trees all around were ready to start the show. They were going to skip the previews and go right to opening night.

Stopping to watch those trees change seemed indulgent, especially in a city with so much to do. So many carts that needed to be lifted up subway stairs. So many trucks backing up into loading zones, so many people already late for their first appointment of the morning, knowing that a chain reaction of lateness would reverberate throughout their day, and probably through the rest of their life.

But I did it anyway. I did it in secret. I sat on a bench with the elders and the displaced, all those people with nowhere to go to, and I watched those blossoms burst open. You would think there would be nothing in real time to see, but I stood up and pressed my ear to the trunk of a tree, and I swear I heard the sugar coursing through it, like I was hearing a Union Pacific trundle down the tracks.

Epilogue

I was recording a song in a studio on an old reel-to-reel machine. Robert was taking photographs. Actually, he was taking one photograph. One long photograph that took him all afternoon to compose. That is sometimes how he did it, not wanting to waste a shot. He would sit there and wait until all the elements were in place. Maybe he did it to save money, if he was using expensive film, but it was almost like he did it to test his own patience. Or mine.

The recording engineer was messing with the machine, a constant process in a studio. Balancing and tuning and calibrating. Something was always threatening to throw the machine off, even a passing satellite that dipped too close to Earth.

I was sitting at the piano, expecting that Robert was going to take my picture at any moment. But maybe he was waiting for me to leave the frame and I was screwing it up. Or maybe I was supposed to smile. Or stop smiling.

From the other room we heard the engineer talking to his assistant about the tape machine, and he said the word "capstan."

"That's funny," Robert said. "Capstan."

"What?" I asked.

"It's a sailing term," he said. "A capstan is a large spindle on a ship's deck. They wrap ropes around it and pull them tight."

"Hmm . . ." I said.

"What is it on a recording machine?" he asked.

"I think it's like a spindle, too. The tape goes around it. Is that right?" I called to the engineer, but he had turned the microphone off and was lost in the guts of the machine.

"On a ship in the old days," Robert said as he stood up, "when men wanted to coordinate their efforts, they would sing a song, some shanty which allowed them to walk in sync." He paced around me. "They would be at sea walking around the capstan, opening the ship's sails."

He stopped behind me. Maybe he was going to take a picture of the back of my head.

"And now *you* sing a song," he said, "a beautiful, heartfelt song about the wide, wide ocean, and the spindle spins, right? And your voice is captured. And it's there forever. We can call it up and listen to it even after you're long gone."

Behind me I heard the click of his camera, and I felt released to move again.

Tour Dates

City	Venue	Date
1. Philadelphia	The Fire	10/3
2. Pittsburgh	Club Café	10/4
3. Columbus	The Treehouse	10/5
4. Cleveland	Grog Shop	10/6
5. Detroit	Warehouse	10/7
6. Indianapolis	Vonnegut Library	10/8
7. Chicago	Yellow Church	10/9
8. St. Louis	Kontrol	10/11
9. Wichita	Fisch Haus	10/13
10. Denver	Larimer Lounge	10/15
11. Salt Lake City	Kilby Court	10/17
12. Seattle	Beery House	10/20
13. Portland	Doug Fir	10/21
14. San Francisco	Hotel Utah	10/23
15. Los Angeles	Hotel Café	10/25
16.Tucson	The Red Room	10/27
17. Austin	The Hole in the Wall	10/29
18. New Orleans	Dragon's Den	10/31
19. St. Petersburg	Absolution	11/2

Tarot	Alchemy
1. The Magician	Calcination
2. The High Priestess	Dissolution
3. The Empress	Separation
4. The Emperor	Conjunction
5. The Hierophant	Fermentation
6. The Lovers	Distillation
7. The Chariot	Coagulation
8. Strength	Calcination
9. The Hermit	Dissolution
10. Wheel of Fortune	Separation
11. Justice	Conjunction
12. The Hanged Man	Fermentation
13. Death	Distillation
14. Temperance	Coagulation
15. The Devil	Calcination
16. The Tower	Dissolution
17. The Star	Separation
18. The Moon	Conjunction
19. The Sun	Fermentation

Novel Notes

I started writing this book at Laura Gibson's apartment in New York City on February 1, 2017, less than two weeks after the inauguration of the 45th president of the United States.

The first piece I moved to a folder on my computer titled "New Book" was the letter in Chapter 65 that begins, "Why is it like this?" It was an email I had sent the previous year to my friend Leslie.

I hoped to write a book that could honor the emotions of that letter and support it with a story. Leslie and I had something inexplicable in a way that I hadn't seen represented in any popular storytelling. What is a love story if the people in it feel like they are zapping each other with a strange electricity, but they don't end up together? If it was real to me, was it a story worth telling?

During a road trip across North Dakota once, Leslie gave me the nickname *Tengu*, after the long-nosed flying creature in Japanese mythology. This was after I had almost drowned in a very cold lake, and perhaps she wasn't sure if I was still fully in the Material World. I think she thought I had crossed over somehow. I searched for a nickname for her for weeks, and then I finally found the word *Hitomi* on a list of Japanese names. I liked it for the longing in the central syllable, and for the English translation: pupil of the eye.

But as I tried to add material to this book in Laura's apartment, all I could think about was the terrifying rise of white supremacy, violence, and authoritarianism in my country. When I wrote, out came memories of being ten years old and riding in a car with my dad listening to Rush Limbaugh on the radio. I thought Rush was a funny entertainer, and because of his influence, I rolled my eyes at feminism and snickered as we bombed other countries. One Christmas, I asked for and received one of his books.

By the time I was twelve or thirteen I awoke to the cruelty of Limbaugh's form of politics, but I never forgot how easy it was for me to slip into joining a bloodthirsty pack based on the charisma of one person. This seemed particularly relevant thirty years later as our country fell into a pool of vitriol as encouraged by a man who was good at riffing in front of an audience.

I tried to write about the emotional component of how we engage with politics, rather than the intellectual quality of it. It doesn't seem like most of us are coming to intellectual conclusions regarding important moral questions.

My first attempts to write this book were personal stories married to certain relevant moments for which I was present: chopping wood at the Standing Rock protests while Leslie worked in the medical tent; reporting for the *Portland Mercury* from the Republican National Convention in Cleveland, where it occurred to me that everything in front of me had no more depth or integrity to it than professional wrestling; watching the second presidential debate—the one where the confessed sexual assaulter stalked around and intimidated the female candidate—on a laptop in Mexico City while staying with the kindest family I had ever met.

This book existed as non-fiction for about a week. I soon switched to writing a novel about a fictional radio host as a way of being more honest about the emotional arcs. However, I couldn't figure out how to engage with politics without it sounding like propaganda. And the one thing I felt the world didn't need was more propaganda. The book was originally called *Gordo*, if you can believe it, but I constantly struggled to find a way to engage with that character as anything more than a straw man to pummel.

Meanwhile, the other characters started to come alive, and I felt more qualified to write about love and loss than about the elimination of the fairness doctrine by the FCC in 1987 (look it up).

I kept that first love letter in the book through every draft, convinced that I could write a story around it. What a backwards way to write a book, now that I've reached the end of it.

A few months in, I got stuck because I really didn't know what I was doing regarding narrative fiction. I took the summer off and read a bunch of classic novels. Before a long road trip, I asked Olivia and Michael for suggestions on what to listen to on audiobook, and one of them suggested *Moby-Dick*, which I had never read. It's hard to pay attention to the intricate language of that book while driving through a snowstorm in Montana, but it had my attention with its very basic plot: *Let's hunt a whale.*

I had been plot-resistant in my own writing, but it turns out you need some things to actually happen in a novel. I found as soon as I introduced characters it became rude to ignore them and describe the wallpaper. So I forced myself to talk to them and let them do things, trusting that the story could be as simple as a whale hunt.

I think of *Moby-Dick* kind of like a reference book. You can jump around and skip chapters if you want. Some parts are hilarious and exuberant. Other parts are long, boring descriptions of whale anatomy. Most people don't feel like it's okay to skip pages in a book, but what does it really matter? There's no test at the end. You might as well read for your enjoyment.

One year into writing my novel, I spent the winter in Berlin because a friend had a room in their apartment to sublet. I spent the entire time writing and walking through the streets alone. I tried and succeeded to not meet one person while there, so that I wouldn't get invited to parties, get distracted with social scenes, or fall in love.

Then, back to the States, existing in people's spare rooms, cat-sitting my way around the country. I started teaching writing classes because I couldn't find any other way to support myself while giving every ounce of my brain to this project.

I remember the day I changed the title from *Gordo* to *Hitomi*. It was sunny, and I sat on the deck at Camp Joy. I made sure I saved a duplicate copy. "I'll just try it out," I told myself. Of course there was no going back.

Almost every morning I would wake up and wonder if I had enough empathy and patience to listen to these fictional characters, to represent them fully. I knew that if I didn't do that for them, no one else would.

As I write these words, Rush Limbaugh is receiving the Presidential Medal of Freedom. The First Lady is putting the medal around his neck during the State of the Union speech. The first image that flashes through my mind is that spaceships have decimated Earth, aliens executed the entire government, and they have put on the bloody suits and made pretend that they are receiving awards while the survivors cower in scrap metal shelters. Institutions mean nothing if they are ransacked with brutality. They can't mean anything at all. Maybe they never did. Olivia texts to say that upon seeing this man get the highest civilian award our country can give, she literally threw up.

I remember something someone said around the fire one night at Standing Rock: "This isn't about good versus evil. This is about wisdom versus ignorance."

I try to think of what wisdom I can give to the ignorant people causing so much pain. So much of it is what I learned from writing this novel: Release yourself from affectations. Believe oppressed people when they say they are in pain. Identify your own invisible privileges. Keep diving deeper to have more empathy for every man, woman, dog, and tree around you. Write letters to those you love and say how you really feel. Keep arranging beautiful words on a page for its own sake. Keep noticing the smallest things. Keep going.

— Nick Jaina, February 4, 2020

This book was written here

New York City, NY (Laura's apartment, David's apartment, Milk & Pull Bed Stuy) • **Chicago, IL** (an apartment in a luxury tower) • **Ft. Atkinson, WI** (Café Carpe) • **Austin, TX** (Laura's house, Sa-Tén, Houndstooth Coffee, Charm School Vintage) • **Wichita Falls, TX** (9th Street Studios) • **New Orleans, LA** (Meghann's house, Satsuma, The Orange Couch, Cafe Envie, Siberia) • **Wichita, KS** (The Ffarquhar, Wichita Public Library, Reverie Coffee) • **Fort Collins, CO** (The Alley Cat, Wolverine Publick House, Mugs, Max's house, Kris-ta's house) • **Boulder, CO** (Cherryvale, Rachel's house) • **Pueblo, CO** (Gypsy Java, Desi's house) • **Salt Lake City, UT** (The People's Coffee, The Fellow Shop, Hannah's apartment) • **Tucson, AZ** (Exo Coffee, Time Market, Five Points, Sarah's house) • **Silver City, NM** (Javalina, Tranquilbuzz, The Type Truck) • **Questa, NM** (Gaea's house) • **Crescent City, CA** (Front Street Inn, Perlita's Authentic Mexican, Flint Ridge Campground) • **Point Reyes Station, CA** (Historic Lifeboat Station, Point Reyes Public Library, Toby's Coffee Bar) • **Jenner, CA** (Russia House #1) • **Guerneville, CA** (Higher Ground Coffee) • **Monte Rio, CA** • (Craig's house) • **San Rafael, CA** (Aroma Cafe) • **Sacramento, CA** (Sacramento Natural Foods Co-op, Insight Coffee, Mom's house) • **Berkeley, CA** (Alchemy Collective Cafe) • **Oakland, CA** (Awaken Cafe) • **Emeryville, CA** (Chelsea's house) • **Nevada City, CA** (Foxhound Coffee) • **Mt. Shasta, CA** (Black Bear Diner) • **San Francisco, CA** (Mara's house, Jennifer's house, Rise and Grind Coffee, Outer Avenues Grocery) • **Davenport, CA** (Whale City Bakery) • **Boulder Creek, CA** (lille aeske, Mariel's house, Chris' house, Allison's house, Camp Joy) • **Ben Lomond, CA** (Coffee Nine) • **Felton, CA** (Wild Roots) **Santa Cruz, CA** (Hidden Peak Teahouse, Whole Foods on Soquel,

Dorota's house, Kate's house, Verve Coffee) • **Aptos, CA** (Linda's house) • **Los Angeles, CA** (Corrina's house, David's apartment, Rick's house, Psychic Bunny, It's Coffee, Coffee Bean and Tea Leaf on Wilshire—no, the *other* one) • **Jacksonville, OR** (Forty-Five Coffee, Christina's house (not *that* Christina) • **Grants Pass, OR** (Black Bear Diner) • **Eugene, OR** (Michael's house, Sweet Life Patisserie, Townshend's Tea, Eugene Public Library Downtown, Meraki Coffee, Vero Espresso, Amazon Park) • **Corvallis, OR** (Lainie's house) **The Dalles, OR** (The Riv Cafe) • **Pendleton, OR** (Great Pacific, Pendleton Center for the Arts, Bev's house) • **Olympia, WA** (Olympia Coffee Roasters) • **Port Townsend, WA** (Olivia's house, Velocity Coffee, Better Living Through Coffee, Port Townsend Public Library, The Food Co-op, Seal Dog Coffee) • **Whidbey Island, WA** (Turquoise house) • **Seaview, WA** (Sou'wester Lodge) **Astoria, OR** (Street 14 Coffee, Blue Scorcher, Kelli's house, Elisa's house, Israel's house) • **Seattle, WA** (Stumptown Coffee, Caffe Vita, Ingrid's house) • **Anchorage, AK** (Rustic Goat, Writer's Block Bookstore, Charlie's house, Alysia's house) • **Sutton, AK** (Sutton Public Library) • **Palmer, AK** (Vagabond Blues) • **Cantwell, AK** (JP's Coffeehouse, Rose's trailer) • **Berlin, Germany** (Collette's apartment, Café Behring) • **Copenhagen, Denmark** (Copenhagen Airport, Coffee and Donuts) • **Mexico City, Mexico** (Diana's house, Lardo, The Backyard) • **Portland, OR** (Extracto, Nectar, Heart, Affiche Gallery, Matt's house, Amanda's house, Meara's house, Dave's house, Corporeal Writing, Crumpacker Family Library, Mt. Tabor Park, Powell's on Hawthorne, Powell's Downtown, Soma Taproom, Guilder, Elevator Cafe & Commons, Rain or Shine Coffee House, Water Avenue Coffee, Seastar Bakery, Albina Press on Hawthorne, Pieper Cafe, Whole Foods on Sandy, Miss Zumstein's, Seven Virtues, Cathy's house)

Acknowledgments

Thank you to Chelsea Coleman for saying yes to everything and turning all energy into love. Thank you to my parents and my brother for making so much of everything possible and for showing me stability and discipline. Thank you to Jennifer Lewis for stepping in at a moment of extreme disappointment and vulnerability and saying, “I think I can help you,” and challenging me to go deeper with this book, tie more things together, and write better. Thank you to Leslie Orihel for reading the earliest of drafts of these words, which were originally just letters typed out on a phone in apartment lobbies and backs of cars, and for once saying, when I was in an apartment in Berlin doubting my abilities, “You GOT this.” The line, “Drugs will make you miss someone before they're even gone,” came from her, along with so many other things. Thank you to Olivia Pepper for altering my view of the entire universe. References to tarot and plants are thanks to Olivia's tireless research and philosophy. Frameworks for creating ceremony and prayer come from her as well. Thank you to Stelth Ulvang for all the laughter and games and late-night drives around the country, and the tireless, unpaid (sorry) work you've done to promote my books and my everything. Thank you to Jessie Carver for finding me an editor, a copyeditor, answering so many questions about line breaks and printing, and selling my books at so many different events. Thank you to Rose O'Hara for insights into nature, the police state, and chemically-altered adventures. The Florida information comes from Rose, especially the mangrove trees, getting shot with saltpeter while picking up oranges, and the details of the belladonna flower. Thank you to Dave Depper for endeavoring to like as many things as possible. Thank you to Nathan Langston for so many conversations about so many wild and wonderful things. Thank you to Emily Coletta for being such a great companion in Whole Foods all around the country. Thank you to Karla Starr for being such a great role model of a writer and a reader. Thank you to Laura Gibson for providing that first place to start writing. Thank you to Sarah and James Mackessy for supporting crazy whims and making them a reality, and for the wild wonder of Spektrum.

Thank you to Gaea McGahee, Brittan Ashford, Lori Englert, Shanthi Sekaran, Meghann McCracken, and my dad for reading advance copies of this book and giving valuable feedback.

Thank you to all my friends, students, associates, and allies around the world. My favorite thing is a deep conversation on a couch while we look out the window wondering if it's going to rain. So many people have said encouraging words, interesting phrases, displayed affection or curiosity for something small and humble, and that has sustained so many quiet days in the marathon of novel writing.

Thank you to anyone who has crossed my path.

(You might also enjoy Nick Jaina's 2015 memoir, *Get It While You Can.*)

About the Author

Nick Jaina was born in Sacramento and has lived for a spell in New Orleans, Portland, New York, and maybe Colorado. This is his first novel. His memoir *Get It While You Can* was a finalist for the 2016 Oregon Book Award. He performs in living rooms, libraries, churches, bars, galleries, and anywhere people listen. He currently lives in Oakland.